The Country Doctor's Tale

Middle East Literature in Translation
Michael Beard and Adnan Haydar, *Series Editors*

Select Titles in Middle East Literature in Translation

Castigation
Sultan Raev; Shelley Fairweather-Vega, trans.

A Cloudy Day on the Western Shore
Mohamed Mansi Qandil; Barbara Romaine, trans.

The House of the Edrisis: A Novel, Volume One
Ghazaleh Alizadeh; M. R. Ghanoonparvar, trans.

The House of the Edrisis: A Novel, Volume Two
Ghazaleh Alizadeh; M. R. Ghanoonparvar, trans.

The Man of Middling Height
Fadi Zaghmout; Wasan Abdelhaq, trans.

The Pulse of Contemporary Turkish: Poems from the New Millennium
Buğra Giritlioğlu and Daniel Scher, eds.;
Buğra Giritlioğlu, trans.

Salt Journals: Tunisian Women on Political Imprisonment
Haifa Zangana, Christalla Yakinthou, and Virginie Ladisch, eds.;
Katharine Halls and Nariman Youssef, trans.

Tracing the Ether: Contemporary Poetry from Saudi Arabia
Moneera Al-Ghadeer, ed.

For a full list of titles in this series, visit https://press.syr.edu/supressbook-series/middle-east-literature-in-translation/.

The Country Doctor's Tale

Mohamed Mansi Qandil

Translated from the Arabic by

R. Neil Hewison

Syracuse University Press

This book was originally published in Arabic as طبيب أرياف (*Ṭabīb aryāf*)
(Cairo: Dar el Shorouk, 2020).

Syracuse University Press
Syracuse, New York 13244-5290

First Edition 2026

26 27 28 29 30 31 6 5 4 3 2 1

Publication supported by the generous donors to the SU Press Gift Fund.

For a listing of books published and distributed by Syracuse University Press, visit https://press.syr.edu.

ISBN: 9780815612025 (paperback)
9780815657644 (e-book)

Library of Congress Cataloging-in-Publication Data

Names: Qandīl, Muḥammad al-Mansī author | Hewison, R. Neil translator
Title: The country doctor's tale / Mohamed Mansi Qandil ;
translated from the Arabic by R. Neil Hewison.
Other titles: Ṭabīb aryāf. English
Description: First edition. | Syracuse : Syracuse University Press, 2026. |
Series: Middle east literature in translation
Identifiers: LCCN 2025024522 (print) | LCCN 2025024523 (ebook) | ISBN
9780815612025 paperback | ISBN 9780815657644 ebook
Subjects: BISAC: FICTION / Literary | FICTION / Small Town & Rural |
LCGFT: Novels | Fiction
Classification: LCC PJ7858.A53 T3313 2026 (print) | LCC PJ7858.A53 (ebook)
LC record available at https://lccn.loc.gov/2025024522
LC ebook record available at https://lccn.loc.gov/2025024523

The authorized representative in the EU for product
safety and compliance is Mare Nostrum Group B.V.
Doelen 72, 4831 GR Breda, The Netherlands
gpsr@mare-nostrum.co.uk

Contents

The Country Doctor's Tale

1

Black fields, as far as the eye could see. Burned land, smoke rising from its fissures in sinuous lines. It was like the aftermath of a battle just ended. I gazed horrified. What had brought war to this place? I heard the voice of the farmer sitting beside me, who had sensed my bewilderment though I had not said a word. "It's what's left of the sugarcane, sir. After it's cut, we don't pull up the stubble, we leave it in the ground and burn it. This black ash is the best natural fertilizer."

I turned and looked at him for the first time. I didn't know when he had sat next to me. His face was all wrinkles and creases, like the cracks on parched land. He smiled in embarrassment, knowing he had broken into my silent mood. I nodded to him without a word and turned again to stare out of the window. There was no curiosity in me at all to get to know this new world—it was enough that I was being sent here. I was simply angry and bitter, and everything was stifled inside of me. The bus was packed out with people and animals: men, women, children, goats, a few geese, all jumping about with the motion of the bus as it bumped up and down and emitted alarming noises from all its joints. It trundled along, leaving the black fields and following a wide irrigation channel. Again, I heard the man beside me speaking. "It's called the Ocean Canal. It starts from the Bahr Yousef and passes by the edge of our village."

I couldn't keep my derision to myself. "This irrigation channel . . . an ocean?"

"That's what we call it," he replied diffidently, "and we sing about it too. It's the biggest one there is."

I held my tongue; I didn't want to vent my fury on him. But he was incapable of silence: he knew I was a man of education, coming from one of the gloomy cities whose people didn't easily open up to outsiders, but I was a stranger who didn't understand anything of what I was seeing. To me, it was all just expanses of green. I didn't know the types of crops or the times for planting or harvesting. He went on giving me snippets of information, without waiting for me to respond. I didn't want to know—I wanted this world to remain mysterious and unknown to me until the time came to leave without looking back. The bus shook violently as the road dived down with it toward the edge of the Ocean Canal and stopped just before we plunged into its dirty water. Wearily, I asked the man, "When will we get to the village?"

"Any minute now the tops of the palms will appear," he told me confidently, "and under every palm grove there must be a village."

The sky was still gray and empty, but then clouds began to gather and take on a crimson tinge. I didn't want to arrive after dark, but the bus kept to its slow crawl. I had left home early and traveled by train and service taxi, and finally everybody at the stand in the town advised me to take the rickety bus that they called The Fairest of Them All—because it was better than the donkeys and the crowded service taxis, and it was my only hope of reaching this remote village. I nodded off for a few moments and when I jumped awake, I saw the crowns of the palms in the distance, drawing closer. I turned to the man beside me, who nodded in affirmation. The nightmare village began to appear, the end of the line for all the passengers, after which the bus would turn around and head back. The trunks of the palms came into view, then the roofs of the mud houses covered in straw. It was the familiar village scene, unchanged for hundreds of years, inhabited by the same farmers who had cut the stones of the desert to build the temples and the tombs but who were niggardly in their own regard and built the houses they lived in with their children and their animals, and the graves of their forebears too, out of mud—houses that burned under the sun and melted away in the time of the flood.

The bus had no sooner stopped than the animals scrambled to leap out of the windows and the people formed a crush at the door. I waited until everyone had disembarked then stood up weary and sluggish. I could smell the people and the houses and the dung of the cattle. Of course, there was nobody waiting to meet me, and I had to find my own way. I knew what the building I was aiming for would look like: it would not be built of mud, but it could well be dilapidated and on the point of collapse. A line of men sat on the ground, leaning against the walls of the houses, neither moving nor speaking, just staring at the people passing by. Their stares widened when they saw me, carrying my small suitcase. They knew I was a stranger, but not one of them moved to offer me guidance or assistance. Even the man who had been sitting next to me on the bus had disappeared. I would not have to walk far—in this constricted space I knew I would reach my goal before the end of the village. But as soon as I turned away from the narrow alley that led to the depths of the settlement, I found the white building I was looking for. I knew it right away, though it was no longer really white—the dirt and mire that were stuck to its walls lent it a dark hue. It had taken on the characteristic muddy aspect of the entire village, the original white almost extinguished, and it seemed to match its surroundings. It was not dilapidated, but it was deserted and sad, the only sign of life being the plants that climbed up its walls. It stood alone, with an empty space in front of it, beyond which stretched the green fields.

The clinic's location was the best thing about it: alone at the entrance to the village, rather than in the heart of it. Here there would be room to breathe freely, to find seclusion, and to be away from turmoil and turbulent times. I climbed the three steps to the locked door and knocked on it with my fist, producing a muffled reverberation, but nobody answered. I knocked again, refusing to believe there could be no one there, not even the janitor, who wasn't supposed to leave the place. I didn't know what to do. I couldn't just ignore everyone, I had to announce my presence. I looked around but saw nobody. Darkness was extending its shade across the sky and the air was becoming colder. Could I go back? Perhaps I could catch that last bus and escape from this trap. I was about to make a move, but I noticed there was someone watching me, a skinny youth on a donkey standing in the middle of the road. I shouted to him, "Do you know anyone who works at the clinic? Go and tell them the doctor's come."

The lad was struck with panic, I don't know why. He kicked his donkey and made off quickly. Had he understood what I had said? Should I wait for him to come back, or hurry before the bus left? I went back to sit on the dirty steps. In the distance the dogs started barking, seeing off the last of the daylight—they are the best at sensing the light's retreat. Was I to wait until I heard the wolves? The darker it became, the more my fear increased. I had to get away from this frightening place. I picked up my suitcase to go back the way I had come, but then I became aware of a man running toward me. I heard the sound of his rattling breath before I could see his face. A worn-out old man, he raised his head and saw me, then put on a burst of speed as he hailed me, "What an honor! What an honor!"

We were wrapped in the gloom that surrounded us, a darkness that gave us no opportunity to examine each other's faces, but it was clear he was an old man. He held out his hand to me, but I pretended not to see it. I was furious with him, and with the fact that I was now unable to go back. He stood there, expecting me to say something, but I silently gestured to him toward the locked door of the clinic. He hurried to take a bunch of keys out of his pocket and pulled the door firmly open. A moist draft of stale air that had been trapped inside poured out, a mix of the smells of decay and bottles of rhubarb solution. How long had the clinic been closed, I wondered, and why had it been neglected all this time? We stepped through the door and stood in the dark. I heard him say, "Your servant Desougi the Gray! Strange name, isn't it? But I've worked at this clinic longer than anybody else!"

I was fuming and didn't need any more talk. Exasperated, I said, "Isn't there any light here?"

Apparently startled by my words and the tone of my voice, he backed away and began searching around, for what exactly I didn't know. The whole village was without electricity. We had reached the end of the 1970s, and still Egypt's villages drowned in the darkness of a bygone age. Suddenly, he left me and dived into the dark interior. I didn't know what he was doing, but I heard him let out a yell of victory, as if he had discovered oil. He came back with a large mantle lamp—a small gas canister with a round plastic casing on top, in the center of which was the mantle, which would become incandescent when lit. Carrying it like a valuable treasure, he placed it on the table and began his heroic attempts to strike a match. Finally, the fire caught in the guttering mantle, which suddenly glowed with light, revealing the man's features, his dark face with its deep furrows. I saw his eyes, which shone bright as he stared at me, trying to work out what kind of man I was. I was held by his eyes, unable to take in the rest of the scene. He was old, a veteran who had seen dozens of doctors come and go while he remained in place, and it was he who would accompany me on my sojourn here. He had witnessed the founding of the clinic, and he was the first to be employed in it. He would no doubt constantly remind me how, in spite of everything, he had saved me from sleeping out in the open, having seen my tired appearance and my suitcase thrown down on the ground—and he would definitely still be here after I left. He said, "Let's go to the examination room."

Lighting the way with the lamp, he led me to a small room with a metal desk in one corner, a metal cabinet, an examination table, and thick cobwebs that the spiders had been spinning for months. He hurriedly wiped the desk and the chair, and the room was made even more suffocating by the resulting clouds of dust. I sat behind the desk, where I belonged, and Desougi surprised me by sitting on the floor, where he disappeared in the dark and I could barely make him out. My hand was grimy with the thick dust that still lay on the surface of the desk. "This doctor who was here before me," I asked, "when did he leave the clinic?"

"Many months ago," he said. "He wandered off without warning, leaving everything behind him. He seemed quiet at first, then his behavior changed, I don't know why. He became short-tempered and started sending notifications to the Health Directorate about cuts to our salaries for no reason. Then he suddenly left."

I continued staring at him uncomprehendingly. How had matters come to this alarming pass? Was it possible the same thing would happen to me? Apprehensively, I asked, "Were there problems?"

He shook his head. "There's nowhere that's free of problems, but nobody runs away like that."

"Perhaps the work at the clinic wasn't going well?"

"We're like any other place in Upper Egypt, with our good points and bad. You'll find out for yourself. Anyway, you've had a long day, and you must be tired."

I stood up, and he stood up too. Picking up the heavy lamp, he showed me to the staircase that led to the upper floor. "You'll have to put up with your accommodation for tonight, and tomorrow we'll begin cleaning. Watch out for the rats."

The warning came too late. I was startled by their dark bodies leaping down the stairs away from us. I had never seen rats so big. In my alarm I exclaimed, "They're huge!" To which he replied calmly, "Don't pay them any mind. These are field rats—like the people of our village, they're full of air."

I was gripped with terror, and I lost the detachment and cool demeanor that I had been pretending. I wanted to cling onto him or to turn and run away. But we went on up the stairs and I said, "No wonder the doctor before me took to his heels."

"With God's help we'll clean it all up. The place has been deserted for a long time, but now that you've come everything will change for the better."

He swung the lamp around to make sure all was clear and the rats had fled. He inserted the key in the door, which groaned as he pushed it open with his shoulder. He left me to go in first, then came in behind me and closed the door quickly. I stood, nailed to the spot, as he walked around the apartment, searching in its various corners. The light revealed a room with a medium-sized bed, then another room that was empty, a small kitchen, and a smaller bathroom. The apartment was a reasonable size, if uncongenial. He opened a door that led to a small balcony and a squall of cold night air blew in, carrying with it the smell of dust, crops, and dung. I finally caught my breath, looked around, and stepped out toward the open sky studded with stars. I saw the cluster of palms and under them the houses, with smoke rising into the sky and a few scattered lights that were like shining eyes watching me from a distance. I was tired and certainly there was no food of any kind here, but there was a bed that I could throw myself on. Desougi placed the lamp on a table so that its light shone over everything, and began to move toward the door. "I'll leave you to rest, but I won't leave the building."

Astonished, I asked, "Where will you sleep?"

"I'll sleep anywhere," he said indifferently. "I'll lie on the floor and sleep. This is my place."

"You're going to sleep on the floor, on the bare tiles?"

"We're Upper Egyptians. We're used to God's rough ground. We pray on it, we plant it and we accept it without complaint, and sleep on it."

"Go home," I said firmly, "and come back in the morning. I don't need you today."

He muttered a few words I didn't catch, backed away, then left the room and shut the door quickly behind him. Exhausted, I sat down on one of the chairs, no more stable on its legs than I was myself. I could hear the rats gnawing at the bottom of the door, trying to find a gap to squeeze through into the room. I examined the door nervously: the lower part of it was reinforced with a sheet of metal, which the rats would not be able to chew through. That reassured me a little and I began looking around. I left the lamp lit—I didn't dare put it out—and threw myself on the bed and closed my eyes. For the last few months, I had been used to sleeping on a damp floor with nothing between me and it but a blanket—just a blanket full of holes—and only fetid, stale air to breathe. I had accustomed myself to that, like the maggots of the earth—and like all the other maggots inside the cramped cells. They were long days in which I lost all hope, waiting for whatever torture would be visited on me at any time. It wasn't just my body that was worn out, my soul was also under assault: the sounds of the night provoked mortal terror in my inner being. Inspections, insults, violent kicks. I closed my eyes and tried to drive all the images of abuse from my mind. I don't know how I got out of that miserable swamp. Some kind of rare miracle, one of those random pardon orders, just as random as the original detention order, pushed me out of the darkness of that prison clutching my papers: my birth certificate, my graduation certificate, and the permit from the Doctors' Syndicate to practice medicine. But all of that still wasn't enough for me to be reappointed to my old position. The clerk looked at me from behind his desk stacked with files. "All these papers are not sufficient. The most important paper has to come from Downstairs. You need to go Downstairs to obtain the approval."

I hadn't known there was a Downstairs. I went down there thinking I was going to the archives, but this Downstairs was different. It was much cleaner and grander than the upper floors: a red carpet, potted plants, strange paintings on the walls. It was as if they were expecting my arrival: the state security officer who received me had my personal file in front of him. From his position Downstairs, he held sway over all the upper floors. Every decision made in this building had to pass across his desk and was subject to his approval. He was civil and firm. He leafed through my papers and spoke concisely. "It was the people closest to you who gave you away. That's why we're sure of our sources." He didn't name any names, but these few words robbed me of my trust in everybody, even myself. I looked at him carefully as he took my papers from me and said, "You were a troublemaker as a student. You never let a demonstration or a symposium or a wall newspaper go by without taking part. You announced your sedition openly. Prison was only a mild punishment, but your soul is in our hands now."

I remained silent. I felt as though, with his arrogance, he really did have custody of my soul. He shuffled my papers with the amusement of someone playing with a person's fate. "We'll let you go for now. We'll send you far away, but you won't be out of our sight. Upper Egypt is the land of reform and correction for all troublemakers. It's almost like a prison." He laughed coarsely, but I needed a new land, a different place to plant my feet. He signed and stamped my papers, but kept them in front of him, and spoke again. "The first time we give a warning, but the second time we strike. Take your papers and go to your posting. And remember that we've granted you a second chance."

I took my papers and ascended to the miserable offices on the upper floors, where instead of red carpets and potted plants there were asthmatic old functionaries. I signed all the papers they presented me with, and all the pledges of good behavior, and I went off to find out how to get to this village, where I came in search of a world that held no trace of my old memories, without any hope of return or any certainty of landing on my feet.

My wearied body refused to relax, as if I had simply been transferred to a new cell. In the distance, lone wolves howled, and the dogs responded with a hysteria of barking. Between them passed the spirits of the dead. The night wore on and I tossed and turned on a dusty bed. I couldn't tear myself away from that pervading darkness—the dark of the prison was mixed up with the dark of the village night. There were no dreams, but there were nightmares. I opened my eyes with a start and looked around trying to recognize where I was. The lamp light was fading, the mantle turning a dark yellow on the point of burning out, so I quickly extinguished it. The dawn gloaming revealed details of the place. I went out onto the balcony. A gray luminance delicately seeped through the fog that lay on the fields and enveloped the tall palms. Despite the overall stillness, I could make out the figures of villagers leaving their low houses and heading for the fields. They walked in groups one after the other: men, women, and behind them the children and the animals. The men carried their mattocks and hoes, the women carried bundles of food, and the animals walked with bowed heads, knowing that a long day of toil lay ahead of them. At the end of the procession were the elderly, some of them leaning on sticks and struggling to walk, like newly resurrected dead. They all shuffled along at the birth of the light as they had done for thousands of years: a mythical ritual performed with a glory befitting the first moment of creation. I watched them in wonder, unable to move. They proceeded one group after another, in tune with the movement of the world, a cycle completing its revolution throughout a distant history. Not one of them turned in my direction, no one saw me. From my experience of life, I knew what kind of food was in those bundles, nothing more than bread and pickled turnip; even a piece of cheese would appear beyond their means. How did they stay alive year after year on these meager rations? I stood there until their living column disappeared and dispersed among the fields. The grayness receded and the fog took on a pallid red as the gray melted away and the sun's rays began to spread from behind the trunks of the palms. My first day was beginning.

Before I could go downstairs, Desougi beat me to it by bringing me breakfast: a few rounds of bread, a couple of pieces of cheese, and a bunch of arugula. Then he paused before producing from his pocket two paper twists of tea and sugar, which he proudly placed before me. I learned later that these were the most important of items: no gathering could be considered complete without them. I always felt supremely happy whenever I had a glass of hot tea in my hand—the whole time I was in prison I tasted only a few cold drops of it. I sat with a feeling of gratitude in front of the food that Desougi had brought unbidden. He tried to refuse when I gave him a few coins, but I firmly insisted that he take them. I didn't want him to put me to shame on the first day. He went into the kitchen to make tea for me. There was a stove there and a fridge that worked by means of a butane gas cylinder, which we had to ignite via an opening at the back. There were old medicines stored in the fridge, serums against scorpion stings and snake bites that had no doubt expired, but I didn't dare throw them out. I heard a hubbub from below and looked at Desougi, who said, "That's the patients. They heard that the doctor finally arrived."

I went downstairs to find a sea of faces occupying the place: some were sitting against the walls, women were lying on the floor, and emaciated, dirty children were spread around in a variety of poses like in an ancient pharaonic tomb scene. The faces were fixed on my steps on the stairs, as if I were a miracle maker. I hid my old defeats deep inside me and passed through the crowd of faces tanned by the sun. An old nurse stepped forward to push them back and open a way to the examination room, where I found patients filling that space too, all mumbling words that they made sure I should hear—what a good and clever and decent person I was. Flattering words, but groundless: not one of them knew me. From the pocket of my overcoat, I took out my stethoscope, that magical instrument all hold sacred. The nurse said, "I'm Atiyat, I'll be here at your side all the time."

"First of all," I said, "get them out of the room. I can't examine anyone in the middle of this crush."

Another nurse came and started pushing them out of the room, indifferent to their feeble objections. I wondered how many people worked at the clinic, but there was no opportunity to find out. The nurse whose name I didn't know arranged the patients in a long line, the mothers carrying their children in a separate line to the side, and she gave priority of entry to them. She was professional, working in silence with a frightful frown on her face. The patients started coming in. I began by using the examination table to see each patient, behind the folding screen, but the two nurses exchanged disappointed looks that told me I was wasting time and this would take all day: I had to see the patients on their feet and it was enough to simply listen to their complaint, or just to half of it. Sometimes, I didn't even employ the magic of the stethoscope. Gradually, I settled into the work, into their aches and pains and all their illnesses: the ailments of poverty and endless days of hard labor. I wrote prescriptions on the chits they carried without knowing whether I would find the medications in the clinic's dispensary.

A mother holding a skinny, malnourished child—what could I do for him? A young man complaining that his urine was all blood, his kidneys completely wrecked. People suffering from tumors, festering abscesses, wounds that refused to heal—nothing simple. They didn't give in, but they suffered in silence because suffering was all there was to do. Their faces blended together and I didn't know how I would remember them when the time came to dispense the medicines. I lifted my head from the stomach of a patient with serious swelling of the liver and spleen. The symptoms of bilharzia spared nobody: these people were doing penance for their forebears' sins of servility and subservience, with diseases that reached out from the cracks of the earth to the vessels of their blood.

I lifted my head, and I saw her. A different form among all this misery. A brief apparition, dressed in white: a white thigh-length coat, her hands in its pockets as she walked unhurriedly. Her hair was left loose to blow in the breeze from the fields. A slight smile. In a fleeting glance her beauty and her grace, incongruous here, shone. The groan of the patient lying in front of me reminded me of his presence—and she vanished as instantly as she had appeared. I turned inattentively back to the rest of the patients, my eyes wandering. I suddenly recalled the heartbreak that had hit me on the day I was released from prison and the passing face merged with that face from the past whose features I used to passionately adore. It was as if there were one woman in my life with two different faces: neither of them resembled the other, yet I was convinced that it was the same woman. Her expression before I entered the prison had been one of loving farewell; when I came out it was one of rejection, with not a note of feeling, of memory, or of pain. She wanted to end the encounter as quickly as possible. Now, this transient face appeared, a face from before the mask of loathing was donned. I shook my head and went back to examining the fatigued faces and worn-down bodies. I couldn't believe that their numbers were decreasing, but eventually there was nobody left waiting to come in. They must all be crowding around the window of the dispensary. I finally left the examination room, peering in every direction, but there was no trace of her. Had I imagined it all? I took a quick look at the room marked Pediatrics—there was a small weighing scale and height measure, and a small examination table—but it was empty. I was disappointed, but there was no time to search or ask questions.

I headed for the dispensary and opened it for the first time, inhaling the smell of the thick cloud that emerged from it, like a dusty, decaying sanctum. I should have had all of this handed over to me by the previous doctor, making an inventory of the pills, ampoules, and bottles of solutions together, but of course that had not happened. I had taken custody of it in this unorthodox manner and I entered the unknown room alone. Nobody went in with me, because I was responsible if even one pill went missing. I was met by layers of dust and cobwebs, and it was clear there must be many spoiled medicines. I managed to clear away some of the grime to reveal rows of different-sized bottles arranged on the shelves, tin boxes containing pills, and boxes of syringes. I inspected everything quickly—I couldn't check expiry dates, but this was all I had to work with. The one positive thing was that there were plenty of bottles of rhubarb solution, the magic compound that everyone took, whatever the symptoms.

I opened the window on the other side of the room, where all of the patients were gathered beyond its bars anticipating my appearance. Their sufferings had been aggravated by the hours of waiting. Some were sleeping on the ground, deep in the dirt, some were breathing with difficulty. I doubted if these old medications could relieve their pain. Others crowded in front of the window, stretching out their hands with the notes on which I had written their prescriptions. I was aware I could not give them the medicines they needed—it was beyond the pharmacy's means, even if it had had twice the stock. I took the prescriptions I had written, unable to supply what was on them—I cut down on the number of items and the quantities. I knew that the roots of disease were perennial in Egypt, while health was a transitory contingent. It was as though when darkness was created it was made eternal in Egypt, to lie within its earth, while light was given to other places. As I carried on giving out medications, I was short of breath. Fingers clutched at my wrist: they wanted me to see them as individuals, with separate destinies, but I couldn't. They were an undifferentiated mass of misery, which knew that what it was given was less than little, and it had no choice but to be satisfied. They persistently called out their prayers on my behalf, elevating me to a higher level than I occupied—but how could I rise up with all that brokenness inside me, and when this world was empty of everything that I aspired to? I went on handing out the medications, trying to suppress the faint voices of grievance in me. The space in front of the window emptied slowly, as those lying on the ground stood up, brushed the dirt off their clothes, and walked away. At last, I closed the window, but I found myself unable to leave the room. I looked at the tin boxes that surrounded me, at the remaining empty bottles. They had left me no time. If there was anything I could fix, I didn't have the time to fix it. The darkness of the room weighed heavily on me and finally, I went out to find them all waiting for me: the two nurses, Desougi, and two other men I had not seen until now, an old man and a younger one. She was not here—I certainly must have imagined her. Desougi said with some concern, "We'll have to go to the Health Directorate in the town, the medical stockroom there will solve some of our problems."

They were reading what was inside of me, they knew the predicament I was in. Their eyes held looks of compassion and sympathy. The second nurse came forward and said in a low voice, "My name is Aleya. I went up to your quarters and cleaned everything. And don't worry, I put some food in the fridge for you. It's working—a bit feeble, but it's working."

I put my hand in my pocket. She said firmly, "Not now," but I insisted—I didn't want to be indebted to anyone. One of the men introduced himself: Awad, clerk of the clinic. Then the old man: Mahrous, agent in the fight against bilharzia, and the oldest employee at the clinic.

I turned to Desougi, who came forward diffidently. "It's true he was here first, and I was second. And it could be said that this clinic was founded for his sake, because it was President Nasser personally who appointed him."

I looked at him in astonishment. "Nasser . . . *himself*?"

Mahrous bowed his head modestly and said, "It's an old story."

One day, I'll hear this story from him, I thought. The clinic's staff was complete now, it seemed nobody was missing. There was no sign of the transient apparition, and I didn't dare ask. I sat tiredly in the examination room as everyone began to leave, giving their various excuses. It was the bus they called The Fairest of Them All that determined everyone's departure—they had to catch it to reach their homes at a reasonable time. Only Desougi and I were left; he hurried to close all the doors, telling me that he would be sitting on the steps outside the main entrance. Again, I would spend my night alone. I went up to my apartment, which was clean and well ordered, and free of any unpleasant odors. Amazingly, the fridge was humming, and in it were tomatoes, cheese, cucumbers, and on one shelf a can of corned beef. I suddenly felt that I could go on living.

I heard a knock at the door and opened it to find Desougi gasping, "There's a patient downstairs."

Uninterested, I said, "The clinic is closed. They should have come earlier."

"It's a private patient," he said. "Anyone who comes after hours is private. You'll see how pretty their money is."

I wasn't convinced, but sitting alone for all those hours without moving was an uncomfortable prospect, so I went down to see the man who stood waiting for me. He was a venerable old sheikh, not an ordinary farmer. He held a little girl by the hand, and in his other hand was a small glass jar. I looked at him closely, curious—it was clear he was one of the village notables. He hailed me in welcome. "I am Chief Ayoub. The land we are standing on now is my land. I donated it for the building of this clinic. I asked them to name it after me, but they did not. Anyway, all rewards are with God."

I mumbled some words of welcome as I looked at the child, who was trying to hide behind the man's galabiya. He held out the jar. "This honey is first vintage, from my own apiary, unrivaled anywhere."

I tried to politely refuse, but he would not allow the gift to be returned: the Prophet himself would have accepted it. He turned and picked up the little girl to place her on the examination table. "This is my granddaughter. She's been ill for two days, and she doesn't stop coughing. You can examine her yourself."

She was certainly ill. I took her temperature: it was high, her chest was congested. There was no time. I didn't know how she was able to stand on her feet when she was almost delirious with fever. I rushed to the dispensary, where fortunately I found an ampoule that would lower her temperature. I injected it into her thin thigh—she didn't object or shout in pain. I asked Desougi to keep placing wet compresses on her forehead. The fridge in the apartment upstairs wasn't up to producing ice, but at least I found a bottle of cold water there. I put some of it on the girl's head and used the rest to soak the compresses. The grandfather stood there not knowing what was happening around him, or the reason for my alarm. He declined to sit on a chair but instead sat on the floor near the child's feet. She closed her eyes, silently surrendering to the fever that was eating up her body. I stayed beside her, changing the compresses and placing the thermometer under her armpit every now and then.

The mercury gauge dropped: her temperature finally subsided. After a while, she opened her little eyes and asked for water. It was more than I had hoped for and the sheikh almost kissed my hand. I needed to write him a list of medicines he should get from the neighboring town. He tearfully hugged his granddaughter and I felt I had passed my first test—I had kept the little girl's soul from an early death. Happy with what I had done, I remained sitting in the examination room until Desougi returned and put a few banknotes in front of me, small denominations, old but well pressed. Surprised, I asked, "What's this?"

"As you see, the private consultation fee."

"What? You took money from him? He's the owner of the land the clinic is built on and he brought us this jar of honey."

"That was just a gift," he replied coolly. "Work is work. Since he came after hours, he had to pay."

He took his share and left the rest spread out on the desk. I would accumulate many such notes as time went on. In these remote villages there were no large denominations. The banknotes were all old, but they were kept flat and taken care of, being the only ones in circulation. Larger notes were rare or perhaps they were hoarded, far from daily spending. I lazily gathered up the notes on the desk, but I carried the jar of honey with pride—the food of the gods, as the ancient Egyptians had described it.

Today, I would share in the very sustenance of the inscrutable deity of the villages.

The door of the clinic opened again and a new visitor came in, a large man—not tall, but large—with a heavily compact body and a dense mustache. My eyes searched for Desougi, but he had vanished, without a word. The man didn't bother to introduce himself; he just came up to the edge of the desk and said, "I want medicine."

He had invaded my room and invaded my peace. "What medicine?"

"Medicine to fix my head. It's a long night and I must have medicine."

He spoke as though he owned the place. I said, "I only have medicines for the sick, and you don't appear to be sick."

"The problem is my head. The rest of my body's in God's hands. I'm not asking much, I just want to fix my head."

Was he asking for narcotics? I stood there perplexed, not knowing what to do. I felt he had me trapped in the tight space of the room. I shouted for Desougi, but he didn't appear. I said, "I don't have anything like that here."

Pointing with his hand, he said, "You have a room full of all kinds of medicines, and you can't manage a single one for me?"

The hand he was pointing with was shaking. He was clearly making a great effort to control himself and was trying not to disgorge his wrath onto me. His body language was overtly threatening, but I didn't want to give in to him, not on my first day. To be rid of him I said,

"Perhaps in the morning. Come tomorrow, I might be able to find you something."

He stood there considering me, assessing my frame of mind. He realized I was not going to give him anything, and he was not happy. I was starting to feel afraid and I prepared to take on a defensive stance, but suddenly he turned around and walked out. I listened to the sound of his steps until they faded away and I exhaled in relief. I wasn't sure if I had done the right thing, but I picked up the jar of honey and headed to go upstairs. Then, Desougi surprised me by turning up. I shouted irritably, "Where were you?"

"That was the Hawk. I saw him going in. I don't like to meet him, nobody does. He belongs to the underworld of the village."

I yelled at him angrily, because he had left me alone with that man and hadn't given me any warning: "I didn't know what he wanted, or what medicine he was asking for!"

Unfazed, he told me the man wanted anything to make his body sweat, anything he could swallow with a glass of strong tea.

I cursed him silently as I headed up the stairs. I closed the door behind me, praying that I wouldn't have to go down again. It occurred to me to make a glass of tea and sweeten it with the honey—that might calm me down and enable me to sleep without nightmares. I took the glass out onto the balcony and sat there for a few moments before night fell and the brigades of mosquitoes attacked. In the distance, flocks of white pigeons flew around the palms in ever-widening circles, and columns of smoke began to rise from some of the houses. The stillness was pure and the atmosphere was uncommonly serene. That other world, with all its problems, its struggles, and its memories too, seemed far away. The taste of the honey took me back to the taste of the land, the taste of my lost world, and I suddenly felt refreshed. I watched the clouds scudding high overhead, white and glowing with the remnants of a golden incandescence, as though they had been dipped in honey.

I spotted a man walking in the direction of the clinic. I didn't want to deal with any more patients, but he kept on coming, and now I could make him out clearly: it was the man who had confronted me a short while ago, the Hawk, with his stocky build and great mustache. He was coming toward me carrying something under his arm. I was nervous. I didn't know whether Desougi had locked the clinic door securely. He stopped right below me, pretending not to see me, but I knew that he did and that he was aware I was watching him. He took a folded rug from under his arm, spread it on the ground, squatted on it, and laid out the rest of his things. There was something that looked like a primitive firearm: a longish pipe with pieces of iron attached to it. I stepped back, but he put it on the rug and took out something else that looked like a handgun, which he placed slowly next to the rifle. There was also a rather long knife, and in front of all this he arranged a row of brass bullets. I was trembling and didn't know what to do. I was prepared to run inside as soon as he moved to pick one of the weapons up, but instead, he proceeded to take them apart. He broke the gun down into three pieces and with a cloth began to clean it with extraordinary care. He took the rifle apart too and set about cleaning that with the same close attention. He picked up the long barrel and looked through it to be sure it was spotless, pointing it in my direction each time he did so, then he collected his things together and reassembled them. I retreated quickly, ran down the stairs, and called to Desougi, "Go and tell him to come in and see me."

Desougi was baffled. "Who?"

"Who else? The Hawk."

I opened the dispensary with a shaking hand. I selected some medicines for reducing fever, one that was a stimulant, and another one at random, and left the room to find him waiting for me. He observed me with eyes devoid of either surprise or malice. I gave him the bag of pills and said, "Take these to swallow with some tea."

Before he could say a word, I turned around and went upstairs, furious at myself, shamed by my moment of weakness. This thug had succeeded in frightening me. I closed the door loudly and went back to my glass of tea. It was cold and the honey tasted bitter.

2

The clinic was closed for the day and I stood waiting for the first departure of The Fairest of Them All as the breaths of morning still covered the fields. Desougi stood next to me and a line of men sat leaning against the wall—had they been there all night? We plunged into the crush of passengers to find seats for ourselves. We needed to reach the Health Directorate early, before the functionaries vanished, or they ran out of medicines. We were lucky to find two seats and I sat next to the window. I was bored as the bus remained stationary, greedily swallowing more people and animals, but just as it started to pull out, I saw her—her white clothes, her hair knotted behind her ears, her slender build, her recognizable gait—as she walked in the direction of the clinic. So, I hadn't been imagining things. She was no phantom, no specter, no apparition and I was neither ill nor a hostage of my memories. My eyes were fixed on her as the bus carried me away. I turned to find Desougi staring at me. "That's Farah," he said. "Didn't you see her at the clinic?"

I shook my head. As usual, he had read my thoughts. He went on to tell me that she was the only clinic employee who was from the village itself, which was why she came to work early and left early, while Atiyat and Aleya came from the town.

I closed my eyes and didn't respond. No need to reveal myself to him. Would I see her when I returned? I opened my eyes again when we were out of the village, among the broad fields, on the edge of the muddy canal. The journey progressed with stops and starts, as we passed forgotten villages, low houses, and farmers who had not ceased working for long years past yet still could not keep hunger away from their homes. We emerged onto the highway and drove parallel to the Ibrahimiya Canal. Then, the first scattered houses of the town appeared. It was a modest town, half its streets unpaved, but at least it had electricity, and its nights were not gloomy. We went straight to the Directorate's medical stockroom. Of course, they paid no attention to the inventory of medicines I presented to them: there were many items they didn't have, and there were others that I didn't need but that I had to take. Desougi whispered that I should not give in to what they were trying to force on me, that they were typical functionaries who would only back down in the face of threats. I said, "I don't have any authority to threaten them with." To which he replied, "So act as if you do."

I went back to them belligerent and irate, yelling that the clinic had been closed for many months, that all the medicines it had were totally spoiled and had turned to poison, that I would go to the managing director in person, that I was even capable of going to the provincial governor, and that I would notify the Doctors' Syndicate;

they were the cause of all my problems and any delay would multiply those problems. Desougi nodded his head in support. And strangely, they dropped their self-importance and their refusal to cooperate. They offered me more items, and in greater quantities. One crate of medicines turned into three. I acquired syringes, rolls of cotton wool and gauze, and serums for scorpion stings and snake bites. I signed the receipt papers in astonishment—the inventory had tripled and they were asking me whether or not I was satisfied. Desougi rushed off to hire a cart, pulled by a bony horse, onto which we loaded the crates of medicines. He loaded himself onto the cart too: it would take them all to the clinic. I couldn't ride along, naturally. Instead, I would spend the day puttering around the town and leave at the end of the day with The Fairest of Them All. I wanted to hang around, buy a small radio from a store, eat grilled pigeon at a restaurant, keep walking until I reached the banks of the Nile, where the desert hills stood on the far side, and sit by the muddy waters for hours. The flood was in its first days and igneous silt was still suspended in its waves. I read the newspapers I had bought, which turned out to be from yesterday, but the news was much the same. The story that caught my attention was about the conversion of a prison into a museum. This was strange news indeed in a country that had been addicted to the opening of prisons, and stuffing them full of all kinds of people, for centuries. I searched for details in the other papers, but the story was written in the same official wording. I was bored but I didn't want to move. I watched a lone fisherman throw his net again and again with no result. I thought about everything that had happened in my life. I was this lone fisherman with his empty net and this job was my last chance to avoid roaming the streets unemployed.

I walked to the bus station and pushed myself through the crowd of passengers, who let me past easily to find a seat by the window, and once again I became immersed in the green of the extensive fields. I kept watching the edge of the horizon, waiting for the tops of the palms to come into view. The Fairest of Them All bumped up and down and, as usual, made perilous halts on the edge of the canal and crossed half-collapsed bridges until the palms appeared, and the slumbering village beneath them. It was nearly evening, though the birds were not yet done with their circling. I found Desougi waiting for me at the clinic, sitting in the dark, not lighting the mantle lamp until he knew I had come in. I took delivery of the crates of medicines and put them in the dispensary without sorting them out—I might do that tomorrow or the day after. I went straight up to my apartment: it was important to take my shoes off, sit on the bed, and listen to some music on the little radio. This had a magical effect, creating a kind of familiarity with the place. I felt the need for the voice of Fairouz, and I fiddled with the dial searching for her. But a great hubbub rose up from downstairs, all the birds circling the clinic flew off, and Desougi began hammering on the door. There must be some kind of emergency. I saw his pallid face as he yelled, "Someone's been stung by a scorpion! The whole village is here."

My heart sank, but fortunately I had brought some tropical disease serums back today. I hadn't been in a hurry to put them in the fridge, but perhaps they could save this life before it was lost. I went downstairs and found the person who had been stung spread out on the ground, a young man barely twenty years old. His face was sallow and covered in sweat and he was drawing breath with difficulty. The room was packed out, with all the residents of the village crammed into it, and it wasn't easy to make my way through them. The situation would be worse when the venom spread to the rest of his body. I shouted at them all to go away and leave him room to breathe, but nobody moved. I took the lamp and went to the dispensary to search the crates for the scorpion serum. I was agitated and my fingers were trembling. I was racing against time, but I couldn't keep myself together. I raised the lamp with one hand and searched with the other, afraid they would all burst in on me at any time. I heard their shouts and the women's screams coming from outside and was aware that things could get out of hand at any moment. There was a knock at the door, which I ignored, but it came again. I headed to open it and to yell in the face of this obstinate person on the other side. I raised the lamp and opened the door just wide enough to shout through it, but I saw her face, radiating light with a shy smile and shining eyes. She was not wearing white but had a shawl of red plush over her head. She fixed her gaze on me and asked, "Do you need help?"

I gulped drily, put out my hand, pulled her quickly inside, and closed the door. We were suddenly alone in this confined space and I was closer to her than I had ever hoped to be. Before she could object or complain I gave her the lamp and said quickly, "Lift it up high so I can find the medicine."

She took it and came so close to me that I could feel her shoulder touching mine, a simple contact that calmed my nerves. I bent over the crate and began taking everything out. In no time I found the box of serums and exclaimed to Farah, "Here it is! Now it's just the ephedrine injection."

She gave me an encouraging smile and moved with me to the second crate, shining the light so that I was able to find the ephedrine easily. We cried out together in relief and I said, "Let's go before the venom spreads."

She carried the lamp and walked ahead of me. Silence reigned over all and the crowd parted before us. The youth was alive, although death was much nearer. His heart was still beating, but weakly. I put a blanket over him and brought the lamp close to his face. I told Farah, "Get them all out of here."

I began to give him the serum slowly. I heard her voice as she spoke to them quietly but firmly, ushering them outside without upsetting anybody. Even the distraught mother and the stricken father went out and she finally managed to close the door of the examination room. She came and stood close beside me. I checked his eyes to see the size of his pupils: they were small to the point of vanishing. I needed to give him the stimulant to make the muscles of his heart work harder and pump more blood through his depleted body, so that he could fight off the numbness caused by the venom. After the injection his pulse became somewhat stronger, his pupils stabilized without shrinking further, and the shadow of death receded a little. I felt her breath on the back of my neck and heard her timorous voice ask, "Will he survive?"

I turned to her. She was so close to me that it was hard to bear. Her face was pale and her eyes were wide. I lowered my gaze, to resist the urge to touch her. "It's too early to say," I told her. "We have to monitor his pupils and his pulse, and I'll give him more ephedrine."

She averted her face and moved away from me a little. Fearfully, she said, "Nobody survives a sting like this. Dozens of children die from scorpion stings every year."

She rolled up a piece of gauze to mop the sweat that had collected on his brow. "Who is he?" I asked. "And why did the entire village come in after him?"

"His name is Barakat, 'Blessings,' and he is indeed a blessing. A good young man, it's not right that death should take him suddenly like this. He's still doing his religious studies at the Azhar Institute, and he's the one who gives the sermon at Friday prayers. His talks are as popular with the women of the village as with the men."

Uncertainly, I asked her, "Is he related to you?"

"In this village," she said simply, "we're all related. Even the Copts are related to us to one degree or another."

She smiled and smoothed a wisp of hair back from her forehead and said, "I must go out to them. They won't leave until they're reassured that he's alive."

We were still at the beginning, and death had retreated only slightly—his breathing was heavy and his pulse raced. She went out to them. I took off my watch and put it on the desk in front of me—I had to keep a careful eye on the time until I gave him another injection. I heard mumblings outside, but I didn't know whether she had succeeded in sending the people away. The patient still had his eyes closed, but the sweat on his forehead had dried. I took his pulse and sat down again to wait. It had been a long day, but I didn't feel tired. In front of me lay a soul suspended by a narrow thread that was on the verge of snapping. Farah returned as I was giving him the second injection. She was nervous, but she closed the door behind her and came closer to look at him for a moment before turning to me questioningly. I said, "As you can see, all that sweating has dried up, and the swelling of his tongue has gone down. He can breathe more easily now."

Her face shone. "I didn't think he would survive. The sting of the yellow scorpion always leads to the grave, but you saved him. It's like a miracle."

She sat facing me. I said, "There's no miracle. He was ill and we happened to have the treatment to hand."

"Death is easy in our village," she said. "We die for trifling reasons. That's why the saving of a life here really is a true miracle."

The sound of the young man's breathing reached us, quiet and with no rattle in the throat, as I asked, "What do you do in the clinic?"

"You ought to know—I'm in Family Care."

"Why don't you work with me in the examination room?"

She stared at me in astonishment, her eyes wide but radiating an ambiguous desire; eyes innocent in the extreme but concealing secrets. Perhaps she was no ordinary village girl? She possessed the magic of the female sex and its temptations, even if not deliberately deployed. But I had taken a long stride in her direction, and I had no intention of backing down. "Tonight, you've proved that you're good in an emergency."

She inclined her head and said, "As you wish."

Perhaps she was thinking about how the other two nurses would react, being both older and more senior. I didn't want her to fight that battle, so I would have to give Desougi clear directions on the matter. I looked at the young man laid out like a corpse. His eyelids were open and he was staring at me with fixed, glassy eyes, but his breathing was quiet and regular. Once again, I was conscious of her beside me as she whispered, "Are you going to give him another injection?"

"No need for that. I think the danger has passed. Go and tell them to bring a donkey to take him home."

I felt her hand grasp mine and squeeze it. It was small and warm. "May the Lord preserve you, you're a really good man."

She said it in a hot whisper, her slender fingers still pressing my hand. A strand of her hair escaped from under the shawl of plush and fell over her face. In an instant she pulled her fingers away from mine and adjusted the shawl on her head. I stared at her, dazzled. It was too much, all this beauty and meekness. How was it that I was accorded such closeness, such contact? She must have been feeling it too. Who could believe this was only our first meeting? I let her leave the room quickly and beyond the door arose the men's cries of "God is most great!" and the ululations of the women. They burst back into the room, Desougi shouting angrily at them. The mother grabbed and tried to kiss my hand, which I pulled away from her with difficulty. Several of the men came forward to pick the young man up and I warned them to do it gently. One of them lifted his limp body over his shoulder. The boy's glassy eyes stared at everybody without any real sense of their presence. He would sleep and wake up sound and healthy. I went back to looking at Farah, who was standing in front of me fastening the plush shawl around her face. Her cheeks were rosy, as though some of the red of the shawl had leaked into them. "You've done a beautiful thing for us," she said. "May the Lord reward you."

And before I could say anything, she turned around and went off with everybody else: my eyes followed her as she caught up with them. Desougi stood beside me watching them and muttering. "Garbage! I didn't get a single piaster out of them."

At this point I didn't care much about the money either way. But one of them came back: different in appearance but nevertheless a villager, he wore a light-colored galabiya under a lightweight coat—I couldn't see the colors properly. Desougi snorted irately. The man held out his hand and introduced himself. "I'm Master Abanoub, the village tailor."

I shook his hand, which was rather soft, and his skin was not tanned by the sun. He came closer and went on. "I know they didn't pay anything, even though they kept you up late into the middle of the night."

I shrugged my shoulders, unconcerned. But he didn't want to stop talking, or to leave. "They're poor, and you won't ask them for anything, so would you allow me to compensate you?"

I was astonished. "Who said I would accept compensation?"

He laughed. "I'm not talking about money. I'm talking about what I'm good at—I'll make you a white doctor's coat, with your name embroidered in blue thread. A gift from me."

"I don't need a coat. I have everything I need."

"Please don't embarrass me—wait until you see the coat and judge for yourself. Have a good night."

I watched him as he walked away. After such a strange evening, I went up the stairs alone, threw myself on the bed, and sank into the darkness of sleep.

I woke late and went sluggishly downstairs. The clinic was crowded, patients sitting everywhere, some lying on the floor. I felt guilty and made for the examination room with my head bowed: I had to make a quick start. Farah stood waiting for me, without the red shawl of course, but instead with a white headscarf, and a gentle smile. There was a crimson rose on my desk. There was no need to exchange morning greetings: I felt as though we had been together since yesterday. The patients began to come in straightaway and her presence gave me more confidence in dealing with them. Throngs of sick faces, gaunt bodies, and ruined skins—ancient ailments, cultivated in the cracks of this land, that neither medication nor talisman can cure. They don't know exactly what they are suffering from, they just have the feeling that they are not deserving of life. They can only complain to the point of entreaty and accept any medicine, even if it is ineffective. In between all these cases, and despite the lack of time, I didn't stop talking with Farah. She asked me with the wonder of a child, "Are you really from Cairo? Have you always lived there? How big is it?"

It was a vast city, I told her, full of all sorts of places and all kinds of times, and I had lived in them all, in the worst of its places and in the strangest of its times.

She didn't understand everything I was saying. Without realizing it, I wanted to impress her, but I didn't talk to her about Cairo's prisons, the black mark of that city. She went back to her questions. "Have you been abroad? Have you been on an airplane or crossed the sea?"

"Perhaps two or three times," I said.

"Oh, how I envy you! I haven't even left this village. The distances are short and the graves are close; we have to pass by them any time we go anywhere. . . . This is where my end will be, and the end of the world."

A bird in a cage, with not enough air to help it fly. "But at least you've gone to nursing school."

"The school is in the nearby town. I went and came home on the same bus at the same time. I don't know a single street there. I always come back to this village, and I don't think I'll ever leave it."

One patient went out, another one came in, and still we talked. She liked to talk, despite the crush of patients; perhaps she was making up for long days of silence, or perhaps she just had no one to talk with. A patient came in suffering from chronic asthma, a child with measles, a woman suffering from the cruelty of her husband, a large man with incontinence, several children with malnutrition, day after day—and in front of them all we built a parallel world together, purely platonic at first, of course. Throughout the few morning hours, among the dozens of patients' faces, we met, we talked, we touched involuntarily, we prescribed medicines, and we spread a wave of new, positive energy through the old clinic. She was a straightforward young woman who had never left this small patch of land, though she had a passion for the vastness of the world and wanted it in the palms of her hands. Every morning, I encountered her luminous eyes and her sweet, shy smile. She stood at my side and didn't leave me until the clinic closed for the day. She was good at giving injections, finding hidden veins with ease, and reassuring patients with simple words. When I went upstairs alone to my quarters I would imagine her beside me, continuing our morning conversation. Was it possible she might sometime leave the clinic behind and come up to my rooms? Her presence at my side had made me hunger for intimacy, and rather than just granting me a little companionship, she had set off a craving in me for the touch of a woman. In spite of these conflicting feelings, I maintained the formal distance between us, the physical space at least. I was aware that there were eyes fixed on us, waiting for a misstep or a slip, and behind this was a forceful rage that I did not see at the time: a blaze that burned in the hearts of the two silent nurses, and perhaps in Desougi too.

I heard the sound of his fist knocking on the door and his hoarse voice saying, "There's a patient waiting downstairs, Doctor."

Afternoon patients were the source of his true happiness, as they paid whatever he asked. They preferred to buy their medicines elsewhere and were looking for a measure of privacy. I went down to the courtyard of the empty clinic. Desougi was standing near the door and in the corner sat a woman wrapped in black, nothing showing of her, not even her face. I motioned her toward the examination room, where she looked worriedly back at Desougi, and asked me to close the door. She raised her hand to remove the shawl that was hiding her face: she was a woman of average age, still youthful, her face not without beauty and with some touches of makeup, which was unusual. It was clear that she had possessed a generous measure of good looks. The years had taken some of that with them, but what was left was still noticeable. She didn't rise or sit on the examination table. She wanted to talk first, though she didn't want to give me her name, and she hesitated a little before telling me that she was experiencing severe nausea every morning and that she could no longer bear several kinds of food. She also felt a heaviness in her breasts. These would all be normal symptoms, had it not been for the degree of confusion and fear she manifested. I said, "You're married, of course."

She shook her head. "My husband died two years ago."

I started on the list of normal questions—there was no way to stop. "What about your period? Is it regular?"

She paused briefly, hesitant to answer, and glanced at me, perhaps wondering whether or not I was to be trusted. Reluctantly, she said, "It was, but it stopped two months ago."

This then was the dilemma that had pushed her to come to me. I looked at her and she looked back at me briefly with inquiring eyes before lowering them. I said, "I don't think there's any need for you to lie on the examination table."

Almost whispering, she said, "No, no need for that. I know what it is."

For the sake of something to say, I continued, "This morning sickness, the pain in your breasts, and the interruption of your monthly cycle are unmistakable signs."

"I know, . . . I know."

She looked at me again, the marks of dread showing more clearly on her face. There was nothing I could do for her and I didn't know what she was expecting from me. We remained silent a while, until finally, she said, "My belly will grow and everyone in the village will see it. It will be a scandal."

"What's the problem? Why don't you marry, so that it all becomes legitimate?"

She struck her hands on her thighs. “He can’t, and I can’t. Nobody wants a baby. You have to help me, I’m still in the first trimester.”

Taken aback, I said, “What do you expect me to do?”

She was almost in tears. “I want some medicine that will help me, to make my blocked blood flow.”

My voice began to rise. “I have nothing like that here. What you’re asking is outside my specialization and my abilities, and besides all that, it’s against the law.”

“Please, lower your voice! His ears may be at the door.”

I suddenly felt pity for her, aware now of the extent of the predicament she had fallen into, the moment of weakness for which she would pay a high price. I whispered, “Look around the village, but in secret. There must be an old woman who can help you to empty your womb—there’s one in every village.”

Her tears flowed and she said in despair, “She’ll expose me.”

“She won’t,” I reassured her. “It’s her profession to cover up scandals, not to expose them. Pay whatever she asks and she’ll keep your secret.”

She looked at me pleadingly. “Don’t you have any other solution?”

I shook my head and helped her to stand. She covered her head well so that her face didn’t show. Desougi regarded her with curiosity as she crossed the hall of the clinic and went down the steps that led to the forecourt. I stood at the door and watched her go. At the far side of the forecourt, I caught sight of someone observing the clinic door, and I recognized him from his clothes and his yellowish coat: it was none other than Master Abanoub—not carrying the white coat he had promised me, but watching the woman cross the open space in the direction of the village. He looked around warily, then followed her at a distance, taking no notice of me. I heard Desougi shouting in my ear, "Who's that woman?"

Sharply, I replied, "What business is it of yours?"

The next day, in the middle of our consulting hours, the mount of the umda, the village mayor, came. We had finished seeing most of the patients, but nobody had received their medications yet. Desougi came in to announce that the umda's mount had arrived to take me to his house. I didn't know the umda and had not met him. All I knew was that he was the only man in the village to own a car—a Mercedes, though an old model. I had sometimes seen it flashing by the clinic, raising the dust, with a bunch of barefoot children running after it. Without paying much attention, I said, "Is he ill? He has a car, so why doesn't he come here?"

I realized I was annoyed. Perhaps because he was the only person who owned a car in this remote village. Or perhaps because he was treating me like one of his subjects—which was why he thought it was sufficient to send this mule. Desougi was alarmed. "He's the umda!"

His tone revealed that the umda was the absolute ruler of the village and nobody dared to gainsay him. I said, "He can wait until I've given out the medicines."

Even more alarmed, he shouted again, "He's the umda!"

I didn't reply. I entered the dispensary, closed the door behind me, and opened the window to everyone.

As usual, they were waiting for me, more sick and miserable than ever. I was not in a hurry, nor was I parsimonious, even when an old man leaning on a stick, who I had not seen before, came forward. The crowd parted for him respectfully and he said, "Give me something for a headache."

He had no prescription, and I had not seen him in the examination room. Someone volunteered to say that he was Sheikh Abdel Barr, "our blessing."

I gave him what he asked for and he repeated many prayers for me in his tremulous voice. Eventually, I closed the window, content with myself. When I left the dispensary, I found Desougi standing nervously. He had brought a pile of berseem clover for the mule to keep it quiet—I could only smile. I said to Farah, "Get the box of dressings ready. You're coming with us to the umda's house."

I caught the stupefied looks in the eyes of the other two nurses, who suppressed their anger with difficulty. Even Farah stared at me in disbelief, then hurried to fill the box with rolls of gauze, pieces of cotton wool, and empty syringes. She ignored the two truculent nurses and went ahead of me to the door. Desougi carried my bag and walked behind me. The umda's representative approached, leading the mule, but I shook my head—we would go on foot. We passed through the uneven streets of the village, myself in the middle, Farah on my left, and Desougi somewhere or other. Farah was embarrassed and looked constantly at the ground as she walked. She didn't want to see anyone, even though everyone could see us. They all watched us in wonder, and more than one of them greeted us audibly. The village houses seemed stuck fast together, their walls supporting each other—if separated, they would all collapse—and covered with straw: a single match could set the whole lot alight.

Desougi pointed to a tall, white house looming behind the trees. A mix of awe and curiosity appeared on Farah's face and, as if whispering to herself, she said, "I've never been into this place. I've never even been near it."

Desougi nodded in agreement. It seemed to be an area forbidden to all. A white wall surrounded the house, with an iron gate that produced an unsettling sound. There was a tall mulberry tree in front of the door, its berries scattered on the ground. We climbed a few marble steps. Desougi, whose self-assurance had evaporated, whispered, "You lead the way, Doctor. You go first."

I couldn't understand the secret of this fear, but it was the norm: the natural terror that Egyptians feel when confronted with any sort of ruling figure, a kind of servility latent within their genes, an inherited chromosome in need of surgical removal. I knocked with the iron doorknocker that hung on the door and it opened immediately—it seemed the umda had been standing behind it. I knew who he was, even though this was the first time I had met him: a large man with a thick mustache twirled at the ends, and with piercing eyes. In a booming voice, he said, "You kept us waiting, Doctor."

I muttered a few words about the crowds, the clinic, the many patients, and he responded, "Of course, it's a sick village. You're to be excused because you're new, but here nobody keeps the umda waiting."

His tone was cold, and sharp as a knife. He made way for me to enter, but didn't bother to receive the others. We went into the main hall of the house: a spacious reception room stuffed with old furniture covered in velvet, red and dusty, and on the walls, photographs in heavy, overwhelmingly black frames—old faces, all resembling the mayor, with the same thick mustaches and penetrating eyes, his family history full of dread. I turned to find Desougi and Farah shrunk into a corner of the hall: it appeared that the umda didn't see them at all. I stood silently as he gave me the opportunity to contemplate the pictures. Their intimidating force even penetrated my own soul. How was it possible for this great ruler to reign over this small village? When I looked around, I found him watching me. My body seemed tiny in front of him. I swallowed and said, "I see you are not sick."

"May evil be far from me," he said hoarsely. "I'm as healthy as a lion in a jungle."

I continued staring at him, until finally, pointing upstairs, he said, "It's her, she's not in a good way. She's lying down up there. We'd better not waste any time and go up to her."

He gathered the skirts of his galabiya and rushed to climb the stairs. I had to hurry after him, signaling to Desougi to stay where he was and to Farah to follow me. She had still not recovered from her fright, but hugging the metal box of dressings she hesitantly came up behind me. We walked along a corridor with many closed doors, into one of which the umda burst without knocking. I didn't dare to go in after him. I heard him saying, "The doctor's here," and angrily he bade me enter. It was a big room, dominated by a large bed, and a number of mirrors suspended on the walls. I didn't take in the rest of the room's furniture, as my attention was caught by the woman sitting on the bed. At first sight I thought she could not be the mayor's wife, though she might just be his daughter. I looked at him to confirm my assumptions. His features soured as he observed the makeup and bright red lipstick she had applied to her face and she returned his gaze with indifference. Her eyes widened in annoyance when she saw Farah coming in to stand in a corner of the room. She pointed at her and said, "Who's that?"

"She's my assistant. She's always with me when I examine women."

I said this clearly for the umda to hear. She seemed to be a petulant, spoiled girl, and I could not tell what was wrong with her just from looking at her. She turned sharply to her husband and said, "The doctor has taken everything into account. You can leave us now."

He was taken aback, but she stared hard at him. He gave her an angry look, hesitated a little, and then left the room, not forgetting to close the door behind him. She turned to us and said, "You're not going to examine me. My whole body hurts, but I'm not in real pain. You have to listen to me."

I hesitated. "I'm not a psychiatrist."

"There's nobody here but you?"

She got up off the bed and moved toward Farah, who still stood, frightened, in the corner of the room. "What I have to say is very private. You mustn't be here."

"She can't leave," I objected. "The umda is outside."

She grasped Farah's hand and pulled her firmly toward her. "Come with me."

She led her to the door of a side room that I had not noticed before, pushed her inside, and commanded: "Keep quiet."

She shut the door before Farah could say a word, turned the key, and faced me. I began to feel afraid. I didn't know if the umda was listening at the door, though I was sure he was capable of it. But she sat on the edge of the bed and said quietly, "I want some poison."

Trying not to gasp or show any sign of surprise, I said, "Do you plan to kill yourself?"

"That might be my next step. First, I'll try it on my husband the umda."

She seemed terrifyingly serious. "I'm just a general practitioner," I said. "I only have cures for fever and diarrhea."

"Isn't there anyone who can rescue me from this dreadful life?"

I remained silent. All I wanted was to get away from there. She went on, "I brought this on myself. I'm the third wife, as I expect you know. Neither of the first two walked out of here. He used them both up in this place, maybe on this bed."

"You don't look like you're from the village."

She shook her head. "Of course not. I came from the town. We were seven sisters, living in a small apartment, with one bathroom. You can imagine the crush for the bathroom every morning in that cramped place. All I wanted was a private bathroom to myself. Can you believe that was one of the main reasons I married this man?"

I had no idea where this conversation might lead us. "So, what's the problem? Instead of a small bathroom you have a whole house."

"This isn't my house and never will be. That man makes me ill: every touch spreads a sickness in my soul. My body's drying up."

Warily, I said, "How are your relations in bed?"

"Worse than you can think. I have a panic attack every time he comes near me."

She quickly began to unbutton her dress, to show her breasts plainly. They were covered in blisters and scratches. "Do you want to see the rest of my body? It's all like this, and this is all I get from him every night. Not to mention the endless frustration and craving. You must do something for me."

"You could ask for a divorce."

"If I dared to do that," she asserted, "I wouldn't leave here alive."

"I'll prescribe you something to ease the physical pain and some antibiotics."

"Is that it? Is that all you can do? Don't you care about this constantly deprived body?"

Now she was talking openly. I removed the stethoscope from my ears and took a step backward. She looked at me and went on. "It's the first time we've met but I've heard about you from the women who come to the house.

They whisper about all kinds of gossip—you can know everything about the secret world of the village from them. That's why I wanted to see you."

Suddenly, she stood up and grabbed hold of me. "Do something for me! Either give me poison or make me feel that I'm alive!"

I could feel her body shaking as she tried to cling to me. I slipped from her hands and moved away. "The examination is over."

I went to the locked side room and, as I heard her angry abuse, turned the key that was still in the door to find Farah directly behind it. I pulled her briskly by the hand and we walked across the room, taking no notice of the insults, which had become quite obscene. We saw the umda at the top of the stairs—far away, but there nevertheless, and he could have heard every word said in the room. He watched us go down the stairs, apparently not particularly concerned as he asked me what was wrong with her. I said, "Overexertion and strain."

Surprised, he exclaimed, "And where did all that come from?"

I stopped briefly to pull out my prescription pad and write a list of fortifiers, making sure they were all imported products and thus expensive. I hurried out with Farah at my side, while Desougi lingered behind to negotiate with the umda. We went down the steps and were soon alone outside the wall of the compound. I finally caught my breath and looked at Farah's face to find it pale. I said, "That's not a house, it's a lunatic asylum. A psychopathic umda and a nymphomaniac wife."

"The whole village is sick—and all these people are walking dead."

We set off together through the streets of the village. Although all eyes were on us, Farah walked on confidently, but once we were beyond the mass of houses and the barefoot children, she came a little closer to me and said quietly, though I heard her clearly, "If I hadn't been in the next room . . . would you have done it?"

I turned to her and our eyes met, but she couldn't hold the look for long. She pursed her lips, and her face reddened vehemently. I said, "How could I do anything when you're listening in on us and when the umda is standing at the top of the stairs ready to pounce? More importantly though, I don't like . . . that type of woman."

She stared into my eyes. Could she read what was in them? We went back to walking in silence—something had occurred between us that didn't need words. The world of mud houses ended and we found ourselves out in the open, with only the green fields stretching away around us. It was the season of berseem clover and the thin stalks swayed in the wind. Above us, some unfamiliar white birds flapped their wings. We thought they would fly far away, but one of them came down to the ground and stood with its long legs in the middle of a small patch of water and mud in front of the clinic that never dried up. It stretched out its neck and thrust its beak into the water. As she watched it, she said in a whisper, "The egret's hungry and it's searching for a worm in vain."

We were nearly at the clinic when she suddenly stopped. I stopped too and contemplated the red of her cheeks. Did she want to apologize for her question? She didn't, and instead surprised me by saying, "So, what type do you like?"

My mouth went dry. It was difficult to answer right away, I had to think before saying something I would be unable to take back. Finally, I said, "You should look at yourself in the mirror."

She stared at me uncomprehendingly, then the redness flushed her cheeks again. She swallowed with difficulty, and I too felt my mouth was dry. She lowered her head quickly and walked hurriedly to the Family Care room, shutting the door behind her. Should I go after her? Strike while the iron was hot or leave her to take in the shock of my confession? Perhaps she was just now looking in the mirror to be sure of what I had said. I stood watching the egret, which had despaired of finding any appropriate food, and was flying off. Desougi arrived and sighed with relief when he found me standing there. He said, "I barely got the consultation fee out of him, the tight-fisted man. He didn't want to pay anything. He wanted us to pay! He thinks we're his slaves and we should give him tribute."

He handed me a few banknotes, which I shoved into my pocket without counting them. I knew he had taken his share before giving the rest to me. Suddenly, from inside the clinic, women's screams arose. The sounds of a fierce quarrel. I rushed inside and Desougi followed. The three women were caught up in a violent row, their arms entangled, the braids of their hair coming loose. Each one of them was pulling at the locks of another and they were shouting insults and screaming. I intervened and barely managed to extricate Farah from their grasp—the internal cauldrons of their rage were boiling over. I pulled her forcefully to the examination room, her face covered in scratches, and went back to the others in a fury. I didn't want to know the reason for the fight, but old Atiyat screamed in my face, "Ever since you arrived here you've favored her over us!"

Aleya, more prudent, said, "In an important visit like that you should have taken one of us."

"I'm going to submit a complaint to the Health Directorate!" Atiyat yelled rashly.

She was talking nonsense, and she knew it. I remained calm and said, "I will suspend you both from work myself and refer you to the Directorate for investigation. We're not in the street here."

They instantly quietened down. Aleya picked up the thread of calm and said in reproof, "You must treat us fairly."

I scoffed. "I'm not your husband and you're not my wives. Go away now and there'll be more to say tomorrow."

I stood there, hand on hip, until both women had collected their things and left. I went back in to see Farah, while Desougi stood on the steps outside. She was still crying quietly, her head bowed, her hair disheveled, and her headscarf thrown on the floor. I hesitated a little, then put my hand to her head, stroking her hair in an attempt to return it to its natural state. She didn't resist or move her head away, instead surrendering to my touches. She calmed down and stopped sobbing. "I didn't do anything to them. The minute I came through the door they leapt on me for no reason."

I smiled. "No, it's the oldest reason in the world—the jealousy of women."

She raised her face to me, so I took my hand away from her. "Why?" she said. "They're older than me, they've been here longer, and they have more senior positions."

Instantly I said, "You're more beautiful."

She gasped and froze, as if my words had scorched her. She moved away until she was pressed against the wall. I felt I was unfairly harassing her, putting her in a position she didn't want to be in. She said, "I'm very late, I have to go."

The situation had changed to the extent that she no longer felt comfortable being alone with me. I said, "Not before you take what's yours."

She looked on in surprise as I took a note from my pocket and held it out to her. She shrank back even more and moved farther away from me. I said, "This is your share of the umda's wealth. Desougi wasn't going to leave without relieving him of some of his money."

At last, she smiled, but she refused to take it. I insisted and our fingers engaged until she finally gave in to my urging and took the money. Suddenly, she stood on tiptoes and touched her lips to my cheek, a light touch like the brush of a butterfly's wing, like a flash of light, like the dissolution of a cloud. I put my hand to my cheek in wonder and when I opened my eyes I found she was no longer in front of me. She gathered her things quickly and left the clinic. I stood, unable to move, then I walked slowly to stand beside Desougi, who was perched on the steps like an old hawk. I watched Farah's back as she slowly receded, trying to gain control of herself and keep her gait steady.

Before she reached the main street of the village, someone appeared out of the blue: a tall young man, thin as a stalk of sugarcane. She waited until he caught up with her. She walked on, and he walked with her. He was a step behind her, but they were together, so that the sun having descended from high in the sky made two long shadows of them that met at the end: two shadows with one head. I stared at them and Desougi's sharp eyes followed me. "Who's that?" I asked.

"That's Eissa," he said simply, "her husband."

I failed to hide my shock and I couldn't help shaking, it was such a surprise. "She's married?"

With a hidden note of derision, he said, "All this time beside you in the examination room and you didn't know she was married?"

I tried to conceal the effects of the blow. "She seemed too young to be married."

Desougi's tone was neutral. "We're in Upper Egypt, Doctor. He's her cousin, it's his duty to protect her."

I retreated quickly and went up to my rooms alone.

3

It didn't seem that The Fairest of Them All was about to show up. The passengers muttered as they assembled at the edge of the village and some were weary from waiting so long. They sat on the ground, leaning against the walls of the houses, unintentionally joining the line of the men looking for work who were always present at this spot. The waiting animals took their place to one side on their own: goats and newborn kids, rabbits in their palm-frond coops, geese peering with their long necks from reed baskets. I felt the morning dew damping my hair. The Fairest of Them All didn't appear and somebody said, "The bridge must be down."

I didn't know what this meant. I was holding my bag and standing stupidly among them. More than one person tried to explain the reason for the delay to me: the bus, before it came here, went around several other villages, crossing more than one damaged bridge over a number of canals and drainage ditches. Some of these bridges were well beyond their life expectancy, their floors full of holes that looked directly down at the muddy water, and most of the drivers were afraid of taking the risk, preferring to turn back without finishing their route and wait for the bridge to be repaired. Thus, the village became cut off, isolated from the rest of the world. Voices rose as they assured each other of the situation, which was a normal occurrence that happened every few weeks. Like a defeated army, they began gathering up the items they had brought with them ready to travel and retreated one after the other. Even the animals left, and I was surprised to find myself alone there, apart from the line of unemployed men sitting behind me.

I had turned my back on the clinic, giving myself a few days' holiday to go to Cairo. I had finally found the courage to return to the city I hated, but circumstances were denying me the journey. Should I go back to the clinic? When would I be able to leave again? I was alarmed at being cut off from the world—despite the fact that I had come here to escape from it, with a feeling of dashed hopes: confinement always tasted good. I left the line of the unemployed and headed for the clinic but found Desougi walking toward me: he had seized the opportunity to send all the employees home and close up. This made me feel guilty, like everything was hung around my neck. He was surprised to see me. "The Fairest of Them All didn't come, did she? It happens a lot. Please, sit at the clinic, Doctor. Let me arrange something."

Leaving me no opportunity to ask questions, he turned and walked away quickly. I took a few trudging paces. There was nowhere to sit but on the steps outside, and I sat there defeated. I wished he hadn't gone off before letting me into my quarters, my last refuge. The passing farmers gave me curious looks. Had I been in too much of a hurry in deciding to go away? Should I have taken things more slowly? The cold wind that blew up from the neighboring fields felt chillier by the minute: I started shivering and wished I could go inside and hide under my quilt. I heard a clamor approaching. It was Desougi on a motorcycle, riding behind someone from the village. They stopped right in front of me and Desougi jumped nimbly off, clenching the skirt of his galabiya in his teeth. "This bike will take you to town."

I didn't understand. I looked at him, at the motorbike, and at its rider. "Masoud will take you on the back," he explained, "and get you to town in half the time it would take the bus."

I looked on dubiously and Masoud interjected, "I know the way well, sir. Every day I take half the village to town and bring them back in the evening."

I was uncertain. I couldn't imagine that this was a reliable means of transport. "Isn't it dangerous? The road's full of pits and potholes."

"I know it like the back of my hand," he said confidently. "Come on, sir, don't hold me up, I'm giving you preference over the other customers."

In confirmation, Desougi added, "I told him to take care of you. He won't drive as crazily as he normally does, he'll get you there just as you please."

I didn't want to look like a coward in front of them, so I warned him, "You'll drive carefully."

He said, "Just do as I say and we'll arrive safely."

He was businesslike. After taking my bag and strapping it on the back of the motorbike, he sat on the seat and asked me to sit behind him. I was embarrassed to touch him, but it was clear that he had been expecting that—he was wearing a loose galabiya and allowed me to cling onto it. He set off promptly, leaving me no chance for second thoughts, and as soon as we were out of sight of Desougi and the clinic he took charge. "I'm sorry, but we have to hurry. With The Fairest of Them All out of action there are a lot of customers."

I barely suppressed my screams as the bike roared at full throttle, flying off without touching the ground. The tops of the palms disappeared, the green fields receded, and we passed by unknown villages and houses. A thin, sunken line of water appeared as we proceeded along the bank of a long canal into which any awkward move might pitch us. He followed tracks that were new to me, narrow and perilous, though always passable. The level of my terror only grew. We encountered no cars or buses, just other crazy motorbikes carrying people as terrified as I was. The wind, blowing cold and carrying the smell of manure, filled the driver's galabiya, inflating it like a balloon, and it was as though we really were flying. But we rose in the air only to quickly come down again, the tires sinking deep into the dirt ground. We were clouded in dust on all sides and there were times when we couldn't see a thing. It was no use screaming: the driver would return to the village later to tell of the cowardice of the clinic's doctor, so I just had to hold on until this nightmare was over. The bike made a great leap and I found we were on the asphalt road that led to the town. I couldn't believe he had made it here so fast. He said, "You're a special customer. I usually have two or three of the farmers on the back, but I'm doing this trip just for you."

He maintained his insane pace even after we reached the streets of the town—frightened people scattered in front of him and I heard the screams mixed with the curses. "We've gone past the bus stop and the train station," I pleaded.

"What do we want with them?" he replied confidently. "I'll take you to the Peugeot service taxis, they're faster."

Exhausted by all the bumps in the road, I capitulated. He stopped in front of a driver whose Peugeot seven-seater was covered in dents and I asked Masoud if he knew him.

"He's my brother."

"Is he as reckless as you?"

He laughed, revealing yellow teeth. "I'm the most sensible one in the family."

But sensible had no place here. The car zoomed off once it had filled up with passengers, weaving relentlessly along the highway between enormous trucks, allowing no one to overtake it, and swerving at speed around the buffaloes that lazily crossed the road while the driver continually gesticulated threateningly at everyone. I closed my eyes and tried to sleep and forget that I was traveling in this flying coffin, but I remained alert because the car's momentum exceeded the limit at which relaxation was possible. I asked the passenger next to me the name of the broad canal that we were traveling alongside. He said,

"That's the Ibrahimiya Canal" and the driver added dryly, "It's full of all kinds of cars." It was a bad joke that made me turn my head to concentrate on the monotonous landscape. Then I fell asleep.

I woke with my head resting on the shoulder of the passenger sitting beside me, who had borne it patiently, and found the lights of Cairo and the swarm of cars all around us. The air was hot, dust-laden, and replete with the smell of exhaust fumes. My lungs were full of dirt before I had even exited the service taxi station to find a cab to take me to my single room, which was as it had always been: cramped and dusty, a mess of books and dirty clothes, slogans written on the walls. I exhaled as I sat on my old bed. It was an uncomfortable room with bad memories, but it was all I had, and I had to spend the long night there. I didn't want to contact anybody, or see anybody, or think about anybody. I had not come to the city to run away from anything but was searching for things—old things that refused to be wiped from my memory.

I slept only a little. I went down to the street and got into the first taxi that came along, telling the driver, "Take me to the Citadel."

He gave me a vexed look, which was typical, and didn't bother to put the meter on, which was also typical. I sat in the back seat and looked out of the window to avoid talking with him. The city had changed, even though I had left it behind only a few months previously. This was the second time I had seen it changed, more crowded, uglier—when I was released from prison it was hostile;

now it seemed indifferent. The taxi left the modern city and entered the cramped neighborhoods that wrapped themselves around the Citadel. Old palaces, mosques, public water dispensaries. The choking ring that was felt only by those who had endured the experience of the prison in the heart of that rocky fortress. The taxi passed through the street between the two great mosques, and there was the Citadel, high and alone, the Muqattam Hills behind it blocking the horizon. I climbed out of the taxi at a set of worn limestone steps and began the ascent, this time on my own feet rather than in a prison wagon. I reached the inner courtyard of the Citadel, where high walls built of square blocks of rock surrounded me. The ground was covered with limestone paving too and it was as though I were moving in the midst of a mountain of stone and lime that had been shaped and rounded out and filled with mysterious passageways to become a fortress. I followed the signs to the awful place that had opened its doors made from sycomore wood to transform into a museum, having been a pit of every kind of human terror. At last, I stood in front of the arched stone entrance. For the first time, I learned the location of the prison: I had not seen it, even when I had entered it as a prisoner inside the dark, suffocating wagon. Thousands may have passed by here without knowing that behind this entrance lay a genuine section of hell. My heart quaked and I felt the cold that had begun to creep into my extremities. I stood there unable to take the few steps that would lead me inside: if I went in, I might not be able to leave. The guards of old were watchful, whether Mamluks or state security, they were always in place. They kept me hidden from the light of the sun and God alone knew when they would release me. I looked closely at the scratchings on the stone gateway. They must have been made by the prisoners of times past. When the prison wagon passed through this entrance there was nothing but darkness; even the small skylight in the vehicle's roof was covered by an iron grill. I was cast in a corner, under the eyes of three security agents, who prevented me from making any movement and never stopped beating me. When they raided my room, it was the middle of the night, their favorite time. There were many of them, both inside and outside the room, as if they had come to arrest the whole neighborhood, not just me. They threw my papers everywhere and shook out my books looking for any documents that might be hidden in them. The officer looked at me with contempt. "What do you do, boy?"

I wasn't a boy, I had just graduated from medical college. I said proudly, "I'm a doctor."

The officer shrugged his shoulders scornfully. "You're lying of course. Communists like you are all unemployed."

He signaled to the security agents to bring him a pile of books which he examined for documents. He held up a paper in his hand, his attention drawn to a stamp that he looked at with disgust. "What's this?"

"That's the seal of the Doctors' Syndicate. It's my license to practice the profession of medicine."

His fury was extreme, as though he thought I had said this to spite him. He held the document by its edges and enjoyed slowly tearing it up. "From now on, you have no profession. You'll honor us with your presence for the rest of your life."

He gestured to the agents and the police conscripts and they tore into me. The punches and kicks came from all directions and I was unable to either resist or return them. I couldn't even catch my breath. They dragged me down the stairs with my nightclothes over my face, my body hitting every step. I was the only prisoner on this occasion, as the iron wagon passed through the night. They took me out after hours of being thrown around, knocking into the wagon's metal sides. When they had closed the iron gate, more blows rained down on me, as well as abuse referencing my mother—"son of a" this, that, and the other. Still now I could feel the pain of those blows as I passed through the gate, even though I was walking in on my own two feet, and of my own free will. My feet were not bare as they were that first time, nor was my body bloody, beaten, and humiliated. I walked with my back straight, passing uncertainly by the guards who were there, expecting them to make some devious move, to lock the doors behind me. Until this moment I really didn't know why I had come to this place. Why had I voluntarily reentered the walls of this nightmare? What was behind this burning desire to see the cell I had been imprisoned in? I still knew my way to it and there was plenty of sun, reflecting off the glass fronts of the exhibition cases, behind which were models of the torture instruments used in the prison, lying there motionless and harmless. One was the whip that used to come down on my back to start the proceedings off; next to it the bastinado frame and the cudgel, and on another side the "torture bride," to which prisoners were strapped for lashing—all the tools of intimidation were to hand; fortunately, others were kept behind a glass screen, away from our bodies. Elsewhere there were newspaper clippings of the most notorious crimes that had shaken Egypt—naturally, my case was not among them. It would have been the height of triviality to publish it, despite the effect it had left on me. I walked along a narrow passageway on the first floor of the prison, which consisted of three floors, each floor containing four wings, each wing having ten cells. My cell was the second on the third wing. I couldn't stop myself peering into the first cell. Inside was the wax figure of a prisoner thrown on the floor. The cell was bare, without a single piece of furniture, no chair, no bed, not even a mattress. Succumbing totally, the effigy was as wretched as we all had been. I moved on to the neighboring cell and the trembling spirit of the prisoner that had been planted inside me awoke, the spirit that shivered at the footsteps of the guards in the middle of the night. I gripped the bars of the window and looked down at the tight space of the cell, which was all I had to move in for the longest months of my life. Unfulfilled yearnings and cravings, waiting for a visit that never came. Absolute isolation, unshared with anybody. Interrogation only made it more lonely: cryptic questions, fanciful accusations, meaningless trips between cell and interrogation room. And everything subject to the mood of the interrogator: sometimes he was so sympathetic that I thought he would release me the next day, but mostly he was angry, heaping all kinds of accusations on me, leaving me in despair and convinced he would not let me go until the end of my life. All this with no facts that I could deny or evidence I could refute. The real torture was the privation, the feeling of being alone in the universe, with no one to offer me a helping hand. A lost star in a vast galaxy, I could fall into a black hole without leaving any trace. I put my hands on the door of the cell and stared hard, as if I would discover myself still in there, and was surprised to find that the door shifted under the pressure of my touch. It opened wide with a loud creak: this was the sound that had killed me with fear, meaning that punishment was on its way. And although the door was thick and made of steel, it didn't shield me from the sounds that came in from outside: the screams of those being tortured to admit to things they hadn't done, the echoing howls of the lonely, hungry wolves in the cemeteries nearby. It was as though I had been transported to another world far from the sun, a cold, dark world. I walked into the cell—every couple of steps brought me to a halt at a solid wall. It was narrow and suffocating. How had I lived in it without it crushing my chest? I didn't stray far from the door: I was afraid it would be closed by evil forces and I wouldn't be able to get out. Had I left any trace of me behind? I searched the wall for dates, names, scratches, signs, attempts to hang onto hope. I went on looking for something related to me and, in spite of the darkness, I found some small letters carved in my handwriting: "Faten," her name, and next to that her birthday. In that miserable time, I had remembered her, even though she had not come to visit me. She wanted to but couldn't—that was the excuse I gave myself. But nobody else had visited me either and yet she was the only one I thought of. Behind me I heard a rough voice. "How did you get in there?"

I turned to face the speaker, a police officer, tall and broad, with the same domineering delivery they all had. I said, "The door was open and this is a museum, isn't it?"

"But it's a prison," he said brusquely, "and it will remain a prison until it's torn down."

He walked forward a little and took hold of the steel door. He moved it, saying, "If I close this door on you, can you guarantee it will open again?"

I looked at his face for the first time and I recognized him: he was one of the prison guards. His footsteps in the outer corridor alone were enough to evoke fear and if he opened the door in the middle of the night that meant the worst. In a subdued voice I said, "I was imprisoned here."

He stared at my face for a while. "I remember you. You're the skinny medical student."

I objected. "I wasn't a student; I was a doctor."

He waved his hand contemptuously. "Whatever you were. Since this museum opened, you all come here: ghosts emerging from their graves, politicals, organizers, saboteurs. They're nostalgic for the moments of pain. It's a shame this fine place has been misused and is now filled with the dead."

I protested. "We are not dead, and we are not ghosts."

"But you refuse to move with the times. You prefer to live in the past, however painful. I'm going to send a report to the authorities. They should shut this place down again, we don't need to resurrect the dead."

He stood aside to make way for me. "Please come out. I will not be responsible for you if I close this door."

The tone of his voice frightened me and I hurriedly left the cell. I stopped to watch him shut the door again carefully. He pointed his finger at me. "Don't come back here. Next time it will be closed, and perhaps it will be a prison once more."

I couldn't finish my visit—I realized I had only come to see this cell and as I went down the stone steps, I found the memory of Faten assailing me. I trembled as I told myself, "It's worth a try."

Up until now, I had had very little rest and I was still in traveling mode. There was no firm ground I could stand on or belong to. I wanted to search for a telephone to make the call that I had come to make, my last chance to escape from the trap of the clinic in the faraway village. I hurried down the steps. I didn't want to let hesitation sap my will. I went to the nearest cigarette kiosk. The old black telephone sat there silent, waiting for me in anticipation. I dialed the number as the kiosk owner watched the timer. It rang several times, as if in a vacuum, as if that other world no longer existed. Finally, I heard her voice. I was surprised that she knew who I was right away. She didn't ask where I had been all this time. Her voice was cold. Perhaps she was startled to hear me saying without elaboration, "I want to see you."

I heard the sound of her breath as she hurried to say, "We've seen each other enough. There's no point in meeting again."

I persisted. "Yes, there is. Come and find out for yourself."

She was silent for a moment before saying, "I thought we were finished."

"Perhaps there was a new beginning we didn't see."

Firmly she said, "I can't leave the house to meet you."

"Luckily, I know the way to your house. I can come and spare you the trouble of going out."

"Let's meet, then," she said quickly. "Just once, and for the last time."

I hadn't wanted to resort to making veiled threats. I knew I had made an unforgivable mistake, but I was desperate. I had made a difficult journey and come close to a grievous death. My future was at stake, and I had been caught off guard by that cold—not simply indifferent—response. Would I be able to change everything just from an uncertain meeting?

She was a fascinating, strange girl when we first met. In that neighborhood of middle-income families, it was striking to see a girl walking her dog at the same time and place every morning. The dog was always wearing a jacket the same color as the dress she wore; when she wore a blue dress, the dog wore a blue jacket—and likewise with red or green—even when the weather wasn't cold. It was arresting, this habit of making the dog a part of her, or like her. It was this that drew my attention, before I was drawn by her quiet, composed beauty. We continued to cross paths like this at the same time every morning, even if it was raining or foggy. It was quite natural to say "Good morning" to her, and even more normal for her to return my greeting, for us to stop for a moment and exchange small talk so that each became acquainted with the world of the other, for us to become connected, to make promises, to share a first kiss in secret, to wear silver rings, and to feel passion, desire, and hunger.

The café wasn't crowded when she finally turned up. Elegant, tall, she walked casually, as though she were not over an hour late. She stood at the door, hesitant to enter, but she caught my eye. We stared at each other for several moments, then she began to come toward me as her expression changed, becoming sterner. She sat directly opposite me. On the table was a half-full glass of lemon juice, which I had drunk for its bitter taste while I waited. "You're threatening me?" she said.

Her tone was as cold as a blade and I saw the end of the encounter from its first moments. "I wanted to see you," I implored. "It's been so many months since we last met."

"And nothing has changed."

"Everything has changed," I countered hotly. "The old world has been turned upside down and receded far away. The only thing left is my love for you."

She looked at me incredulously. Her hand stirred on the table, formed a fist, then relaxed. I noticed a mark on her ring finger, a white indentation that went around it. Had she been wearing a ring? Had she taken it off when she came to see me? I shook my head and she remained silent—she didn't feel the need to speak, didn't say she loved me, or she hated me. But, despite all the coldness in her voice and her remoteness, here she was sitting in front of me, in the very café that had heard our fervent words and seen our trembling fingers as they intertwined. I felt the rustling of our knees as they touched under the table. I said, "My circumstances are changed now. What separated us, my experience in prison, is a thing of the past. Now we can recover our relationship in a formal way."

"How?" she asked, astonished.

Quickly I said, "By marrying."

She burst out laughing, a loud, harsh, scornful laugh. Other people sitting in the café turned to stare. I felt embarrassed: this was her answer to my suggestion. I looked at her and she looked back at me defiantly. How had time circled around this far? How had pledges of love turned into derisive laughter? She said, "And you'd take me as a bride to that old room of yours?"

I tried to inject some warmth back into our conversation, which was moving toward a dead end. "I got my job back and I have my own place to live, above the medical center. And the salary has turned out to be quite good. We can marry there and stay for a few years until we can buy an apartment here in Cairo."

She was calm. "You mean you want to take us back to square zero—the square of unrealistic dreams."

Was I carrying a quiver of empty dreams, more than necessary and beyond belief? The waiter came and we ordered more lemon juice. She didn't get up and leave, at least she would stay and finish her drink. She said, "Can you guarantee that you won't go back to prison again?"

"I've learned the lesson well. I've left politics forever."

"But politics won't leave you. At any time, whether you've done anything or not, they'll be following you."

"I spent terrifying days in prison. I don't want them to come back."

She observed me for a little while and I thought she felt for me, but with genuine bitterness she said, "You still don't know what happened to us because of your arrest."

Startled, I said: "I never mentioned your name in any interrogation or even hinted at any relationship with you."

"But they knew about it, knew about me. They know everything. They didn't arrest me, but they didn't stop invading my life and my family's life. They were a true nightmare. They would arrive without warning, at any time, searching for nothing. I don't know exactly what they were looking for, but they never left empty-handed. One time they took a pile of books, including books that were precious to my father, and papers that had nothing to do with them. Another time they took the radio that my father used to listen to the Qur'an station on. And all through these oppressive visits they didn't stop questioning me. They asked endlessly about your name and the officer asked me countless questions about you, about your life, about your friends, the same questions, the same answers, without end, time after time, until my father became ill and I was shamed in front of my family."

In a choking voice I said, "I'm sorry. I didn't know."

"There are many things you don't know. I had to do something to keep my father well and to cover my disgrace."

She stopped speaking to hide her agitation. She took a sip from the glass of lemon juice, then busied herself opening her bag. She rummaged in it for a while before pulling out and holding up between her fingers a small ring for me to see. The café lights were reflected in its shiny surface, the illusive and glittering colors of a spectrum. She said, "I didn't want you to see it on my finger, but anyway you had to know."

My heart sank. "Are you really married?"

She put the ring on her finger and said, "Almost. I wanted to tell you, but there was no opportunity until you telephoned. Perhaps that's the reason I came to see you."

Paralyzed, unable to even begin to react, I said stupidly, "Do I know him?"

"Is that important? As my father says, . . . he's a groom who didn't turn me down. And he was also my last chance, before they raided our house again."

A thought suddenly struck me. "Is he one of them? A policeman?"

She pursed her lips and ignored the question. I said, "My God, he is one of them! Maybe even one of the ones who raided your house."

Again, she didn't respond. She turned away slightly, to gaze at the wall of the café, which was covered with foreign movie posters, full of images of false love, beautiful faces that had never experienced any kind of real loss. She said, "Everything's over now. I have to go."

She didn't wait for me to reply and then started to walk away. I wanted to grab her arm and force her to sit down, but I remained seated, numbed. I didn't leave the café for a while and then I walked the streets among the people and the cars, hearing nothing and seeing nothing. It was a city I no longer belonged to and I had to get away from it, fast.

4

After hours of grueling travel I found The Fairest of Them All at the bus station ready to depart. The village was no longer cut off as I had left it. There was no need to spend the night in a hotel in the town, I just had to climb aboard the bus until it started on its way. It was completely full of people and there were no animals—the town's market had swallowed them up, down to the last chicken. All the seats were taken and the aisle was crowded too. With difficulty, I managed to stand on one foot, but then one of the farmers got up from his seat and said clearly, "Please sit, Doctor."

Every head turned toward me and their voices rose with exhortations for me to take a seat. More than one person stood up, making space beside the window, squeezing themselves onto one seat to leave me a reasonable amount of room, and they pressed me until I agreed to sit down. I was no longer alone and abandoned as I had been a few hours ago. They talked a lot and I listened to their gripes and chatter as The Fairest of Them All bumped up and down with the potholes in the road. The wide canal that they call the Ocean appeared, and the palm groves, the fields of berseem clover, the piles of manure, and the huddled mud houses. Somebody brought out a box of halva and began passing it around and I realized that I was in need of something sweet after the bitterness of my trip. I laughed for perhaps the first time in days. My soul healed and my wounds eased and when the final cluster of palms came into view, I felt that I belonged to this place more than to any other. I said goodbye to them and disembarked, carrying my small bag and heading for the clinic. The smell of the village filled my nostrils. I passed by the crush of people and the houses to find myself in the clinic's empty forecourt. The door was open and a bony donkey was tethered to a stone, which was odd and worrying. I climbed the steps apprehensively and Desougi seemed to be waiting for me. He called, "You've come at the right time, Doctor."

It was as if he knew all my comings and goings. Next to the wall, on the floor, lay the withered body of a farmer, curled up and breathing with difficulty. Beside him was a woman dressed in black, equally emaciated, sitting silently with her hand on her cheek. Desougi said, "This patient came yesterday from one of the nearby hamlets and he's been lying here like this waiting for you."

"Do you mean he spent the night here, on the bare tiles?"

Desougi nodded. "He didn't have the energy to leave and go home and I couldn't throw him out."

I went over to him. His face was very jaundiced, and his lips were dry. His body was cold and sick. He had lost all ability to resist the death that was overtaking him.

Together, Desougi and I carried him to the examination room. He was almost in rigor. I took out my stethoscope quickly, putting my hand on his chest, and asked, "What's the matter with you?"

His wife came forward and broke her silence. "He won't be able to tell you what's wrong with him, sir, but just look at this . . ."

She presented me with a bottle, full to the brim. "This is a sample of his urine."

It was not urine, it was murky pus with strands of blood in it. The dark liquid of jaundice, as though his kidneys had disintegrated and turned into this awful mixture. I looked at his exhausted face, from which the disease had sucked all the lifeblood. I measured his pulse and listened to his heartbeat. His body had reached a stage of the illness that could exist only in Egypt. I didn't know what I could do. I hurried to the dispensary and took out all the medications that I thought might help: tinctures, pills, injections. I gave him an injection to bring down the fever and another one of penicillin and asked Desougi to go upstairs to my rooms and fetch some food for the two of them and make them some hot tea. The wife unknotted some old, crumpled money from the end of her headscarf, but I refused to take anything from her. I cautioned the man to take the injections and the medicines regularly and to come back and see me again in two weeks. We helped him go out. He was incapable of riding the donkey in the standard way, so we hoisted him up to lie across its back, his head and arms on one side, his legs on the other. His wife grasped the rope that led the animal and walked off slowly. I expected him to slip off the donkey at any moment, but his body continued to swing until he was out of sight.

I went up to my rooms and realized how exhausted I was. I had not had enough sleep to make up for the frustrations I had faced, and I wasn't sure I could ever make that trip again, or even whether there had been any point to it. It seemed like a journey to a strange world, another planet that I was no longer capable of living on. I threw myself down fully clothed and sank into a sleep devoid of dreams, without the need for any artificial relaxant. I woke with the first light of dawn and watched the morning procession to the fields, filling my lungs with the air they were breathing. For my breakfast I ate the remains of the food in the fridge—it was almost spoiled. Only the glass of tea saved me.

When I entered the examination room Farah was there, smiling at me in welcome. I ignored her smile, putting on a serious face as I received the line of patients. I immersed myself in their problems and the symptoms of their irremediable illnesses. Farah was standing to my right, then she moved to my left, but still I didn't see her. I avoided her shining eyes and her pale face and I didn't ask her for anything or enter into conversation with her. I almost replaced her with another assistant, but when I saw the faces of the two brawly nurses, I changed my mind. It was difficult to do anything in front of the succession of patients, who had all put up with their ailments during the time I was away. At some point, she grabbed the sleeve of my coat, or failed to hand me the stethoscope, but I was determined not to see her. My rage at her had not abated. Finally, the long line ended, and she made a show of tidying the papers before going with me to the dispensary and for a few moments she and I were alone in the examination room, away from everyone else. She stood in front of me as I went to go out and said quietly, "What's happened? Are you angry with me?"

Exasperated, I said, "Why didn't you tell me you were married?"

"You didn't ask," she said. "And I didn't lie."

I had to leave her to go and give out the medications. I read the prescriptions and fulfilled them absentmindedly. There was always a husband somewhere, and a woman concealing a secret. I was almost finished when there was a knock at the door. It must be her, and she must have chosen this inappropriate time to explain things. I dealt with the remaining patients before lazily opening the door. It was not her. It was somebody else, wearing a white galabiya under a yellowish coat, clean-shaven, with a trimmed mustache. He opened his mouth in a broad grin and said, "I've brought the new coat."

Farah was not in the examination room, and apparently had left in a hurry. But the white coat had been placed on the desk, ironed and folded. Abanoub picked it up and presented it to me, smiling. "I hope it's the right size."

I had not thought he was serious and would keep his promise. I looked at him uncertainly, but he opened the coat out in front of me, and I saw the letters of my name embroidered in blue thread on the pocket. It was elegant and gleaming. I touched the material admiringly. Abanoub insisted I try it on. I didn't know how he had managed to sew it to my size with such precision. I felt I looked good in it, though there was no mirror in the room. I smiled and said, "I like the coat, but I must pay for it."

He smiled. "It didn't cost me anything except the price of the material and that was very cheap. The important thing is winning your friendship."

"I am a doctor for all, and perhaps I can be a friend of all too, . . . but I can't accept anything for nothing."

He sat in front of me in silence. I knew right away that he wanted something but was hesitant to ask. I really did like the coat, and I had no intention of taking it off. It only remained to know what he had in mind. "I don't think you're sick, Abanoub. Is it your wife?"

He answered haltingly. "I've never married and it doesn't look as if I ever will. I'm a Copt, an only child, and I don't have any family. My parents died when I was young and there's no Coptic family willing to marry their daughter to a solitary tailor like me."

I didn't understand a thing and I didn't know why he was telling me his life story. I tried to find words to express my sympathy for him, but my patience ran out, and I said, "I don't understand what you want from me."

He paused, then said, "There is a woman who is sick. She's getting worse by the day and she needs your help."

"I don't see any problem. She can come to the clinic in the morning or in the afternoon and I will conduct a complete examination."

He hurried to say, "She did come to you. Perhaps the circumstances weren't the most favorable for seeing her properly."

"I don't recall her. What was she complaining of?"

He was still reluctant to speak, and silence took over between us. Then, he came to a decision and said, "She was pregnant and her husband died a year and a half ago. . . . She was in a real dilemma."

I remembered her at once, and how she pleaded with me for a solution, her craving for a medication that would help her to bleed and empty her belly of the fruit of an error. I said, "What's her name?"

He yielded. "Jalila."

I didn't need to know more. I remembered that I had seen him following her at a distance, that I had asked her if she could marry the man she had indulged herself with, and that she had said it was impossible. I looked at him closely. "It was you, wasn't it?"

He lowered his head. "I'm ready to do anything for her. I offered to convert to Islam, but that's pointless—her family wouldn't accept me, nor would the rest of the village."

I was annoyed with her and with him and with the whole community. "And so you left her to her fate."

His body shook as he wept and he begged me, "Please, go to her. She's unable to walk and can't come to the clinic."

His tears had moved me, but I was at a loss. "How can I go when I don't know her house and you won't be able to guide me there?"

Quickly, and as though he had prepared his answer in advance, he said, "Isn't Farah a nurse here? You only have to ask her about the address and she'll take you."

He left hurriedly, turning his face away so that Desougi didn't see his tears. I stayed on alone, wearing the new coat. This good-looking young tailor was living his own private tragedy, sentenced to solitude. He had sown his seed in the belly of a stranger, and this could lead to him being killed, and her too, if the story came out. His image remained with me as I went upstairs and threw myself on the bed. I could have taken off the coat and forgotten all about him, but in the morning the matter still troubled me. Farah came in early, but she was distant. She didn't know whether I wanted her in the examination room or not, but I couldn't imagine being with one of the other nurses, so I indicated that she should accompany me and I won a small smile from her. After seeing a few patients, I found the opportunity to say to her, "When the morning session's over, you'll take me to visit a patient in the village, Madame Jalila."

She looked at me in surprise. "Which Jalila do you mean? The wife of al-Mansouri, the trader who died?"

"I don't know her husband's name, but yes, she is a widow. She came to the clinic once before."

"How did you know she's ill?"

I didn't elaborate. "She sent someone."

We went back to examining patients. The clinic wasn't busy and we finished at a reasonable time. I prepared my medical bag as Desougi watched me, curious and expecting to accompany us. But I asked him to stay behind at the clinic—Farah and I would go alone. We went out and she began showing me the way. She said, "Her house is a bit far. It's bigger than the rest of the houses in the village, one of the few that's built of red brick."

We walked on, eyes watching us as expected, but no one spoke. When the way narrowed and we were closer to each other, I found myself asking her out of the blue, "Where is your husband?"

She was flustered for a few moments and the red blush appeared on her face. "Somewhere around here. Maybe he can see us now, but he doesn't interfere in my work."

I felt myself becoming more aggressive. "Do you have children?"

She shook her head. I went on with my questions. "When I first saw you, I didn't imagine you were married, you seemed too young. How long have you been married?"

She didn't speak for a while, then said, "Two years. He's my cousin. We marry young here and grow up together."

A little derisively I said, "Is there no divorce?"

"There is death."

The road broadened ahead of us and we had to walk farther apart. We crossed over a dirty drainage ditch and now the contiguous mud houses came to an end, houses of red brick standing separately among the crops instead. We noticed there were men stationed sporadically along the road. They wore dark clothes, with black scarves around their heads that almost obscured their faces. They watched us pass by, not one of them moving.

In a quiet voice, Farah said, "They frighten me. Their eyes are full of evil."

She didn't tell me who they were, perhaps afraid they would hear us, but we continued walking until we reached the first house. She knocked and nobody answered. I came forward and knocked harder, still with no result. She looked at me. "Should we go back?"

"She's expecting us. Does she live alone? Is there no servant in the house?"

I don't know what I was thinking but I pushed at the door and it yielded and opened wide. I said to Farah, "Perhaps she left it open for us."

I asked her to go inside; she hesitated, and I pushed her in gently. She stood in the hall and called out to Jalila quietly and uncertainly, then raised her voice, and the echo rang around the walls. I caught a glimpse of the sumptuously furnished interior; signs of wealth and comfortable living. Farah turned in a circle and finally signaled to me to go in. When I joined her, we both heard a feeble moan coming from one of the rooms, as if alerting us to its location. Farah went ahead and pushed open the door of the room. I followed in the dark and the sound of the moaning grew louder. There was an oppressive smell, putrid air full of the stink of illness, sweat, and spoiled food. The room was empty of all furniture except for a mattress on the floor, on which lay a black, groaning bundle. Farah knelt down next to it, pushing away the remains of the food scattered around. She pulled back the black wrap to reveal the face of Madame Jalila as I had not seen it before, pale yellow and covered in sweat. She was breathing heavily and looking at us with fixed, unseeing eyes. Farah put her hand on her brow and cried out in alarm, "She's burning up!" I sat beside her to measure her racing pulse and listen to the rapid palpitations of her heart. I exclaimed to Farah, "We have to bring down her temperature immediately."

As a professional nurse, Farah knew what she had to do. She quickly brought cold water to bathe Jalila's face and extremities and prepared the necessary compresses, while I hurried to give her an injection to bring the fever down. Her blood pressure was low and her heart was weak and she seemed to be falling into shock, which could kill her. I didn't know how she had sunk into this state. How could she have left the rest of that spacious house to crawl into this cramped little corner? Was she running away, or seeking protection? And why was she so totally alone? Had she gone ahead and had an abortion? And were these the symptoms of puerperal fever? She needed sulfonamide tablets and I had not brought any with me. In my mind I went over the conversation we had had in the clinic and what Abanoub had said about her doing something serious. She must have found out where the old woman was and gone to see her. I inspected the mattress she was lying on: it was wet and covered with blood stains and it gave off a rank smell. She must have chosen to lie on this isolated mattress so that she could throw it away later. I said to Farah, "I want to examine her genital region."

She gasped. "What? She has to give us permission first. You know it's a private area."

"I know. I'm aware of her condition and I know what's wrong with her. I have to see if she's hemorrhaging internally."

She wasn't sure. "Can't we wait until she's conscious?"

"We could wait, but she could also die before she revives."

She went on staring at me. I didn't want to reach out and remove the woman's clothes myself, she had to help me with that. She closed her eyes as if reevaluating the situation, then opened them and stretched out her fingers to pull down the cover, revealing a blue plush dress, crumpled, clinging, and spotted with dark stains. I gestured to Farah without speaking and she slowly and hesitantly pulled the dress back, exposing the woman's thighs, then lifting it higher. She was not wearing underwear, but her private parts were not visible: the whole area was covered in a great patch of congealed blood. Farah gasped. "Oh my Lord! What's all this bleeding? And how did you know there was something like this?"

"We have to clean her well. She may still be hemorrhaging."

Farah stood up, having regained the courage to move around once she knew the house was empty. She came back carrying a large washing tub of water and some towels. Slowly, we began to remove the accumulated clots together. We leaned over her, cleaning this area as if we were preparing a channel for life to enter her body. It was clear she had found the old woman who rescues village women from their problems and keeps their secrets, but it was also clear that the old woman had not been gentle with her. White appeared at the top of her thighs, then her pubic hair, trimmed and cared for. We continued to clean away the clots until her vagina showed clearly: it was swollen and flushed and full of coagulated blood. There was hemorrhaging, but had it stopped? I looked at Farah inquiringly, but she was still in shock, operating mechanically as if she was unaware of what she was doing. When she saw me staring at the vagina, she grabbed my arm as if to warn me. Her face was pale as she said, "Let's leave her alone. Her body is a wreck and she might accuse us of something."

I freed my arm from her grip, spread the palm of my hand, placed it on the woman's naked belly, and pushed down. I pushed hard while watching the opening of the vagina. Nothing came out and I sighed with relief. The hemorrhaging, the main danger, had stopped. I heard her weakened voice saying, "What are you doing to me?"

Farah jumped back in alarm and pressed herself against the wall. I looked at the woman's face: her eyes were fixed on me and she was startled and unable to move. I quickly covered her up to reduce her embarrassment. She said, "Are you trying to rape me?" I shook my head and smiled reassuringly at her. She looked at me as she tried to regain full consciousness. "You're the doctor. He sent you, didn't he?"

"Your condition is serious. You've lost a lot of blood and you probably have an infection in your womb. You need to be transferred to a hospital."

"What can I do?" she said weakly. "You know I can't. My fate is determined and written."

She was silent for a while as she caught her breath. "My husband's family are watching me. If they suspect what happened, they could kill me."

I couldn't hold back. "Why would they treat you so violently? Why are you so afraid of them?"

"Since my husband died, they've been trying to get their hands on my house and my money. They believe my inheritance is theirs by natural right. So, they're waiting for any slip, . . . waiting for me to fall."

She stopped speaking, exhausted. She turned her head to look around her, perhaps to be sure there was nobody but me, but she shrieked in alarm when she found that Farah was there in the corner of the room. She tried to get up but fell back strengthless. She looked at me as though I had deceived her. I said, "It's all right, she's my assistant, a nurse at the clinic."

Her terror didn't abate. "But she's from the village, she'll expose me."

Farah crawled closer to the woman and said, "I won't say a single word. It's my job to guard the secrets of every patient."

She wasn't convinced. I said, "What matters is that you're not well. Your treatment is beyond my capability. You need a blood transfusion and an intravenous drip, and you need care night and day."

She muttered feebly, "They'll kill me."

Her eyes closed for a while. On each occasion with this woman, I stood powerless in front of her. Her life was suspended by a delicate thread, and I couldn't preserve that thread if she resisted. Was her fear of them greater than her desire for life? There was no use in discussing it with her, she might die before I could convince her. I stood up, ready to leave. I had said everything I had to say. But in a sudden move she reached out to take hold of Farah's hand and pleaded, "Please . . . don't leave me."

Farah turned to me in confusion. The woman was dragging us into her personal life, making us a part of the tragedy she had created. I said to her, "That's impossible. She's a government employee; she doesn't work in private houses."

She was panting and trying to catch her breath. "Don't you see I'm dying? They're out to kill me."

She turned her head away from us and closed her eyes. I knew her temperature had gone down. I measured her pulse and heartbeat: the danger of coma had receded a little. Everything was more or less normal, but weak. Farah looked at me and asked quietly, "Are we leaving?"

"We have to. We've stayed here longer than we should have."

I collected my instruments, and she packed the box of dressings. We could hear the woman breathing regularly and quietly. We walked slowly out of the room and passed through the empty house, which was dark, like a vast tomb, watched over from somewhere by the angels of death. Before we reached the outer door, Farah stopped me. "I'll come to her. I'll give her the medicine, and I might be able to bring her some food."

"You don't have to do that. It's her that's refusing to go to the hospital."

"She's not an animal. She's a soul of God's creation, and we must help her to keep living."

I put out my hand to touch a finger to her cheek, feeling a surprising kind of gratitude toward her. It was a grim and difficult situation and she had automatically done the right thing. She took hold of my finger and gently removed it, but the feel of her skin stayed with me. We left the strange house and when we reached the old drainage ditch, she stepped away a little, saying, "I'll go home this way. No need for the villagers to see us going back together."

She hurried away, hugging the box of dressings, crossed the bridge, and disappeared in the maze of houses.

When I arrived at the clinic, I found Abanoub standing at a distance waiting for me. He came up to me quickly and I indicated he should follow me into the examination room. Desougi watched us, almost dying of curiosity. I closed the door firmly and looked into Abanoub's frightened face, the face of a desperate lover without the means to defend his love. I whispered, "Let's not mention her name at all."

He nodded in agreement and I went on, "As I told her, her condition is very serious. She needs a blood transfusion and an intravenous drip, and she should be in a hospital." He was on the verge of tears. "I offered to hire a car to take her by night to the town, but she refused."

"Even taking her in an ordinary car could start the bleeding again and it might kill her."

"What can we do?"

There was nothing to do but wait for a miracle. That is the solution in Egypt when it's a matter of life and death. I wrote him a list of the medications she needed: sulfonamide, antibiotics, fortifiers, and multivitamins. "I don't have these things. You'll have to go to the town and get them quickly: we may be able to go some way to saving her and I'll find a way of getting them to her."

"Can I go and see her?"

"Of course . . . if you're thinking of suicide."

He put his hand into his pocket and pulled out a number of banknotes, saying: "I don't know how to thank you."

"Keep that to buy the medications—I need them fast."

He set off running for the bus stop.

The next day when I came down to the examination room, I found a bag with the medications I'd requested. "The tailor brought these early this morning," said Desougi. "What's going on? Why did you send him to buy them, not me?"

I didn't reply, but his objection made me realize that the woman's secret was still safe. Farah came a little late, panting, her face flushed. I talked with her at the back of the examination room. In a hushed voice she said, "She's still alive. Her temperature was up, so I gave her another injection."

"Any fresh hemorrhaging?"

"I don't think so. I didn't check. But she's very weak and she didn't eat anything."

I gave her the bag of medications and said I would write down for her how to use each one.

"I'll do it. But you have to know that the house is being watched: there are men watching me come and go."

I had felt that on our first visit and my concern grew, but we could not abandon her now. I told Farah to take the medications to her and I would deal with the patients at the clinic on my own. I talked with Farah under their eyes, though far from their ears, as if we were weaving the threads of our own little conspiracy. I was setting aside the shock of discovering she was married and was contenting myself with the fact that she was a good soul, with her readiness to help and to put others first. I watched her as she took the bag and walked out of the clinic. Under the gaze of the men observing that house she was treating a woman who had had an abortion, was convalescing, and was facing death at any moment, but with little discussion she was doing what she had to do, motivated by an innate sense of generosity. Atiyat came up to me and asked angrily, "Where are you letting her go off to?"

I held myself back from blowing up in her face. "That's not your business and you can send a complaint to the Directorate if you like."

She went away vexed and I got on with seeing the patients alone as Desougi too gave me perplexed looks. I noticed Abanoub's face outside the clinic, appearing and disappearing behind the faces of the patients, and I signaled to him that all was as well as could be expected.

My own state of nervous tension endured and I wanted to go and take another look at her, but at the same time I didn't want to attract attention to her condition and had to be satisfied with the reports Farah gave me every morning. Her body was responding to the antibiotics and her temperature had dropped. After a few days she was able to move around and she was asking for food. Farah smiled one morning when she told me that she had taken a bath by herself and washed away whatever discharge, congealed blood, and other signs of illness were left on her, that her body, while still lacking vigor, was building up resistance, and that she wanted to see me to thank me herself. I didn't want to be rash and expose her to more conjecture, but I felt she needed another visit, at least so that I could see her standing on her own feet.

But it was a visit I wasn't able to make, because it was a strange morning, filled with a mysterious clamor that reached us from inside the village. We looked at each other questioningly. The sounds were out of place in the quiet village morning; perhaps there was a violent altercation for some reason or other. But the patients at the clinic couldn't wait to find out and started slipping away before I had examined them. Confused and not knowing what was happening, I looked at Farah. Desougi couldn't control his inquisitiveness, leaving without my permission, and going into the village. All work stopped at the clinic, as the noise came closer to us, and the patients left one after the other. I stood at the door, Farah standing near me, and we looked at the main road leading from the village. The fronds of the palms swayed and the birds broke off their circling and flew away. Then, they all appeared: a greater jumble of people than I could have imagined—they must have been hidden away inside the houses or maybe even down in burrows I knew nothing about. Barefoot children collecting stones from the dust, women screaming, some with their hair loose, and men running backward and forward holding sticks, or carrying mattocks, or picking up rocks. The throng pushed on until it reached the open space in front of the clinic and still I understood nothing. A revolution? An uprising? Then, everything became clear. In the midst of these rings of storming humanity there appeared a person riding a donkey, the only one riding among all the others on foot. He was riding backward, his face toward the tail of the donkey and his back to its head. They surrounded him, screaming at him and hitting him with sticks, or throwing mud and stones at him. Finally, I was able to recognize the face of Abanoub the tailor, humiliated, beaten, his head cracked. An entire village pouring out its wrath on the head of a single person, piling all its sins on him, screaming with all their might, "Infidel! Infidel!"—as if they had discovered for the first time that he belonged to a different faith. I moved in his direction, wanting to intervene and rescue him, but Farah grabbed my arm and shouted, "Don't interfere! They're enraged and won't distinguish between him and anybody standing by him." I stood frozen. I didn't understand what was behind this tempestuous fury. Desougi returned panting and said, as though establishing a truth of the universe, "They caught them together!"

I said, "Make sense! What's behind this fight?"

He pointed to Abanoub. "They saw him go into the house of Madame Jalila and they broke in after them. They say he was violating her."

I looked at Farah as the mass excitement increased. They reached out, trying to pull him off the donkey. If they had managed to do so they would have torn him to shreds, but a strange figure stepped in, a diminutive person who couldn't see what was under his feet, stumbling and almost falling. Farah called out, "It's Sheikh Abdel Barr, the sheikh of the mosque!" He stood in front of them holding his arms high in the air, shouting, "Stop! He's a dhimmi, a protected person, one of the People of the Book!" Nobody took any notice.

But a bearded youth—who may have been the one I had treated for the scorpion sting—came from nowhere and yelled, "He's a licentious Copt who violated the sanctity of Muslim womanhood!"

They all became even more worked up. The umda was not to be seen, nor any of the village guards. Sheikh Abdel Barr stumbled, fell, got up, and shouted, "Let him go! Let him go!"

In spite of the agitation and the excitement, some of the young men succeeded in pulling the donkey away to the road that led outside the village, hitting it on its rump so that the animal quickened its pace a little, and freed itself from their crushing mass. The donkey fled running, but Abanoub still faced the mob, and they threw mud and rocks at him and didn't stop chasing him until he reached the village boundary and turned toward the cemetery. They left him to disappear from sight. Sheikh Abdel Barr fell to the ground from all the effort. They carried him across the square to me, as he struggled to breathe, and laid him on the examination table. I asked them all to leave: the place was too crowded. I turned to the sheikh. His face was still flushed but his breathing had eased. I listened to his heartbeat and his rapid pulse. "Did you see what happened today because of Madame Jalila?" he scoffed. I said, "Yes."

He shook his head as he whispered, "They defended her honor more than she did herself."

5

Before the morning mist dispersed, I stood on the balcony watching their early parade to the fields, which always impressed me despite its daily occurrence. The tresses of the palms swayed softly, and the white birds shook off the dew from their wings. Sounds echoed from far away, perhaps the lowing of a cow, or the faint barking of dogs. But nothing disturbed this clarity and the gentle peace that accompanied the rising of the sun. Where had the cries of savagery gone that had rung out the day before? How had they lowered their voices and their heads and changed their masks so quickly? They had stripped off the mask of naivety, then the mask of entreaty, then the mask of violence, before returning to the mask of meekness. Was it possible that Farah was one of them, able to change masks so easily?

When I went downstairs, I found the clinic crowded with the sick. Their faces had recovered their old features, with their former suffering and still their insistent pleading. Farah was late, but I didn't ask about her, and I began seeing patients without her and without requesting help from the other nurses. Weak and feeble patients as usual, without the strength to cry out or object. When I had finished with half of them, she came in, out of breath. I thought, How did you dare to go there after the events of yesterday? When the current patient left the room, she said, “I wanted to see her and to find out what really happened.”

“And what did really happen?”

“She’s as she was. Getting better slowly. Her one mistake was to contact Abanoub. I don’t know how, perhaps via one of the servants, and it must have been her who gave her away. She just wanted to see him and be sure he was all right.”

“What did they do with her?”

“Nothing at all. But they burned down the tailor’s shop with all the cloth that was in it. If he’d been inside, they would have burned him too.”

Surprised, I asked, “Are they ignoring what happened? Have they forgiven her?”

“Here, nobody forgets, and nobody forgives.”

I began dispensing the medications, reading the patients’ faces behind the window. Had they been part of the raging throng? I didn’t think the medicines would be enough for them or contribute to their cure—they were a lost cause. I heard a loud knock on the door and Desougi said quickly, “There’s someone from the Health Directorate who wants to meet you. He’s waiting for you in the examination room.”

An unexpected visit. I hadn’t officially taken that holiday—had someone reported my absence from the clinic? I finished dealing with the rest of the prescriptions and went to see him. A middle-aged man sat waiting for me; the vehicle he had come in was a small delivery truck, parked in front of the door. He didn't seem to be a senior official. He gave me a bundle of papers, asked me to sign them, and gave me copies. I leafed through them quickly: a new project to trial a treatment for bilharzia, the curse that had made its home in the land of Egypt for thousands of years and was not inclined to leave. I walked with the man to the truck and Desougi followed. He handed us two large tins containing the new bilharzia pills and a medium-sized wooden box that the man himself carried in and placed in front of me on my desk. He made me sign another pile of papers, and I looked at the box dubiously. "What is it?"

Excitedly, he said, "A microscope! You won't be able to discover the presence of parasite eggs without it. You know that, of course."

When everybody had gone, I sat down to study the papers and scientific booklets the man had left behind. The medicine came from Germany—naturally, we didn't know how to treat ourselves. It was a magic dose to be taken just once orally and the patient would be rid of that wretchedness, their body expelling the bloodthirsty worm. It was successful where every other medication in history had failed, a miracle that we were in urgent need of. The man who first discovered the disease and gave it his name was a German, and it was another German who would help us overcome it—and between the two, we had paid an enormous price with our livers. I went upstairs but I couldn't sleep, so I reread the information then went down to the ground floor again and took out the microscope, adjusting it and organizing the as yet clear slides and counting up the pills in the tins, the number of doses, and the number of patients that could be cured. My mind eased a little when I made the decision that we must begin with the children. We could save this generation that had not yet enjoyed its share of life but was paying the cost of its inheritance with its blood.

I woke early in the morning, despite having stayed up late, and found myself eager to make a start. I asked Desougi to hire a donkey to be with us the whole day tomorrow, and I would send a quick letter to the school principal informing him that we would be coming to examine the pupils. The two other nurses took no notice of my enthusiasm: they had seen any number of health campaigns and knew what they resulted in, but Farah followed wide-eyed. She came close and said quietly, "Can I go to the school with you?"

She was looking at me with her shy, blushing face, and perhaps she was hoping that nobody but me had heard her. We had not spoken since the previous morning. I felt that I had come to depend on her more than I should—and there was the possibility that she might become ensnared in the same mishap as Madame Jalila. But here she was coming back again to stand beside me. I looked at the two nurses and I couldn't imagine myself walking alongside either one of them, so all I could do was to nod in agreement.

The school was situated outside the village, on salty land that was no good for cultivation, and the way to it was quite far, passing through fields thick with maize: this was the crop most dreaded by country folk, because any murderer could lie in wait for his victim among the tall stalks and kill them in cold blood, and because any fire that started in it could spread and burn down entire villages. Our expedition began first thing in the morning. Desougi led the donkey at the front, with the microscope and its accoutrements in one panier and the two large tins of pills in the other—three pills were enough to save a young soul from the clutches of the bilharzia worms. Farah walked beside me. We didn't touch, even purely by accident, and when at one point she stumbled, I kept my distance. I watched her as she regained her balance and we carried on walking. The morning breeze passed through the thick leaves of the maize, producing cryptic mutterings that caused a person to shudder. I heard Farah's voice talking, and at first I thought she was talking to herself, but when I moved a little closer I could hear her almost whispering, "He's my cousin and I had no choice but to marry him. It was all arranged, even before I was born. There was no young man who would dare to ask for my hand and my cousin wouldn't risk looking at another girl. Nothing could change the established agreement between the two families."

She paused to breathe. I tried to say something but couldn't. She swallowed and went on quietly. "Eissa—perhaps you know that's his name—dropped out of school after the primary stage, while I continued up until nursing school, but this made no difference. And even when he couldn't find a permanent job and he turned to seasonal work as and when it came to make a living, that changed nothing either. He was still my cousin, and I was still his wife."

I sensed she was on the verge of tears. I wished I could hold her hand, but Desougi and the donkey were in front of us, and either one of them could have turned around at any moment. I said, "You don't have to explain anything. We work together because you're a very efficient nurse and that has nothing to do with your family life."

She looked at me in surprise. "So why did you get angry when you found out I was married?"

In Heaven's name, what could I say to her?

The school wall appeared ahead, as if it had materialized from out of nowhere. The janitor opened the gate to let us in and hurried to notify the principal. I was amazed to see this number of children—boys and girls, dashing about and yelling in excitement—and I knew at once that my decision was the right one, because the school was there to serve more than one village. To reach it, the children crossed dangerous fields, unsurfaced roads, and bridges full of cracks and holes. They all came to this isolated school to learn and they had a right to receive treatment and save their young flesh from being weakened by blood loss. The principal came out to welcome us, embracing me, and crying out, "Are you really going to stop them urinating blood? It's a terrible thing. Every day when we clean the bathrooms we find blood everywhere. They don't stop bleeding, Doctor."

I pointed to the two tins I was holding. "I have a new medicine. I hope it will be efficacious."

He put his hand on my shoulder, seemingly to walk me to his office. He said, "They're naughty children. They skip school, they don't pay the simple fees, and they tear the books to pieces. But even so, I feel sorry for them. Their parents are poor and miserable. They wake them up in the morning and make them walk long distances on these dangerous paths to come here and learn something, and we don't even provide them with a meal."

He was still pulling me to go upstairs with him, but I stopped and worked myself free. I said apologetically, "We have work to do."

He objected. "Don't you want to sit and at least have a glass of tea?"

"Your hospitality is appreciated, but first we must put a stop to all this blood loss."

Farah knew very well what to do. She set up a table in the schoolyard and put the microscope and the two tins of pills on it. Then she stood the pupils in two lines, one behind the other. They took the cups and came back with their urine samples—the whole place smelled of urea. I took a few drops of each sample and put them under the lens and was immediately struck by the sight of the eggs with their attached spike—clear, sharp, and shocking—wriggling against the background of the pale urine. By means of this spike, the egg implants itself in the internal tissues and penetrates these children's bodies, making them bleed. I looked into the face of the child in front of me. Giggling and twisting his head in embarrassment, he told me about swimming regularly in the water channels and was astonished by my warnings not to. He pointed to his classmates and said they all swam in the water. The little egg with the pointed tip was immersed deep inside the bodies of all of them. The samples shivered under the lens—or was it me that was trembling? The children came one after the other and the eggs varied slightly in size but were always present, secure and comfortable as they carried out their destructive work through year after year. I gave them the pills, hopeful of breaking this hellish cycle. What was the anti-bilharzia team that was working with me at the clinic doing? Where did they go with the snail poison that they went out with every morning? I didn't need to continue testing: I had gone through more than half the children and they were all infected, and as the accompanying instructions said, I must give the pills to all of them. And perhaps I ought to give them to the principal and the other teachers as well. It was a draining and depressing day. I felt like the smell of urine was emanating from my own body. I couldn't drink the tea that the janitor brought me and when the principal asked me how things were going, I immediately said, "Worse than I expected. I've finished with half the pupils and I'll come back tomorrow to treat the rest."

We retreated with our donkey, the remnants of a defeated army. In wonder, I asked myself how we had been able to live all these years while hemorrhaging all that blood. We walked on along the path through the maize and I heard Farah saying, "Every day I dream of having a child of my own, but after what I've seen today I've begun to feel really afraid."

"It's not fated that your child should suffer from this disease."

She said, "It looks like it's the fate of all of us." And she went on, genuinely sorrowful, "I don't even know if I'm capable of bearing a child or not."

I reached out to hold her hand and she didn't try to pull away, leaving her fingers trembling in mine. She needed someone to cling onto. I watched Desougi as he hurried far ahead of us with the donkey. We walked more slowly and I wished the world would disappear completely. I said, "Don't worry about a thing. There are still days to come for you and for the child you hope to bear."

When we emerged from the passage through the maize, we let go of each other's hands and left sufficient space between us, but her warmth remained in my hand. I thought of my sweetheart in our early days, when her hand never left mine—a feeling of absolute security. At the beginning of creation there was not sorrow enough, and regret was born only when the time of deliverance came.

Farah went off to her house and her husband, and Desougi went to return the donkey to its owner and didn't come back. I sat alone in my quarters and nobody came. I recalled my trip to Cairo. I would not go back there for a long time and it was here that I must search for the tranquility of my soul. But when I laid my head on the pillow, I saw the filaments of blood dancing in front of my face, and they stayed there dancing all through the night.

I woke early, but even so, I found Farah waiting for me, a bewitching figure at this early hour, enveloped by wisps of morning fog as if she were emerging from a diaphanous world. She stood leaning against the wall, watching me as I approached. I wanted to take her body, to join it to my own, enclosing it in my arms. I stood, lost in front of her, close and so far away. Her face was different; tired and worried. Her eyes were red and ringed in dark shadows from lack of sleep. I put out my fingers to touch her and she shut her eyes. She opened her mouth to speak but closed it again in silence. The sound of the donkey, announcing its presence outside the clinic, startled us both. I moved away quickly, she adjusted her stance, and the unforeseen magic moment evaporated. Desougi arrived from the world of reality, carrying the equipment for testing and the tins of pills. We walked behind him, into the passage between the maize stalks, silent and shivering in the morning cold. I looked at her out of the corner of my eye, not daring to ask. I wanted her to speak, to seek support in me, but we walked a little apart. The school wall came into view, the pupils waiting for us, and the principal standing with a long cane in his hand. After I had tested just ten of the pupils, I decided to give the treatment to all of them, and whichever teachers wanted it. After several hours of work the schoolyard was empty, but Senior Arabic Language Teacher Mr. Omar, as he had introduced himself, remained standing with me, talking about general matters, and complaining about the things we all suffer from. He didn't take the pills, but he looked at me seriously and said, "Do you think you'll succeed?"

"I hope so. All the trials that have been carried out on this medicine demonstrate its effectiveness."

"The problem isn't with the medicine. The problem is with us as Egyptians. Throughout our history we've been repeating the same mistakes without letup. We don't learn from any experience and we turn our backs not just on others' experiences but on our own as well. Those children who took the pills today, it will kill the hidden worm inside them, and they'll be cured temporarily, but they'll jump in the canal again, a new worm will pierce their skins, they'll bleed anew, and all the deadly symptoms will come back."

"I know that. There are other efforts to clean the canals where the bilharzia snails are found."

His derisive response took me by surprise. "I know how they clean the canals, particularly that Mahrous who works under your auspices at the clinic. Have you seen how he works? Have you thought of going out with him on his rounds of the canals?"

I shook my head stupidly. I hadn't once thought to go out and see this for myself. Mr. Omar went on speaking without abandoning his ironic tone. "He uses the molluscicide powder in an innovative way: he doesn't go near the reeds that the snails attach themselves to, he spreads a small amount of the powder on the water and waits until the dead or dazed fish float to the surface, then he collects these fish to sell in the market—and that's the end of his mission. That's how the fight against bilharzia is waged, and this probably happens with all the canals. That is the campaign as it's been carried on for decades: dead fish—perhaps you should try it, to know what it tastes like?"

I stared at him stunned and unable to offer any defense. I said, "Does he really do that?"

As he turned his back to leave, he said, "You need to find that out for yourself."

I thought to occupy myself gathering up my equipment but found that Desougi had taken it and left. Glancing at the children now running cheekily around me, I went out of the school feeling confused. There was no Desougi and no donkey, only Farah standing waiting for me. Her face sad and enchanting, she spoke for the first time since the morning. "I didn't want you to go back alone."

What a strange day this was. Why should I be surprised at the way other people acted with me? We walked side by side, separate but not far apart. Suddenly, she was talking to me about Madame Jalila, about how sad she was that she had lost the precious gift that fate had placed in her belly. Then, she said, "If I were pregnant like that, I would never give up what was in my womb, whatever the circumstances."

The open land came to an end, and we entered the fields of maize, the place where she had let me hold her hand. The maize stalks secluded us from the world, a seclusion fragile but real. At that moment I was overtaken by a precipitate kind of forwardness: I seized her hand again, turned her face toward me, and said with resolve, "Now tell me: why this sad face and the tearful eyes?"

She looked ahead and then behind, wanting to be sure there was nobody to see us. She didn't remove her hand from mine but said, in a quavering voice, "It looks like I will never have a child."

I pressed her hand. "Why do you say that?"

"Eissa, my husband—I found out he passes blood in his urine. He hid it from me for a long time, until yesterday when I confronted him about it."

"You know now there's a cure."

"For years he's been too weak to ejaculate. My belly will remain empty."

I pulled her to me suddenly, impelled by desperation, by recklessness, by abstruse signs, by a tyrannical hunger. We left the narrow path and at once we were among the maize stalks, surrounded by the rough, broad leaves that cried out to me, "In God's name, stop!" I didn't stop. I took her in my arms and searched for her lips, going from her cheek to the end of her nose, then her lips, cool and trembling. She tore them away from my mouth and cried, "You'll bring scandal on us both!" I kissed her again so that she could not make a sound, and to soften her lips a little. She resisted, but not to the extent of pulling her body away. I could feel it warm and shaking. She gasped, "Please, Doctor! I'm really scared." She did not embrace me and she did not relax, but her face stayed close and her lips remained accessible. It was all very strange. I didn't try to take my folly further and do more—I didn't put my hand on her breasts or push my leg between her legs. But I kept firm hold of her and went on kissing her as she went on asking me to stop. Her body slumped and she became unable to stand on her feet. I continued holding her, but she was having trouble breathing and I was afraid she would faint. I helped her to lie on the ground and sat close to her, watching her chest as it rose and fell and her face that had gone very pale. I sat without uttering a word, just hoping that no one would pass by and find us in this shameful state. Then I implored her, "Get up, Farah, I don't want anybody to see us like this."

She raised her head but didn't look at me. Her breathing finally eased, and the color returned to her cheeks. She struggled to her feet and stood dusting off her clothes. I tried to help her, but she signaled that I should leave her alone. I watched her walk away and I walked behind her, with some distance between us. How angry was she? Would she report me to her husband, to the Health Directorate? And what would our working relationship be like after this? Had I been foolhardy? Had I been aggressive with her? Had I ruined everything? I realized I had turned in an instant into a frightened mouse.

The clinic was completely empty, as I entered apprehensively. Desougi must have gone to return the donkey, but where was she, and where were the other two nurses? I went upstairs and lay down, recalling the taste of her lips, the one positive thing from today's events—she had resisted, and muttered words of refusal, but I always found her lips. My own lips never fell on her cheek or her ear, or even her neck, but her lips were always there. She didn't turn her face away, and she didn't try hard to avoid me. She didn't kiss me back, but she did remain within reach. Even at the end when her legs would not support her, she collapsed only from overexcitement. I couldn't picture the consequences of what had happened, but it was a step I had been wanting to take from the first moment I had seen her.

The next day I hesitated a little before going downstairs, but Farah wasn't there. Desougi told me that her husband had come to tell us she was ill. I looked into Desougi's face, trying to divine whether he knew anything about what had happened the day before, but it revealed nothing. I said, "I want to see Mahrous, the bilharzia worker."

"He's a senior employee, very senior, and he sets his own agenda."

"Ask him to kindly include me in that agenda."

I busied myself with the patients, but my mind was preoccupied. I expected Farah to come in at any moment, whether smiling at me or railing at me—whatever she did would be acceptable. I was more or less confident that her husband wouldn't appear and wouldn't dare to rebuke me. His proper course of action would be to lie in wait for me in the maize fields and bring me down with a shot from a primitive weapon, but this was not his way—all he had done was come and ask for her to have some time off. She wouldn't tell him, or else how would they face each other? It seemed she preferred to put things off. I finished seeing the patients and she had not shown up. I went upstairs and searched my radio until I found a distant Lebanese station broadcasting an announcement about a battle between armed factions, interspersed with the songs of Fairouz. Then evening came on. This is the best time, when all creatures settle down and another of God's days comes to an end without problems. Then, there was a knock at the door, and it was Desougi. "Mahrous has come to see you." Angrily, I thought, why hadn't he come in the morning? But I realized how canny he was: he knew there was an issue and he preferred to come after everybody had left. I told Desougi that I would go down to him. I changed my clothes as I planned in my head what I was going to say so that I didn't blow up in his face. I went downstairs but found the clinic empty. They were outside, in the forecourt, sitting on the ground in front of a lit fire. I went out to them, and they made room for me on the blanket spread on the ground. There was a soot-covered pot of tea. Gone now was the formal meeting I had anticipated and there was no longer room for a scolding. The old man was cleverer than I had thought. Desougi put sugar in the three glasses, ready for the first pouring of the tea. I sat facing Mahrous, pondering the features of his old face as the flickering flames played on them, and thinking he must have passed retirement age years ago. I said, "There is a complaint about you."

He put his hand into a bag beside him and pulled out a cob of maize encased in green leaves, which he began stripping away to reveal the shining corn underneath. He put the cob on the fire and rearranged the burning brands around it. Finally, he responded, unconcerned, "You mean this talk about using the snail poison to catch fish? You can see it's nonsense—nobody's going to eat poisoned fish."

"But that doesn't prove the complaint wrong. I was at the school yesterday, and the day before, and I found that all the pupils, all of them, are infected with bilharzia."

With light scorn he said, "And did you think I was going to fight this endemic disease all on my own, with a handful of yellow powder? All these endless canal banks and drainage ditches need a full army, bigger than the national border guard, not one old worker like me. You're talking about a problem going back hundreds of years."

"At least you should be doing your duty."

"Please, Doctor, don't talk to me about duty. I'm older than you and I've seen corruption everywhere, since the earliest days. Perhaps you don't know that this clinic was built for my sake, after I sent a complaint to President Nasser and he responded to it. All the villages around here are bigger than us, and closer to the main road, and some of them even have a police station, but none of them have a clinic like we do."

I prepared myself to argue with him, and force him to listen to me, but he placed another cob on the fire and Desougi poured the second round of tea and passed me a glass. I asked in wonder, "I still can't believe it: how can a friendship exist between a man like you in this remote village and the man who ruled Egypt with such absolute authority?"

He looked into the flames, took a breath, and sat back. He seemed to sink into a distant time. "I only came to know him when we crossed the sand of Sinai on our way to fight in Palestine. Of course, I knew him before that: I was an insignificant orderly and I was afraid to go near him. He had a piercing look that was intimidating and his features were hard. He was an Upper Egyptian like me. No, he was graver and sterner than me. He had been wounded in the head in an earlier battle, but he was determined to return to the war again. I was attached to the battalion that received the orders to go to Palestine and I was one in the long line of soldiers who had no idea about war. I didn't dare to approach him until after we reached al-Arish, when we discovered that there was no transport to take us to Rafah, at the Palestinian border. These simple mistakes we make in every war, and after each defeat we don't give any weight to them. We make a mistake and then carry straight on. In that war perhaps we should have retreated, but we saw columns of Palestinians expelled from their homes that they had lived in for thousands of years: children, widows, old men. We wanted to go to war for their sake: they were unbearably miserable and broken."

I was caught up in the story as I drank the tea and ate the grilled maize. "Was Nasser the commander of the battalion?"

"He was a captain, but he was the staff officer of the battalion. Everything was supposed to pass through him, from the weapons to the rations. The commander was General Sayyid Taha, who was a brave Nubian officer, the Black Panther as they called him. He managed to make an agreement with a Palestinian travel company that had a number of buses to take us to the front."

I opened my mouth in astonishment. "You went to the front in tour buses?"

He laughed. "That's how it was, and that's how I came to know Nasser. He was sitting in the seat in front of me, and he said, like you, 'What kind of war is this? At the Suez Canal we proceeded with the permission of the British, and at the border all we find is tour buses.' And when he turned around, he only found me. He thought there were officers sitting behind him, but it was just a simple soldier, which was me. He laughed out loud but stayed where he was, and he said to me, 'You'll be with me from now on. You'll be my orderly, but you mustn't repeat a word I say to anybody, whoever it might be.' I was with him once we reached al-Falouja and stayed with him through the days of hunger and siege."

"Did the siege last long?"

"Five full months. And the truth is that the siege began the first moment we reached Palestine: they fired on us when we were at the gates of Gaza, but we managed to enter and occupy al-Falouja, a position that divides Palestine in two. If we had managed to hold it, we would have won the war, but we were not strong enough. Despite the weakness of our weapons and the shortage of ammunition, we repelled several attacks. I lived with him through long days of hunger and no more supplies reached us. We went into the neighboring villages, searching all day for food, returning with just a few bags of wheat. A third of the Egyptian army was encircled and starving. We were surrounded by bands of men who we thought knew nothing about war, but we found out later that most of them had taken part in the war in Europe and came to us well prepared. They exploited our mistake of pushing into the heart of Palestine without securing our lines of communication and they cut off all our supplies. Even the planes that tried to reach us, they brought them down or forced them to ditch the supplies in the sea. Nasser and I shared a single plate of boiled wheat. I wanted to leave it all for him, but he insisted on sharing it with me. 'You brought the wheat, how can I eat it alone?' he said. From then on, the Jews held us under siege. In all the battles we fought against them they continued to surround us. They were still a handful of gangs and we were still ignorant, disorganized, and liable to defeat. And then after the war was over and Nasser had become president, I wrote to him asking for a position, and all he gave me was this job. We had seen death together and had lost the war together, but he won everything, and here am I tramping up and down canal banks, asked to do more than I'm able to do, and accused of dereliction and catching poisoned fish. Is there anything else you want to know?"

My voice choking, I said, "No, nothing else."

The tea had boiled over and the cobs had burned. Desougi had been listening earnestly and it was clear that he was hearing this story for the first time. From far off came the howling of wolves, followed by the persistent, frenzied barking of dogs.

The following day there were more patients than usual and I hadn't yet started seeing them. Perhaps I was unconsciously waiting for Farah, but she didn't turn up. Desougi was there as always and out of the blue I asked him, "This man Mahrous, he's old and debilitated, why doesn't he go into retirement?"

"Many doctors before you tried to make him retire or at least to have him transferred or investigated, but they failed—because as soon as the management opens his file they find the Republican Decree with the signature of President Nasser. That's enough to put an end to anything, even retirement. No one dares to pension him off."

I tried to get on with examining patients, but I could no longer contain my need to know. "And what about Farah?"

He was surprised. "What about her? I haven't seen her since the day before yesterday. She must have come down with bilharzia."

"Haven't you spoken with her?"

"How can I speak with her if I haven't seen her?"

I smiled to myself—so far, nothing had happened—and said, "Send the first patient in."

I dived into the details of the patients and their symptoms, which had developed and become harder to treat. One of the two nurses came to help me, I don't know exactly which one, I didn't look at her face, and I didn't say a thing to her. I missed Farah's presence beside me and wished I hadn't been so reckless with her. I finished seeing the patients and dispensing the medications. They accepted my simple medicines gratefully. Death cannot get the better of us and we multiply despite the elements of ruination all around us. Everybody left, and only Desougi remained—always he was there. We sat outside the door of the clinic. The sky was clear and cloudless, the sun warm and joyless. I didn't know what I was waiting for, but I didn't want to go up to my room and stay there alone until the next morning. I wanted to know where she was, where her house was, but I didn't dare to ask. I needed some crazy stroke of chance, but there was no alternative to the long wait until the next day came.

A hubbub arose, coming from the end of the road—three old wagons drawn by three skinny horses, whose bones protruded as they strove to pull the vehicles loaded with piles of baggage and reed baskets. Some women walked alongside them, their appearance strange, unlike the women of the village. They wore bright-colored, patterned clothes, and their hair was uncovered and wild, a halo of black encompassing their faces made up with thick powders. Right behind them walked another group, this time of men, some of them banging douff drums and swaying to their rhythm. I looked at Desougi. "Is it a wedding?"

He said with clear distaste, "That's the Gypsies. They come every year and pitch their tents outside the village."

"What do they do?" I asked in wonder.

"Shameless stuff. Dancing, singing, other things. All shameless."

Leading them all was a lofty woman, towering over everyone, stepping confidently, her prominent breasts thrust out. She moved her feet slowly, placing each foot carefully in front of the other, walking like someone accustomed to knowing where their path lay and being in the lead and followed by others. Her untidy hair was tied in a red band that made her head glow in the afternoon sun. I watched her as Desougi watched me with sharp eyes, perhaps wanting to know what kind of woman I found attractive. The woman stopped abruptly, raising her hand for the whole parade to come to a halt. The horses snorted from their exertion and the men paused from banging their drums. The woman turned and looked straight in my direction. Did she see me, or had something else caught her attention? She left the procession and came toward me with the same slow steps. I could see her features clearly: large eyes, a small nose, copper skin, full lips, a slender chin with a line of blue tattoo, and the bundle of unruly hair that the red band was attempting to rein in. She stood in front of me with a hand on her hip and her breasts jutting forward. "If you're the doctor of this clinic, why don't you give me some medicine?"

"What kind of medicine?"

"As you see, this endless traveling from God's land to God's creation—my life is slipping away on the road."

I felt sorry for her. She could have been more beautiful if she had left behind the hardships of the trail, and if she had tempered her gaudy garb. I couldn't refuse her request, especially while she pleaded with those eyes. I went into the clinic and she followed me inside as Desougi stood furtively at the door. Opening the dispensary, I asked her, "Why don't you all stop roaming and settle somewhere?"

She laughed. "We're Gypsies. We own nothing but the shadow of the trees, as they say. Our only freedom is to roam and our destiny is to die by the roadside."

"What have you come here for?"

"The same as in the other villages, we give them some joy and happiness. As you see, all these villages are dismal. From all the bowing down their heads are full of silt."

I selected some fortifiers for her, and other medicines for headaches and strain. I gave her some of the pills and told her how to take them. She took hold of my hand and said, "My name is al-Jazya. Why don't you come and see us? We'll pitch our tents outside the village. The sound of the drums and the shawms will lead you to us. I don't dance or sing, I only tell stories, all the stories of the world."

"I can't promise you."

She laughed again. "They all come. Some come openly, others secretly, but they all come."

She pressed my hand in thanks and returned to the line of Gypsies, who stood waiting for her in the same order. I watched as they marched on until they disappeared and the sound they made went with them. I felt I had to go up to my quarters and observe the village from my balcony. I saw the birds circling around the heads of the palms, migratory birds that had come from afar and that could return whenever they wanted, not bound by the earthly obstacles that turned the place around us into a prison, or by suppressed cravings and desires. I realized that the hungry cells of my body had awakened since I had touched her and my lips had fallen on hers.

A few patients came—I went down and went back up and then the silence of the night took over. All the doors of the clinic were closed until the next day—which came, while Farah still did not. It was a sad, gray morning in the examination room and I was surprised that the sun was shining normally outside. I saw the clear malice in the eyes of the two nurses who came one after the other to help me in the examination room and as usual, I couldn't tell them apart. I knew they had different names, but together they just made up a mass of dull white. Before I went into the dispensary I asked Desougi quietly, "Is she still ill? Did her husband come today?"

He said tersely, "Nobody came."

I stood alone in the dark of the dispensary. I could hear the clamor of the patients outside the window, complaining about the delay. After a while I realized this silent isolation was a waste of time and I opened the window, giving out the medicines without speaking. I could no longer distinguish their identical faces and there was no face among them I wanted to see. I closed the window quickly, everyone went away, and silence reigned. The two nurses were out of my sight, busy with some of the mothers who had come with their babies. Desougi stood at the door to the room. "Eissa wants to see you."

"Who's Eissa?"

He pointed to the clinic forecourt. "The husband of Nurse Farah. He's standing outside."

I straightened up. Why didn't he come in? Was he going to say something he didn't want the others to hear? He stood tall and thin as a single stalk of maize—ah, the maize! He was wearing a blue galabiya, but not the type that the farmers wore. I didn't shake his hand. I walked around him a little before standing in front of him. Now, I could finally inspect him properly. We were two rivals, even if he was not aware of it. But he didn't scream or yell or threaten me with his fist. He didn't do that. He looked at me with hollow eyes—perhaps he had not slept all night—and said, "She's very ill, as you know. She has a fever that makes her shiver all night."

Quickly, I said, "Do you want me to come and examine her?"

I stressed the words "examine her." Was this my medical duty, or my impure mind? I was longing to enter her house and see how she lived, what her room looked like, whether he had a place beside her. But he shook his head in refusal. "She doesn't want that. She didn't even agree to me coming here to ask for medicine."

"So what do you want?"

He shuffled his feet, trying to make up his mind between staying and leaving. "I don't want anything. It's true she doesn't know I've come here. I've never seen her in such a bad state as this. I'm really afraid for her."

We shared the same fear. He didn't speak for a moment, then he looked directly at me, and said, "What happened?"

I trembled a little, then said, "What could have happened?"

"Did those two nurses Aleya and Atiyat fight with her?"

I breathed out. "Nothing unusual happened. Illness can strike anybody. Anyway, let her get her rest. I won't mark her down as absent."

He shook his head. "None of that matters. I'm sure the reason for her illness is here in this place."

Before I could reply he turned to leave, but then I said, "So, what is it that you do?"

He paused, startled, then said quietly, "I find work where I can."

I was a little hostile. "Meaning you don't have regular work and if it weren't for your wife's job at this clinic you wouldn't have a bite to eat."

I went back into the clinic, having taken my uncalled-for vengeance. Desougi, as always, was keeping tabs on me—I ignored his questioning looks and went up to my quarters. I listened to the sounds coming from below until they faded and all I could hear was my own breathing. Soon, darkness would fall and then I would hear nothing but the wolves howling and the dogs barking in response. A long night, marked as usual by the biting of the mosquitoes. Night in the village is more oppressive than anywhere else, especially when the smoke rises and forms a dark cloud over the palms, a cruel village that nobody but its residents can endure—but could Farah survive?

With the onset of evening, I thought the day was done, but then I heard Desougi's knock on the door. There was an old woman in the heart of the village with a large boil on her back and she was in great pain. Her sons were downstairs with a ride. I was impatient. "She must have been suffering for a long time. Why did they choose this time of night?" I didn't like stumbling through the dark alleys, meeting rabid animals. Desougi said, "They say the pain has become too much."

I gathered my bag and followed him downstairs. Three men, who looked prepared to launch an attack on the clinic if I hesitated to go with them, were waiting for me. I declined to ride the donkey, preferring to walk. I had never been able to accustom myself to riding donkeys and I could never imagine that these emaciated animals, which had so little to eat, could bear all those burdens. I floundered along the paths while they walked steadily—it was their territory and they knew every obstacle in it. I panted and puffed as they described their mother's condition to me and what was wrong with her. I wanted to yell at them, "Why didn't you say anything all this time, then?" But it's an Egyptian habit not to wake up until the last moment, when we're already on the edge of death. The walls of the house were of mud, but it had a broad hall, lit only by flickering wicks of flame. Many women wrapped in black stared in fear and curiosity, while the old lady lay on a mat on the floor. Time and illness had managed to turn her into a decayed creature of skin and bone. She peered at me with frightened eyes and when I tried to examine her buttock, where the boil was, she mustered some strength and screamed at the men to leave the room. They obeyed without argument. She trembled under my fingers as I determined exactly where I would make the incision. There was no local anesthetic to help me, so I asked the women to hold her tight, and collecting my courage I plunged the scalpel into her flesh—these are the moments that I hate. The pus came out, mixed with blood. Her health didn't allow her to keep up the screaming: she moaned with the pain, then gave up completely. I measured her pulse—she was still alive—and I quickly finished cleaning the wound, though I doubted if it would remain clean with her lying on the ground here in this mud house. I stood up, barely able to see who was around me. I looked down at her body, laid out like a corpse on the ground, and felt I had treated her cruelly, but what could I do?

I didn't want any of them to walk me back to the clinic. I blundered along, Desougi supporting me whenever I was about to fall. It became darker and I could no longer recognize anything around me. I was hungry and thirsty, and I could feel the stickiness of blood and pus all over me. I stopped abruptly as I heard the sound of drumming accompanied by a shawm echoing from far away, an unfamiliar sound making its way to my ears despite the howling and the barking, and the croaking of the frogs. The sound of a flute joined in, then someone playing on an arghoul, and the rhythm of drums. The darkness receded a little and the stars appeared brighter than usual. "What's that?"

Desougi said, as if stating the obvious, "Who else would it be? The Gypsies."

I stood as though I could smell their scent, grimy with the dust of constant travel. I said, "Let's go to them."

Desougi gasped in disapproval. "That's not possible, Doctor. We can't mix with that rabble. They're nomadic vagabonds."

I shrugged. "We're not going to buy from them or sell to them. We're just going to spend a portion of this heavy night there."

We followed the sound. Desougi didn't stop muttering objections, but he couldn't leave me on my own. We walked through narrow lanes, the smell of manure filling my nostrils. Barking dogs chased after us and Desougi bent down for stones to pelt them with. The sound grew louder and the houses near the threshing ground appeared to be awake, women and children sitting on some of the roofs. We entered the broad, open space as if transported to another world.

6

A boisterous world amid the wasteland of the night, a tumult of commotion and light far from the silence of the rural community behind it. Numerous torches lit up every corner of the old threshing ground that the Gypsies had selected the previous day as an area detached from the rest of the village. The light of the flames illuminated all the faces there, making them glow, tainted with the red of life. The wails of the old lady finally left my ears, replaced by the chime of finger cymbals and the beating of drums. Many of the men of the village were there—they had all come without their womenfolk, and the only women present were the Gypsies, naturally, exerting their control over every detail.

The wagons were arranged in a semi-circle at the edge of the space. Red, green, yellow, they were no longer soiled with the mud and dust of the road but were now bright and shiny like the garments of the Gypsies themselves. The women were not going around in rags, as I had imagined, but in clothes that were clean, resplendent, and alluring too. Their breasts and their low necklines stood out. Yearning for these colors, I moved among them holding my breath. The men left their women to do as they pleased, while they themselves were busy with the seesaws and swings made of tinplate, the shooting gallery, and the game of three-card monte. In another corner of the grounds a man was breaking in a wild, untamed horse, which was trying to free itself from the halter around its neck. The man would slacken his hold on the halter a little then pull on it firmly. He held a stick made from a supple branch, striking it on the ground and raising his voice at the protesting horse, which whickered and raised its fore-legs high in the air as though about to kick the man. The farmers watched this primal struggle between the man and his steed in awe, as each tried to impose his will on the other—a heated tussle the like of which they never experienced between themselves and their donkeys or their buffaloes. Desougi and I moved on to another part of the grounds and an incessantly clapping circle, at the center of which was a woman dancing and writhing to the thud of the rhythmic beat. She danced with elan and shook every part of her body, especially her rear end, which excited the admiration of all. I couldn't join in with the clapping. Many of the young girls entered the circle to dance with her briefly and then left. Desougi's anger subsided and was replaced by a smile of enjoyment. He began clapping his hands along with everybody else, engrossed in the dancer's movements, and edging forward a few steps to shake his body alongside her. Around us marched jesters eating fire, and a flock of doves flew up from somewhere, every wing a different color.

I felt someone tug at my sleeve and turned to find an old woman, her hair dyed red and three lines of blue tattoo on her chin. She pulled me by the arm so that I bent down in front of her and she whispered in my ear, "Would you like to have your fortune told?"

I looked at her in surprise. "My fortune? Out of all this crowd, why did you pick me?"

She smiled shrewdly. "That lot have no fortune and no future. They'll live and die in the same place. There's nothing in their fortunes to be read, but you look different."

She pulled me away from the circle, where Desougi remained distracted, absorbed in the dancer's moves. The old woman had aroused my curiosity and she led me to a colored rug spread on the ground. She sat down and I sat facing her. She threw a handful of seashells on the ground and said, "Cross my palm with silver!" I handed over a banknote. She scrutinized it for a moment then put it to her forehead, kissed it, and cast the shells once more. I had no faith in her, but she was a part of the rituals there. She looked at me. "You're lonelier than you should be. You're not in your place, and perhaps not in your time."

I looked at her with interest. "I'm in love with a woman. Tell me about her. Does she have a role in my fate?"

She cast the shells again. "You covet her, but she doesn't lie in your bed. You are hungry for her, but you don't have her."

I knew all that without the need of seashells. I asked her eagerly, "And now, will she gratify my hunger?"

"Appetites can be fulfilled. For every hunger there is satisfaction. It's available here and now, if you wish. We have warm women of all ages. And they're clean, I can swear to that."

I shook my head, but she persisted. "The world doesn't stop at a woman—the women are not alone, there are also children, and men with thick hair."

I felt affronted and stood up ready to leave. I shouldn't have got caught up with her, revealing my secret desires so childishly. She said, "Sit down."

I looked around for Desougi but didn't see him and at this moment another woman stepped in, the towering woman who had walked at the head of the procession, the one who placed one foot in front of the other. She took hold of the ends of my fingers and said to the old woman, "You're a fool. Nobody upsets a physician. Leave him to me, to gain his good favor."

The old woman bowed her head. "As you say, ya Jazya."

The woman pulled me away, gazing into me with those wide, brown eyes that took up most of her face. She patted me on the shoulder. "She's an old woman who doesn't know the fates of men. You'll be my guest tonight."

She led me gently to a tent, which was dirty and much patched, sat me on a seat, and sat down in front of me. "That old woman didn't need to cast the shells to know that you're lonely, a stranger in this place. We Gypsies recognize that from the first glance, because we are the strangers of this world. We don't hate walls; it's the walls that hate us. They always push us toward the open land, which is usually more gentle than human hearts, and receives us without hardship. But that doesn't suit you. You need to cast your seed somewhere and make roots."

"Up to now it seems I can't."

"I could warm your bed tonight, but I'm just a passing woman who cannot nurture your seed. You need an enduring woman. When you see her, take her. Love her as much as you can. Every woman is parched earth—no matter how much love you give her, she will not feel watered."

Farah was certainly not that woman, but it was time for me to sow my seeds. Al-Jazya said, "Come to the big tent. I'm going to give my performance and you will be my guest."

She led me to the other tent and suddenly, there was Desougi following me. We entered the broad pavilion, which was full of people from the village and from neighboring villages. Some sat on chairs, but most of them sat on the ground. One of the women brought me a chair, while Desougi preferred the floor, his favorite place to sit. I declined the glass of barley beer that she offered me and steered the mouthpiece of the narghile away from my mouth, but I paid the price she asked anyway. I didn't like the place, or the company, or the cloud of hashish smoke that was suspended under the roof of the tent, but I remained seated. Everyone had their eyes on an elevated space made up of several wooden boxes piled together with a colored rug spread over them. After a while, we heard the beating of douff drums, then al-Jazya entered, carrying one. She was even taller when she ascended the boxes. She rapped on the taut skin to produce deep, resounding, echoing beats. She looked at the crowd, looked in my direction, and raised her voice over theirs. It was like a tight cord, strong and clear. "The first words we utter: We pray for the Prophet, the Arab Prophet of sweet features, of singular qualities. I will relate to you my story, the story of al-Jazya of the Hilali tribe."

One of the farmers shouted, "We want the story of Abu Zayd."

She rapped her fingers on the drum. "I know you love the story of Abu Zayd, but it's not my story, I'll leave it to the other reciters. My story is about the woman who gave me her name, al-Jazya. Her people were of the Banu Hilal, they were Gypsies like us, older than us, but like us they were impelled by hunger to constant travel, and so I, a Gypsy, tell of the Gypsies, of my people."

Voices in the audience were raised in objection—how could she say this about the noblest of the Arabs? She didn't care about genealogies. She waited a little for all the voices to quieten down, then resumed her tapping on the drum and began to speak, as the tapping became a beating pulse, breathing life into the body of a woman who had passed on hundreds of years since. "She lived deep in the desert, among warring tribes, dry sands, and hunger that threatened all. She owned nothing but her sharp mind and her dazzling beauty. She was the daughter of the prince of the tribe, a tribe of great numbers and meager resources. Their land was good for nothing but burying the dead." She struck the drum twice. "Then, al-Jazya blossomed like a wild flower, opening quickly under the hot sun. The poets began to sing of her beauty and the suitors rushed to her, among them the brave knight of the desert, Diyab ibn Ghanem."

A farmer burst out, shouting, "We don't like Diyab! We're followers of Abu Zayd!"

She beat the drum and spun around, her hair flying out like a sun the color of henna. "This isn't the story of either one of them. Al-Jazya refused all the suitors, without giving a reason. She didn't dare to say that her little heart was in thrall to a one-sided love, consumed by a passion for another knight, Abu Zayd al-Hilali Salama."

The farmers breathed a sigh of relief. Their hero had finally appeared. "But there was an enormous obstacle between them: how could she, the princess, the daughter of the prince, love a black knight, an oddity within the tribe? But al-Jazya had fallen in love with the distinctive color of his skin. Abu Zayd didn't see her, he didn't dare to raise his head and look her in the face. Meanwhile, Diyab continued to pester her—he was accustomed to reaching out and taking whatever he wanted, whether the other person was willing or not. And the one time he kissed her, he made her lips bleed." She rapped a series of beats on the drum, caught her panting breath a little, and looked in my direction. "Oh, my life! How I love that kind of man, the one who wants, and reaches out to take what he wants."

She ceased drumming, struck her breast, and laughed. And the audience laughed—she had captured their attention. She was retelling their old stories, pulling them out of their memory. She drummed again. They pricked up their ears and followed the movements of her body. She carried them along with her wild, uncommon magic, and they liked the way she narrated her story, with the overtones it carried. "Al-Jazya lived like all the other girls and shared their dreams. She would go with them to the well, where she loosened her plaits, removed some clothes, revealed her legs. She came to know the chasing of the boys and she played hard to get, the sweetest game the girls played. She experienced touches and kisses while playing these games, but she never encountered Abu Zayd, by day or by night. All the boys came, even Diyab with all his villainy and volatility, but not Abu Zayd. She wanted him to join in the chasing and the games, but he didn't. And when the time of maturity came, the suitors began flocking to ask for her hand. They came from the Banu Hilal and from other tribes, but Abu Zayd didn't make a move. They offered dowries of silk, of jewelry, of she-camels, but Abu Zayd stayed away. If he had only presented himself, she might have been able to do something. She had a one-third voice in the affairs of the tribe, and her opinion was worth more than a whole league of men. Certainly, her father would have listened to her, at least a little, but Abu Zayd still didn't come forward. So, she did something she had not dared to do before: she sent her servant to ask him to propose to her mistress. But his response was frustrating: 'With my color as it is, who could accept it?' All hope was now gone for her. When the prince of Mecca came to ask to marry her, she agreed without love, and prepared to go away without desire. But drought was creeping up on the tribe: their wells were shrinking, their herbage was shriveling, and their herds were dying. It was time to migrate to another place. Her marriage procession was perhaps the last celebration staged by the tribe. Al-Jazya was as beautiful as it was possible to be, even if she didn't feel so inside, and her wedding cortege proceeded to the prince of Mecca. Walk proudly, pretty beauty, flower of the garden!"

Al-Jazya beat the drum and spun around, flinging out her hair, shaking her rear. She stepped down from the boxes and walked among the audience—who burst into applause—as if she were a bride conducting her own procession to some prince. She paused, panting, and looked at the faces of the farmers as though waking from her dream. There were no more princes, nor brides walking proudly. She ascended her stage and resumed rapping on the drum. "Al-Jazya went to the house of her husband, the Sharif Hashem: a spacious house, silk furnishings, abundant food, a sensitive husband. Yes, indeed, kind gentlemen, the sharif never held a sword except to perform the ardah dance. And it was likewise in the bed: a battle he didn't win because he didn't fight it in the first place—he left the bed cold and clean. God preserve all mustaches, all beards! If you don't win in the battle of the bed, all your battles are lost." She wiggled her behind and laughed and everybody nodded their heads and laughed too. "The sharif fought no battle, as I said, but he let no caravan pass without extracting tribute. He was rich and secure, without fear or hazard, but he was passionless and was unable to satisfy a hungry body like al-Jazya's. In any case, she didn't like the light color of his skin. Some reciters will tell you that she had children with him. I assure you she didn't. And they will say she was happy, but a woman cannot be happy in a cold bed. No mother will abandon her children and no wife will leave her husband unless there are compelling reasons. But the years passed, tedium became customary, and starvation was killing her Banu Hilal people. They were facing a dark fate, especially when their babies began to be stillborn. They had to look for a land that was not full of the graves of children, a new land, and they decided to send Abu Zayd to search for that land: if he perished on this mission, they would not have lost much. But he was cleverer than they were. He asked that Prince Hassan's three sons go with him—her three brothers. They went with Abu Zayd, and he came back without them. He said they had all fallen captive to the king of Tunis, al-Zanati Khalifa. This was stunning news that called for an equally striking response: the whole tribe decided to set out for Tunis, fleeing starvation, and seeking vengeance. In an instant they became Gypsies like us, with no land of their own, and no country to shelter them. They pulled up the pegs, pulled down the tents, and piled their effects on the backs of the camels. How did al-Jazya come to their minds amid the fluster of departure?

"A Hilali woman came riding a she-ass and whispered to al-Jazya, 'They want you to travel with them. You have one-third of the voice of the tribe, and they can't attempt a hard journey like this without you.' Al-Jazya asked her, 'Who sent you to me?' The woman said, 'Who else? Abu Zayd.' She couldn't believe her ears—Abu Zayd wanted her to go with him to that land in Africa, where there were so many men with black skin like his, her weakness! She slept and awoke determined to go. She told her husband she needed to visit her people for a few days. All she asked of him was a fast steed, a sword, and some provisions. Of course, he didn't imagine that she could lie or that she could throw away her marriage for a promise in the wind, and he agreed in spite of all his reservations. She began her journey quickly, and as soon as she reached open country, she gave her steed free rein, leaving behind Mecca, her husband, and the servant on the she-ass. She reclaimed her freedom and didn't rest until she arrived at the campsites of her tribe, or rather what was left of them: the corrals of her youth had turned to ruins and there was nobody there but a handful of old folk and a few skinny dogs. The old folk pointed out the way the tribe had gone. 'You'll see the tracks of their horses in the sand and the dung of their she-camels and you'll smell the odor of those who have died.' She galloped off again, the beating of her heart competing with the hooves of the steed, and at night she slept in the open. On the third day she came upon them. They were tired and hungry, and they were preparing to mount a raid, which would be their habit all along the way: whenever they were tormented by hunger they raided any other tribe—this was the merciless law of the desert.

"Her family received her with jubilation and song. Abu Zayd cast a shy glance full of gratitude, while Diyab looked at her like one who wanted to ravish her, the look of a wolf whose desire never abates. There was the smell of blood too. All who welcomed her and embraced her, the smell of blood emanated from them. But she was excited, searching among the faces for the face she wanted, until she stood before him. His black skin also gave off the smell of blood, but never mind, what mattered was that he had asked for her and she had come. If only he had shown his feelings earlier. But he didn't understand. He went on looking at her foolishly, still not wanting to understand. He was caught up in notions of what was unworthy of a knight and did not have the courage to respond to her desire. He was still the disregarded black knight, but now he was married, and he didn't want to leave his wife. Al-Jazya would never agree to be the second wife, nor to stoop to being the mistress. She turned and left. Her sacrifice had gone to dust, she had brought down her house for nothing, but she was determined to recover. And now . . . let's all take a break."

When al-Jazya stopped speaking she was breathing heavily. I looked at her in amazement. Where did the ability come from to tell this old story that everybody knew by heart from such a different angle? I thought of my own life: no woman had made a sacrifice for my sake. An old relationship had ended in refusal and a new one was far from becoming reality. I thought about Farah. Did she have the courage of al-Jazya, the ability to own her destiny and take control of her life? Al-Jazya came and sat beside me, so close that all gazes were directed at us. She handed me a conical bottle and smiled, "You need a small dose."

The smell of the fermented alcohol filled my nose. I said, "I don't drink wine."

She took a mouthful and laughed, her voice clear. "This isn't wine, it's date arak, the elixir of forgetting and good times. Don't you need to forget?"

Of course, I was in dire need of that, but I didn't want to drink in front of everybody. Wasn't it enough that she was sitting right up against me like this? She whispered, "When I finish . . . you won't leave with those farmers."

"I couldn't," I confirmed.

She said, "I know you're a doctor, you have particular sanitary standards, but rest assured, I'm as clean as crystal—you'll find this out for yourself."

I looked around, fearful there might be someone listening to us. "How did you get to be this bold?"

"I'm a Gypsy, Sir. I was raised on the road and I learned to take what I want. You should do the same."

"Which Jazya are you, the princess or the Gypsy?"

As she made to stand up, she said, "You'll know that when you try me."

She rose and the hubbub subsided. The sellers of barley beer, date arak, and honeyed tobacco gathered their things and withdrew. One of the men handed her the drum after tautening the skin over the heat of the fire and she struck it, producing a deep sound like the beating of a lost heart. The story came to life again and al-Jazya continued on the journey of insatiable hunger. "Some tribes hosted them then quickly turned them away from their land; other tribes harassed them to the point of battle. Al-Jazya was distressed. She watched Abu Zayd beside his wife Watfa and her determination to challenge his folly increased. The tribe continued its crawl, paying no attention to those who fell along the way. Their clothes became ragged, and their sandals wore out, but the walking didn't cease—there were no enemies, no boulder fields, no quicksands. But they were forced to stop when they reached Egypt.

"It was the first time they had faced a giant river. Dividing the land from the south to the north, its brown, surging waves swept away all that stood in their path. On both banks extended fields of radiant green like peridot. Al-Jazya stretched her legs into the water and experienced an overwhelming shudder: after so many long days walking over the hot sand, she felt the tiredness seeping away between her toes. Could they settle on the bank of this fresh river? No, of course not, they must go on to liberate the three brothers held captive in Tunis. Yet they remained a long time, unable to cross the river. The sultan of Egypt wasn't willing to let them cross and, typical of the Egyptians, who obey their rulers blindly, no boat or ship would stop to help them reach the other side. Added to which, they were destitute to the point of exhaustion, and they all felt helpless. As the days passed, their sojourn by the river turned into a nightmare. They could not move on, and they could not settle. It was Diyab's idea, which they acted on immediately, to become troublesome guests: they began by attacking the villages, stealing livestock, breaking into chicken coops, and seizing crops. The farmers along the river owned no swords or spears; they always fought back with sticks and mattocks, and were defeated. They were only good at planting and harvesting, not fighting. Their life was one of stability with their neighbors and they were not used to coming under attack, which is why the Banu Hilal were able to make their lives hell. Even when the sultan's troops came, they were unable to repel the Banu Hilal. But the farmers, without any prior agreement among themselves, decided to solve the problem in their own particular way: when night fell, fishing boats were deployed to help whoever wanted to be transported to the other bank, and they went back and forth between the two banks all night, ceasing only at first light. Even the horses and the camels—they were able to take hold of their halters and take them across the river. Through determination and persistence, the Banu Hilal found themselves on the river's far side. The green fields were behind them and the desert was spread out before them. They had to move on quickly before the sultan knew that the bird had flown and they traveled north toward the coast. After fleeing the sultan of Egypt's troops they faced another enemy: Madi ibn Muqrin, the prince of Cyrenaica, came out to block their path. His lines of horsemen were the final obstacle standing between them and Tunis. The sight of them was frightening and their swords glinted in the sun. The horsemen of the Banu Hilal looked at each other: they were tired after so much fighting. But al-Jazya surprised everybody when she went out at their head. She rode a charger, wore a mask, and wielded a small sword in her hand. She shouted to them that she would take this matter upon herself alone and she galloped off toward the mighty black line. The prince of Cyrenaica had to ride out to her himself, approaching her ready to fight, with his sword raised. She showed no fear, nor the desire to retreat, and her firm stance caused him to hesitate and observe her curiously. She lifted her mask from her face and he gasped in wonder: the coal-black in the snow-white of her wide eyes, the curled lashes, the golden-brown skin, the prominent, full lips. She looked at him and made it clear in sweet terms that her people didn't want war or battle, they wanted only his permission to pass over his land to Tunis. He said he was afraid to allow this in case they double-crossed him, to which al-Jazya replied boldly, 'You can keep me here.' He asked, 'As a hostage?' She affirmed, 'As a wife.'

"She returned to her people, conveying the permission to pass, and the price that must be paid, her marriage to the prince. They all, including her father, cried, 'But you are married!' Indeed, . . . how had this point escaped her when she was negotiating? She selected one of her followers to carry a message to her husband in Mecca to persuade him to swear the oath of divorce on her. And she sent a trusted woman to Ibn Muqrin to tell him that they all agreed to his marriage proposal, but that he must wait. The situation was stalled, but the seed of conflict was eliminated. Ibn Muqrin's horsemen withdrew and in their place came delegations to welcome them, bringing them food. Al-Jazya had proved her presence of mind and gained a victory respected by all—nobody dared to call her to account. The days of waiting were not long: the messenger who had been sent to Mecca returned after a time too short to cross the land of the Nile—perhaps he owned a winged horse?—but he swore to all that he had met with the sharif of Mecca and secured his agreement to divorce al-Jazya the legally valid three times. Everyone exclaimed in relief, there was no need to know the details of the journey, and it was futile to talk of the months of iddah, the prescribed waiting period after a divorce before a woman can remarry. The wedding procession was completed, and the celebrations were held."

Al-Jazya rapped several times on the drum to signal to the crowd that she was pausing from the tale. She was out of breath and perspiration covered her face. Looking into my eyes, she said, "That is a woman—when she wants something she devises the ways to get it, and no one knows the means she will resort to. A woman is the cleverest of creatures when she wishes to be."

She remained standing for a while before remembering that there was a story she had to complete. She struck the drum, spun around, tossing her hair out like the night, then spoke again. "Al-Jazya married and now she had a man and a bed of silk. And the Banu Hilal resumed their endless journey across the sands, along the shore of the sea. But al-Jazya soon had her fill of her husband and went back to pondering her position. All who married her had concerns more important than her—thrones to maintain, rather than taking their ease in her bed. She would become old and decrepit before she found a man who would devote himself to her. News of her people the Banu Hilal dribbled in. They had arrived finally at the walls of Tunis, but they were unable to take it by storm. Al-Zanati Khalifa, the ruler of the city, put his sword to work on them every morning. He killed them and hung their heads on the walls. They had made this long journey in order to dig their graves under the ramparts of his city. She slept assailed by nightmares. What was Abu Zayd's state now? Would he also die under the walls of Tunis? In the midst of her uncertainty a fortuneteller came, who they told her was the best clairvoyant in all Africa. She asked her, 'Who can defeat al-Zanati Khalifa?'

"The woman drew overlapping lines in the sand, unknown letters, and said, 'It is Diyab ibn Ghanem.' She was disappointed and asked, 'And what about Abu Zayd?' The woman replied, 'The sand says Diyab, and none but Diyab.'

"And she left her tired and worried. After long, dry days, an old woman of her tribe came to her, confirming all the bad news: the walls of Tunis were impregnable, there was nobody who could overcome al-Zanati, Diyab had angrily walked away from the war and was content raising sheep, . . . and Abu Zayd was still alive, though his wife had died. It was this news that reverberated in her head—Abu Zayd was now free, with no woman, but he was incapable of bringing the battle of Tunis to an end. She felt that her place was not here, not on the silk, and not underneath Ibn Muqrin. She immediately went to him and said, 'It was I who asked you to marry me, and it is I who ask you now to let me leave. I want to join my people.' He said quietly, 'I was expecting this. A free spirit like you cannot bear to stay long between walls.' Consent was given, and this was farewell. She left Cyrenaica, alone, as he decreed she should be, and arrived at the borders of Green Tunis—though it was no longer green: blood had turned it purple, and it smelled of death. Abu Zayd appeared as though the years had weighed heavily on his shoulders and pushed him to the edge of middle age."

The farmers sitting around me grumbled—they wanted their hero to remain young and strong forever—but al-Jazya took no notice. She rapped on the drum and announced the truth to them. "Abu Zayd was losing his strength, and Diyab was far away, angry at the tribe that didn't appreciate his courage. Al-Jazya wandered around among the remnants of the dream: the defeated tents full of widows and orphans, the severed heads suspended on the walls, her father who was dying. What was the secret of this city, and why did it resist so? Was there a talisman protecting it? She tried to awaken the mind of Abu Zayd, who had always come up with creative solutions, but he was immersed in his grief, not wanting to forget Watfa or the warmth of her body. She suggested he make up for it with her own body, a princess's body that had surrendered itself only on beds of silk, yet she was ready to gift it to him on a rough mat in a tattered tent. But he rejected her again. Why was he blessed with such obtuseness? She was no longer a princess, and he was no longer an outcast knight, they were both equal under the shadow of death. She needed to go down the hill and beyond the tents to the pastureland where Diyab ibn Ghanem was: an aggressive, untamable animal, who was always exploring her with his hungry eyes. Her body shook like it had never shaken before. She asked him directly, 'Are you going to leave al-Zanati to annihilate your people? Return to the fight and you'll receive more than your share.' He said, 'I want you to be my share and my lot.'

"He put his hand on her. He still desired her in spite of all the years: his hunger had not diminished and he was never satisfied, no matter how many women he had. Her whole body shivered as she said, 'After you kill al-Zanati Khalifa . . . I'll be yours.'

"It was a deal she had never imagined she would one day make. His eyes shone and he stood up quickly to hone his sword and saddle his horse. The balance of the war changed as soon as Diyab returned from the pastures to stand below the walls and make his challenge. 'Come down to me, ya Zanati!' The shout reached al-Zanati inside his palace and he knew it was the sound of his fate calling him—all the prophecies were known already, and he was well aware that he could battle anyone except Diyab. He remained in hiding, confronted by the stares of all around him, seeing their suspicions of cowardice and inaction. His virility as a knight was shaken and even his daughters in the palace rebuked him for his lack of courage. But he shrank back, knowing the destiny that awaited him. Al-Jazya herself didn't stay silent. Every day she brought the girls of the Banu Hilal together to bang drums and sing, accusing al-Zanati of cravenness, and calling on him to come down. He was a king and he was a knight, and he could not live with his destiny in suspense like this. So, one day he rose calmly and censed himself and his clothes, forgoing breakfast to conserve his agility. He took up the tools of war and went out to meet Diyab so that he might cease his yelling. He stood in the middle of the field, and as soon as the dust parted around Diyab—big, strong, and fierce—he rushed straight at him, facing his brutish fate. They fought closely, as al-Jazya came with her companions and the drums resounded along with the fall of the hooves and the clashing of the swords like the sound of thunder. The Banu Hilal drew closer, the guards stood frozen on the ramparts, and the birds flapped away. The heated struggle went on, ceasing only as evening fell, when the two knights withdrew to rejoin the fight the following day. It is said that the contest went on for two months, but that is much too long for a battle between two individuals, or even for two armies. It was perhaps on the third day that their fates were determined. Al-Zanati brandished his sword, bringing it down onto Diyab's neck, but it was deflected from its path and fell on the head of al-Khidr, Diyab's steed. The horse nickered, a torrent of blood erupted, and he fell to the ground, taking Diyab with him and covering him completely in gore. Al-Zanati breathed in relief, having changed his fate: he was victorious on the threshold of defeat. He turned to return to his place behind the walls, but a sharp spear pierced his back. Diyab didn't know how it had come to his hand. Somebody must have thrown it to him. Perhaps it was al-Jazya—who else could have done it? Al-Zanati fell dead, finally, and Diyab stood up straight, coated in blood. He cried out to all, announcing his victory: Tunis was now his and he was its king forever. He pulled the spear out of al-Zanati and thrust it into the wall—from now on, all who came in to see him must lower their head to pass beneath this spear. Al-Jazya herself ducked under it as she went to give her body up to him.

"It was a terrible encounter, and an extremely bitter fall. Diyab didn't want to give her pleasure but to degrade her, to make a sacrifice of her to his ascent. She obeyed all his orders and submitted to his cruelty and perverse demands. And when she asked him what he intended to do with her, he told her he was going to marry Saada, the daughter of al-Zanati, and he wanted her to be a servant to Saada. He had turned into a monster in human skin. He couldn't get enough of killing—killing all who might be rivals, and first among those was Abu Zayd al-Hilali."

Now this was too much for the farmers and several yelled, "That's impossible! Abu Zayd didn't die. Diyab wouldn't dare kill him!"

But al-Jazya had stunned them all, assassinating their favorite hero. The cries grew louder. She looked around her, bewildered: there was another outburst—screams and loud voices yelling at everyone, all coming from outside the tent. Everybody stood up in confusion. I looked around, also confused, and saw signs of alarm on al-Jazya's face as she shouted at me, "Run!"

Run from what? And where to? Rough footsteps—I turned around to see legions of police conscripts storming the tent. Dark uniforms, tanned faces. They carried not rifles but thick sticks, which they brought down on the heads of the crowd. Al-Jazya screamed as she disappeared behind them. I felt a great blow on my back and fell to the ground. Dirt found its way into my mouth and nose. I tried to crawl to evade further blows, but hands reached out to pull at me, and I was dragged along the ground out of the tent and thrown down in the open space, under their feet. I wanted to stand but I was afraid of being struck again. The hooves of a horse came close, as though the animal had emerged from the old story, and almost kicked me, but moved away. I heard a coarse voice bellow, "Stand them all up!"

I was poked by a stick, so I stood up, reeling, wiping the dirt from my eyes to see what was happening. There was a police officer on his horse and he seemed to be of high rank—his brass buttons shone bright, as did the metal eagles on his shoulders. The farmers, with me among them, stood on one side, surrounded by police who beat them with sticks when they made any sound. I didn't see al-Jazya or any of the Gypsies. They might have been in another part of the grounds or the police might have taken them away. Everything was wrecked: the tents were demolished, the pennants torn, the torches extinguished. The horse whinnied, angry like its master, who surveyed us threateningly. "What are dirty people like you doing in this filthy place? Prostitution, hashish, alcohol! Where do you think you are?"

The conscripts closed in on us more and more, bringing their sticks down harder on our bodies. The high-ranking man on his horse turned around and said haughtily, "I am the ma'mour, the superintendent, of this district and I'm going to teach you all some manners. Every pleasure is followed by pain, and your pain is going to be at my hands in the district jail."

I felt desperate—they would open the files and discover my dubious past. They would release everyone else, and I would be left to rot in the district jail. No one would know anything about me and no one would look for me. I would join the ranks of those prisoners who die in jail without anyone knowing what they're accused of.

The earth opened up and Desougi appeared, as he always did. He bore the beatings of the sticks, slipped through the hands of the police, and threw himself in front of the horse without fear of being kicked. "Excuse me, Excellency. Please hear me, Excellency."

The officer's fury abated slightly, perhaps through being addressed as "Excellency," and he took notice a little. Desougi hurriedly pointed in my direction. "That man isn't one of them. He's a doctor, the physician of the village clinic, and he passed by here by chance. He has nothing to do with anything—no hashish, no women, he's just here by accident."

The officer suddenly paid attention to what Desougi was saying and looked toward me. He prodded his horse and approached me, inspecting me and examining my clothes, which were soiled. He seemed unconvinced. I was just another miserable Egyptian like the rest of them. He asked coarsely, "You have your ID?"

I reached into my back pocket and fortunately found my wallet, from which I extracted my ID. He steered his horse to stand beside one of the torches that was still alight and read it carefully. He shook his head in chagrin before coming back and tossing the ID in the air for me to catch. "You're a respectable government employee. What brought you to this place? Aren't you concerned about your reputation?"

I picked up the thread from Desougi's words, saying quietly, "It was just by chance."

"You can go. I don't want to see you in a situation like this again."

I lowered my head in shame and walked away, with Desougi walking behind me, and nobody objected. We stumbled through the intertwining alleyways of the village, aiming to reach the clinic before the dark lifted and the approaching dawn exposed us. We didn't exchange a word. I was gasping and unable to catch my breath. When I stepped inside, I turned to Desougi and said, "Close all the doors and go home. There will be no consultations today, not even for urgent cases. I don't want to see anybody."

I went up to my rooms, closed my door, and threw myself on the bed. What had I done to myself? How had I let this happen to me? I stared into the darkness of the room and knew at once that it was the loneliness: this agonizing, cold loneliness that encompassed me. I had no excuse. Al-Jazya's words and the tapping of her fingers on the drum rang in my ears. What if the police had not attacked, how would things have ended between us? I closed my eyes, exhausted, and sank into the dark, with the taste of dirt still in my mouth.

7

For three days I didn't open the doors of the clinic or perform any examinations. From behind my window, I saw them gathering at the clinic door and at the dispensary hatch, shaking their heads sadly before going away. I didn't want to face their curious looks or their staring eyes. On the third day, Desougi came upstairs to knock on my door. I couldn't keep the clinic shut down, or else the complaints would pour in over my head. But I particularly wanted to know the fate of al-Jazya. I said, "What happened to the Gypsies?"

With genuine indifference he said, "They spent their night in the police station. They were let go after the conscripts stripped them of all the money they'd collected. That's how it always goes."

I went downstairs behind him and indicated that he should open the doors and that the two nurses should start their work in the Family Care room. Slowly, the throng of patients began, with their unending complaints and mysterious symptoms. One man came in suffering from urinary retention: his kidney must have contained several small stones, one of which had shifted and was now blocking his urethra. I needed to insert a flexible catheter into his member to remove the stone and with luck it would be expelled as the urethra expanded. It was a disagreeable and painful procedure, and it was done of course without anesthetic. But the patient, with his sallow face and the smell of urea emanating from his skin, was ready for anything we might do. I asked Desougi to bring a little oil—I wanted to minimize the pain as much as possible. Neither of the nurses attempted to assist me, as though they had never seen a man's member before. So, I asked Desougi to hold the man firmly, and his screams rose as I pushed the catheter inside. I didn't hear the door of the examination room open, nor did I sense who was standing beside me until I saw her hand holding the kidney dish under the patient's testicles to catch the first spurts of urine. This was typical of Farah, appearing at just the right moment, and doing her job without false modesty. I slowly removed the catheter and the flow of yellow liquid increased, carrying away with it the small stone that had been blocking the urethra. The man sighed with relief, though when he opened his eyes and saw Farah still holding the kidney dish full of his urine he squirmed in embarrassment. Then he turned to me, bouncing with happiness and trying to kiss my hand; I was even happier than he was—only because she had come back and was standing beside me. She must have heard about what happened with the Gypsies, but she had not hesitated to come—an impressive touch in these sorry times.

There were cries of jubilation outside as soon as the patient went out, at ease now after perhaps days of discomfort. We found ourselves standing facing each other for the first time since we had parted. She wasn't wary of me and didn't keep an exaggerated distance between us. And she wasn't angry with me, because she smiled suddenly and said, "What did you get up to with the Gypsy woman?"

I didn't know how the story had reached her, or in what form. I chose to turn it into a joke—shaking my head, I said, "The police didn't give me a chance!"

She tried hard to stifle a laugh. "Did you like her that much?"

Turning serious, I said, "It's your fault. You vanished suddenly and left me alone, without a word."

Her face went very red and I thought she might take a step back, but she didn't. She composed herself and said, "Maybe if you had asked in the first place."

My voice rose. "Would you have agreed?"

She turned her face away from me, but I clearly heard her say, "Maybe."

Desougi came in, then another patient, who said something I didn't take in, but I picked up the stethoscope and began examining his chest. He went on explaining his condition and I heard neither his words nor his heartbeat. There was a buzzing in my head, a buzzing in the clinic—everybody was moving around and talking at the same time. I wasn't aware what medicine I was prescribing, but the patient was happy enough simply because I had put the stethoscope on his chest, meaning that I had discovered everything that was wrong with him. He left and another patient came in, complaining of congestion in his throat. When he opened his mouth, a fetid smell issued from it. I got rid of him fast, then asked her, "Are you serious?"

Quickly, she said, "The matter's too serious to stop thinking about it or to think about anything else."

The nurse Aleya came in to say that it was getting late. It wasn't late at all, but perhaps they felt superfluous now that Farah had appeared, and they wanted to leave. I immediately gave them permission to go. I wanted the clinic to be empty so that I could properly understand the meaning of Farah's whispered words. I quickly finished with the patients, not allowing anyone to start a discussion, or ask me about any details. I opened the window of the dispensary in order to get rid of them all. They didn't look at the medicines I was giving them as much as they looked at me, in a very annoying way. Their numbers began to dwindle—every problem had its solution, except for the problem of Desougi's presence. Farah went on waiting until I finished giving out the medicines, wanting to talk with me, but Desougi's eyes watched us like a hawk's. The last of the patients left, but another sick case appeared outside in the forecourt, a more serious one: Eissa, her husband. I saw him as I was closing the dispensary window, standing at a distance, solitary and grumpy. I felt frustrated, another chance lost. I went out of the room to find Farah preparing to leave. She turned to me and said quickly, "We can't do anything or say anything in this place."

She went off hurriedly, leaving her words hanging in the air, and joined him. They didn't walk together though—she led, and he followed a step behind, as if he didn't dare to walk alongside her. I watched them for a while before going back inside. There was no one left but Desougi and me—as ever, him and me. In the end, the day wasn't as bad as I had expected: Farah had returned, although too difficult to read, her talk full of overtones I didn't fully understand. I realized I had a hunger and was in need of a woman. Al-Jazya could have been a temporary solution, but would I have been able to bear her dirty bed and her loins worn out on her travels through the wilderness?

At night I went out to a case, the village butcher, complaining of a tightness in his chest. He was reclining in a large hall full of his friends, with a fire burning in the middle of the space, and all of them taking turns to suck on an apple-tobacco narghile. Smoke—there was smoke everywhere, thick and clouding the ceiling. Meanwhile, the sick butcher couldn't breathe, but he was happy to have his friends around him, and happy with the hubbub they made as they used up all the clean air in the room. No treatment would do him any good while he was in this situation. I gave him an antihistamine injection to relieve the congestion in his lungs and pointed out that what was going on around him was the reason for all his suffering, but he wasn't prepared to change things. As we were leaving, Desougi holding the lamp to light our way, I said on a whim, "Let's go to the grounds where the Gypsies were camped."

Surprised, he said, "It's just an old threshing ground and there's nothing there now."

After a pause, he yielded to my whim, and we walked to the edge of the village, despite the barking of the dogs and the howling of the wolves. The place was empty, as he had said it would be, but there were some traces of them left: torn pennants, smashed chairs, a few tent pegs. I walked to the place where al-Jazya had related her tale and sat on the shattered boxes, hearing her voice in my head as she told the story of her spiritual sister of yore. Desougi said, "It's risky to stay here too long, the light of this lamp could attract the wolves."

We walked together through the alleyways of the village. At one point, Desougi stopped in front of a house and, without my asking, gestured to it. It was an ordinary house, similar to all the rest, but he confirmed, "Farah lives here. This is her house—hers and her husband Eissa's."

The house was dark and the windows were closed. There was nothing to distinguish it from all the other houses and if I came here in daylight, I wouldn't recognize it. I stood there without speaking, listening to him talking, but not knowing what he was saying. Then, for no reason, a silence fell between us, and I heard the shadow of her voice reverberating through the walls. Soon, we were walking again, until we reached the dark, empty clinic, where I lay with my eyes open until morning.

But the next day was different—Thursday was always different, being the day before the weekly holiday. Work went on sluggishly and half-heartedly and it was the only day when slaughtering was done, and people—only some, of course—could buy meat, the one day of the week when fresh meat was available. Not many patients came to the clinic. Desougi went off to buy meat and the two nurses soon excused themselves, so that by some miracle I found that Farah and I were alone. I didn't dare to close the door or make any attempt to approach her. I said, "What did you mean?"

As though I was continuing yesterday's conversation, she understood immediately what I was referring to. She said, "Here we can't meet, or even talk. We have to go somewhere else."

A different woman was in front of me now. She was bold, knew what she wanted, and spoke openly. She desired me just as I desired her, but she was more realistic. She had the experience of women's long history of caution and concealment. Puzzled, I said, "How?"

As if she had spent the night rehearsing the words, she said, "We can meet in the town, among the crowds where nobody knows us."

It was clear she had been thinking about the matter, thinking hard. Al-Jazya had been right in her telling: when a woman wants something she finds the way. I looked at her in amazement: this delicate young woman, like an angel free from all worldly sins—her body was now in a tumult of craving. What had wrought such a change? I stared at her as she spoke and saw her as a different person. She went on, "My aunt lives in the town. She had a baby a few days ago and it's natural I should go and see her."

She stopped speaking and she was breathless—this had been very difficult for her. I said foolishly, "Are you going to visit her alone?"

She looked at me in surprise. "You haven't got it yet? I'll be there waiting for you. Close this damned clinic and come and meet me."

She paused, catching her breath, as I gazed at her in wonder. Her face had turned very red and she could not look me in the eye.

I said, "How did you come up with all that?"

Almost inaudibly she said, "Do you want to change your mind?"

Moving closer to her, I blurted, "Definitely not! This is more than I was dreaming of!"

She looked toward the door of the clinic and warned, "Don't come any nearer, and don't try to touch me."

I stepped back a little. I should have kissed her at this moment, when she appeared flushed with desire, but I was afraid of spoiling everything. I said, "And when will we do this?"

Without looking at me, she said, "I'll tell you when, once I arrange things with . . . my husband."

She said this hesitantly, as if trying to dismiss the fact that she was married, then in an instant she turned around and went out through the clinic door. She raced away and I stood staring after her as her feet barely touched the ground, thinking about her surprise offer, and wondering whether it would actually happen.

Over the next few days, we exchanged no words outside of the realm of work, and she even ignored my glances. The patients came in droves as usual, an uninterrupted torrent, and the medications began to run out. I sent a list to the Directorate to provide me with new supplies, but as usual I received no response. I would have to go myself, and I would have to tour the various functionaries' offices to collect the necessary approvals. I told Desougi that I was going to close the clinic and go. I didn't specify the timing, but everyone knew that the clinic would be closing its doors. The number of patients gradually began to fall off and Desougi started to look at me questioningly—why hadn't I made a move? Why didn't I go and bring more supplies? I looked in her direction, but she said nothing, and fixed no date. I watched her leave every day. She walked ahead, her husband a few steps behind her, and I wondered whether she had had second thoughts, whether she was afraid, whether her plan had been uncovered? The only answer was long hours of evasion. But finally, she spoke. She took advantage of the room being empty between patients to say, "I'm going the day after tomorrow. Go a day ahead of me."

I remained calm and nodded silently, turning to the next patient, and after two more patients she spoke again. "The day after tomorrow, five o'clock, in Station Square."

With these short telegraphic communications our exchange ended. Her husband was wandering around in the forecourt of the clinic and she went out quickly to join him, not even waiting until I had finished dispensing the medications. I saw them moving off in the usual way: her in front and him behind. How would it be with me? This latest episode had revealed the strength of her character that belied her delicate frame—she knew what she wanted and she worked for it. I finished up with the final patient and went back to Desougi. "We no longer have enough medications. I'm going to the Health Directorate tomorrow, so we'll close the clinic for a few days."

This didn't seem to arouse his suspicions. "Shall I come with you?"

"Not now. Maybe in a day or two. I'll call you."

There was no reason to prolong the conversation. I went upstairs to prepare my travel bag, secretly shaking. All my relations with women went through my mind: the moment of reaching maturity, at which childish feelings ceased, when the way I viewed the opposite sex changed and my relationship with them altered; the chases and the furtive kisses; the delight of touch and the electrical charges that it set off in the soul; the first moments of passion and the feelings of all-encompassing rapture; the unanticipated separations and break-ups; the experience of a failed connection that left a sense of emptiness in the universe; the unsatisfactory sexual encounters; the fear of whores—though this was a plunge that had to be taken, a test to affirm one's manhood, but an inconclusive one, the whores always overacting, wanting the client to know how strong and stimulating he was, and how capable of satisfying a woman. It was a spurious test, but it instilled confidence—it confirmed that you loved the opposite sex in a sound and natural way—at least until you had a genuine experience, even if this was still unsatisfactory and remained so for years to come.

I left the village early, grateful to The Fairest of Them All for turning up on time. She carried me along easily, as she left behind the grove of palms and the fog that still lay over the top of them. I was surrounded by faces from the village, and their animals. The sun rose quickly up in the sky so that the fog dispersed and the road became visible, while I wished I were not so visible as that myself: they were all staring at me for no reason, or so it seemed to me. Some seized the opportunity to complain of their aches and pains, but I had only one response for them: "Come to the clinic." I didn't know if they were really asking or just trying to draw me out, but I resolved to remain silent. Some disembarked, and more climbed on than had climbed down. By the time we reached the asphalt road the crush was suffocating and there was no air to breathe. I gasped for breath where I sat until we arrived at the teeming bus station, where I hurried away from their throng—I didn't want any of them to follow me. I walked as far as Station Square, where I was to wait the next day, but suddenly I was hit by the question I had not considered until now: Where was the place that could serve for this encounter?

I was a stranger, wandering around in a town where I had neither family nor friends, and I had just one day to find an answer to this problem. I went around in circles. The only way was to take a room in one of the cheap hotels around the square. I knew I would have to haggle hard, but I was prepared to pay whatever might be necessary for blind eyes to be turned. I picked up my bag and entered the first establishment, the Family Inn. The entrance was antiquated, with the walls covered in faded wood panels. A large man stood inside, his face bisected by a mustache that was twirled up at the ends. I gave him my national ID card and said, "I need a room for two nights."

"There are no single rooms. Are you happy to share?"

I hesitated a little. "I want a double room. My wife will be joining me tomorrow."

He pondered my ID card again, pursed his lips, and said, "Your ID says you're single, not married."

"I just got married," I said firmly. "I haven't changed it yet."

He handed it back to me. "Come back when you have the new one."

He was stern, his mustache practically jumping out from his face, but nonetheless I had to try. "I'll pay double the rate."

He was resolute. "I don't do that kind of business. Goodbye, young man."

I withdrew. The situation was impossible and money would not fix it. I stood uncertainly outside the hotel door, not wanting to give up. Retreat was not an option. I faced the same response in the Paradise Hotel and the Dreams Hotel—someone even threatened to call the police, so I slipped quickly out of his way. I was feeling humiliated, but I carried on. I went into the fourth hotel, the Inn of the Honorable Ones—the name alone was enough to send me into a state of desperation and dread. It seemed to be of a lower standard than the others, but all I wanted was four walls. I stood at the entrance a while, contemplating the person behind the reception desk. He didn't look to be the owner: he was emaciated and simply dressed, wearing a singlet under a faded vest. Perhaps I could come to an understanding with him. I went up to him boldly and having taken out a rather large bill before a word was exchanged, placed it in front of him. Without looking at my face he put out his hand automatically, hid the bill under the desk, and then looked up at me with a pale smile. "I want a room for two nights," I said. "My wife will join me tomorrow."

He took my ID card, a conniving grin on his face, and I sighed with relief when he began to enter the details in the ledger in front of him. Almost inaudibly he asked for the name of my wife. I gave him some name or other and he wrote that down in the ledger too. Raising his head, he said, "The hotel is packed out, so the rate is double."

We looked at each other: all cards were on the table. Silently, I gave him the amount he was asking, and he handed me the key. "Make sure your wife comes and goes quietly. No sitting outside the room and don't let the owner of the hotel see her."

He pointed to a photograph that hung on the opposite wall: a large man with a bristling mustache—he looked exactly like the owner of the first hotel, and the second, and perhaps the third. It was lucky he wasn't around, but this man was making his conditions clear. He was a pander who could sniff out the scent of any sexual transaction and I found myself caught in his web. I never thought my desire, my hunger, would bring me to this. The man came out from behind the reception desk and picked up my bag. "Your obedient servant Bastawisi. If you need anything else, I'm at your service."

He climbed a few stairs and led me along a dark corridor to open the door of a run-down room of middling size, pointed to the bed that stood in its center, and winked. "I chose this room for you because of the bed—it's wide and firm and doesn't make any noise. There's no other bed like it in the whole hotel. This is a special service for you. I expect you'll give me my reward when you're done."

I found him annoying, but like any professional pimp he was putting the screws on, and he enjoyed what he was doing. Finally, after much importuning, he put my bag on a wooden stand and left me alone. I sat on the edge of the bed, which was not comfortable: the mattress was thin, and I could feel the wooden slats of the bedframe through it. But there was no alternative and I lay down on the covers. Ahead of me was a whole day of waiting—that is, if things went as planned. I left my bag in the depressing room and went on foot to the medical stockroom of the Health Directorate, where I busied myself with the medication inventories and obtaining the necessary clearances—this would remove any seeds of doubt on the part of Desougi and his ilk. I had a meal in a restaurant, tasty in spite of the modest look of the place, and walked on as far as the shore of the Nile, where I sat facing the desert hills of the other bank. I contemplated the sun as it set, hitting the rocks of the hills and gifting them various colors. I didn't want to focus on her, or on her husband. I was only here because I was entangled in an impossible and mysterious lust that I was trying to satiate, no matter how. I watched the waters of the river as they let go of the daylight and soaked up the dark of night. I walked back to the hotel, where Bastawisi met me with his smirk, rubbing his hands and asking if I was going to spend the night alone. I muttered something and went up to my room. It wasn't easy to sleep—I should have been at the clinic now, anticipating the morning line of patients—but I drowned in nightmares one after the other.

Morning was different: gray and strange for this hot city. I fled the hotel without looking anyone in the face. There was nowhere to go except to the bank of the Nile and its flowing brown waters. I was tense, and my tension would only grow as the day went on. My desire was blind. I wanted to draw this village wife to a soiled bed in a cheap hotel, though she had not been guileless herself—when I took one step toward her she took two steps toward me. Anyway, I carried on with my errands and made sure that all was going well with the forms for issuing the medications. Then, I went to Station Square and sat at an inconspicuous café that allowed a view of what was going on in the square but where nobody would notice me. I scrutinized the faces of the passersby—were any of the villagers here? Was there anyone who could recognize me? Time elapsed slowly, the hands of the clock stood still. Was it really possible she would come? Did she have the nerve? I was still torn between leaving and waiting to see what would happen. I don't know how the time passed as I sat there without moving. Memories of all my earlier frustrations went through my mind, overloaded as it was by unbidden thoughts.

Despite all my apprehensions, I saw her coming. I could not see her face, which was hidden behind the red plush shawl, but I saw her frightened movements: she stopped and looked around, then placed her steps carefully on the ground as if she might be about to fall into a deep chasm. I felt her terror, as I was also terrified. I put some money on the café table, without being aware how much, and stood up. She saw me at once and stood motionless on the spot and I thought she might turn and run. She stared at me from behind her shawl as I continued to move toward her, and she gestured with her hand, spreading her palm, signaling that I should stop. We both stood stock still and it seemed as though all eyes in the square were fixed on us. I turned around, my back to her. My steps were slow and unsure and I paused every few moments to glance back to be certain she was following me. A great distance separated us: the distance between our two worlds—two strangers connected only by the need to touch the other—as if we were not together. My heart was quaking, as hers surely was too. We walked on in this awkward way until we reached the door of the hotel, where I turned and signaled to her to wait. I stepped across the threshold alone and looked quickly around: there was nothing but the colluding smile of Bastawisi and the angry picture on the wall. I hurried back and beckoned to Farah to follow me. The moments of hesitation were over—it was as if she had made a break with her past life—and she followed me inside. Bastawisi watched us with his sly grin and winked at me, but I ignored him. Farah went quickly up the stairs, hiding her face. We headed swiftly to the room and I breathed a sigh of relief when I closed the door behind us.

In the room, after we locked the door, our inexperience with each other was apparent. Farah stood there uncertain, not knowing what to do, as I stood there silently observing her, afraid to make any move that would frighten her more than she was frightened already. She sat on the edge of the bed to calm her gasping breath, pulled the red shawl from her hair to reveal her blood-red face, and looked at me with questioning eyes. I moved nearer to sit beside her, took her hand, patted it, and felt its trembling. She left her hand in mine, suddenly saying, "I'm terrified. I can't believe I'm doing this. It's my first time. And the last too."

"There is always a first time. Don't be afraid of anything. You're safe inside these walls. I know it's not a very nice place, but it's all I could manage."

She almost smiled. "What matters is that we're away from the eyes of all of them. To do something like this we have to be far from all eyes, all the eyes of the village."

"It's Desougi's eyes I'm most concerned about."

I succeeded in making her smile a little, and I used the opportunity to pull the red shawl away from her head. I touched her hair. She grasped my hand—she didn't move it away but kept it where it was. "Let me catch my breath first."

"We have plenty of time."

My fingers ran through her hair, soft and enticing. She shuddered. "Believe me, I didn't come here for the thing that might happen between us. It's different for me—I can do without, I've reconciled my body to that, but . . ."

She waited a while before going on. "Then I saw the way you looked at me, following me everywhere with your eyes. Since I was married nobody has paid me any attention, not even my husband. It was a beautiful thing to see your interest, especially as you came from another world. But deep down I wanted more than that and when you kissed me in spite of myself in the maize field, my body caught fire and hasn't calmed down since."

She spoke with captivating simplicity, her eyes shining as though on the edge of tears. Her desire overwhelmed her. I put my arms around her shoulders and pulled her to me. This time her body would be compliant, it would be willing, it would not be caught off guard. But she shook, through an excess of timidity. I found her lips—this was the best thing: always I found her lips, warm and soft. They took form and melted away between mine. She left them to me and I relished their taste. Her hot breath seared my face, her whole body blazed. She lowered her head, gasping. "I know there's no future for any relationship between us except this moment."

"So, let's take as much pleasure from it as we can."

Removing our clothes was no simple matter—we were shedding the traces of our old life entirely. Years of restraint, decades of inhibitions prevented us from seeing ourselves as we were. We wanted to achieve the state of nakedness before sin, the liberation of our bodies from their constriction. We realized we had not prepared for this moment as we should have done—inexperience kept us fettered in our ordinary clothes, our counterfeit husks. We wore too many things, each one creating resistance with our bodies, and with the long history of concealment. Achieving the point of coalescence was not easy. Her desire notwithstanding, she still instinctively resisted revealing her naked self to me, but then she allowed my hand to roam freely around her body. The whole time, I imagined she might put an end to everything and leave the bed. She remained hesitant, knowing that another body was preparing to plunge into hers, but I finished with every last piece of clothing, and finally succeeded in seeing her gleaming body in all its splendor. Together, we discovered that being naked was the best thing about making love, because it tears away all the differences manufactured by clothes, all the differences and the honorifics, all the fragments of the past and the places that we belong to, and the people who tie us to them; it grants us rare moments of emancipation from the vice of shame, simply transforming us into two blank, pure bodies, brought together solely by desire and the need for repletion. There can be no good sex with clothes on, not just practically but psychologically too, but her body seemed more lush and immaculate than it had a right to be, a body radiant as if untouched by a man before now, inviolate, and never brought to the peak of its ecstasy. I didn't tire of kissing every part of it, as she demurred, then surrendered, then cautiously enjoyed. The darkened room was filled with dozens of colored stars and reflected off her abdomen was a soft light whose source I couldn't identify. I said, "I dreamed of this moment, but I didn't believe it could happen." She said, "I knew from the very first that you wanted me, but it was beyond me to take the risk." I found her lips—always I found her lips. Talk ceased, but the incandescence of her body did not. Her responses were natural, without affectation. She was avid and ardent but as far from banal as it was possible to be. We paused, out of breath, but she was even keener to take the rites of pleasure further. She clung to my neck and said, "Don't go away, I want every drop of you inside me." The intensity of her appetite struck a tremor in me and I contemplated her anew, as though inside her there were more than one woman—every time she surprised me with a different personality. Her eyes were closed and there were beads of sweat on her brow. She had not yet revived from her trembling, she was away in another world. I thought that I would make love to her again, that I would never weary of it. We both became alert at the sound of someone knocking on the door and gasped together in fright. The color drained from her face and she turned pale as if she were about to faint. I pulled myself together, pushed myself up from her, and shouted, "Who is it?" No one answered, but the knocking came again more urgently. I put on the first thing that came to hand, while she wrapped herself in all the covers so that nothing of her was showing and pressed herself against the wall. I went to the door and opened it a crack. There was Bastawisi's face with its unctuous smile. In a colluding tone he said, "Can I do anything for you? Do you need anything to eat or drink?"

I had to restrain myself from punching him in the face. He stood back a little when he saw my expression, and said, "I'm your obedient servant. I just wanted to warn you about the loud noises coming from the room. I was worried on your behalf."

I stepped back from the door and searched my clothes for an appropriate bill, which I took back to him. His grin broadened as he snatched it from my hand. "Don't worry about it—enjoy yourself at the top of your voice!"

I closed the door and returned to her, pulling the covers from her shaking body. She held onto them and looked at me wide-eyed as she whispered, "I was terrified." I stroked her soft body, trying to restore her to the warmth of passion. I took her in my arms, feeling her breasts against my chest. Still shaking, she said, "I thought it was my husband. Not just him, but the rest of the village all behind him." I stroked her hair and whispered, "Nobody knows we're here." I kissed her head and her tresses. She said, "I want to leave." I said, "That's crazy. Where would you go at this time of night? You won't be able to get to the village and you can't possibly go to your aunt. Your place is here, beside me."

She calmed down at last. Assailed by distant memories, she said, "When my mother died, when I was fourteen, silence ruled our house, a heavy silence, like darkness at noon. My father worked in the fields all day and came home exhausted, without the energy to speak. And even if he did have the energy there was nothing between us to be said. We sat silent—all talk had died inside of me. It was to escape that silence that I agreed to be married to Eissa early, but he was the same—silent, and out of work most of the time. His whole life is one moment, repeated. I needed someone to break the silence that surrounded me. At work, at the clinic, I talked with you. I could never speak with those two nurses at all, they're so dreadfully old. Talking with you was good, but it was only now and then, and not enough. I wanted something more: a living child, his body brimful of all the essentials of life, who won't stop wailing and crying and demanding food. That's all I want."

Warmth returned to her limbs, and she kissed me. Everything changed. The pulse of desire was reawakened and flowed through our veins. The impetuosity had cooled, but not our desire, which had become more intimate. Our flesh made contact in many places. We learned the details of our two bodies and became more able to cleave them together to become a single form. As she felt my hand circling on her belly, she said, "I've never been this naked, even with my husband. I don't know how I managed to take all those clothes off." I was surprised. "Wasn't your husband naked with you?" "Not once. Even though we were married, he always kept in mind that I was his cousin. There was always part of his body that was concealed from me. I now know your body better than I do his." At one point, talk faded away, and there was no more need for words. We realized that we were no longer making love of our own volition—it was our bodies that continued to engage with each other in a soundless clamor, with feelings more fundamental than the simple gratification of desire. Love, intimacy, play, and the endless things we did made up for the old disappointments and gathered together all the scattered hopes, allowing us to bear the different hardships we faced: she, the marriage imposed on her since childhood; I, this distant exile following the loss of my past world. She caught her breath, covered her body in order to curb her arousal, and said, "You're so strangely solitary. Are you all alone in this great wide world? Why don't you tell me about your family?" She was trying to get close to me, but without meaning to she was opening my old wounds. I said, "I really am all alone. My father and mother died in a train crash. They were on a short trip to a nearby town, something not worth dying over, but these incidents have become commonplace, and we pay the price of death for the slightest things—they swallow up lives and nobody pauses to inquire as to the reason, as if losing my world in a single blow was an inescapable destiny."

We consoled ourselves with more kissing. There was no need to chew over old sorrows. The peeling walls of this miserable hotel were an insulating barrier against all the realities that deaden the heart. We both glowed in the physicality of the other with new life and a different beginning. As the hours of the night passed, an intimate connection was born through the pinnacle of unceasing rapture. One encounter was not enough, and a single night was a short life for thirsty bodies. I didn't know whether she was rocked by the same sensations, but we dozed off each holding fast to the other, making love in the deepest darkness without waking, unaware of whether this was dream or reality. Despite everything, daylight took us by surprise. Sunlight slipped insistently through the gaps in the window. Farah turned away from me, but she remained naked, her body visible, the light imparting to it a sort of fresh grace, primed for an early-morning act of intimacy. We had already done this without barriers or reservations. The moment of climax was our property, to be summoned simply, and spontaneously. She tried to conceal the satisfied smile that beamed from her face and the luster that radiated through her skin, embarrassed at having given free rein to her desire. She put out her hand for her fingers to play in my chest hair. "We have to go our separate ways now, and no one knows if there is hope of a meeting to come or not. Could we . . . ?" She left her question open. I moved the hair away from her face. She appeared especially ardent in the light of day. I began kissing her, then covered her with my body. She gasped in submission. "This is the best way to be sure that every drop of you is inside me." I didn't know what she meant, but certainly we locked together once again, each having become an expert on the other's body, knowing where excitement resided and where yearning lay. I was filled with renewed energy, as if we were joining together for the first time, and she received me with craving and longing. Neither of us wanted to reach the point of fulfillment. We heard sounds of life outside and were jolted by a knocking at the door of the room. I knew it was that damned Bastawisi. I didn't want to argue with him, but he had put me off my stride. I threw on some clothes and opened the door. I saw his grin and his yellow teeth. "Forgive me, I didn't want to interrupt anything, but the hotel owner is coming now. If you're planning to stay on, you'll have to keep to the room all day, but if you were thinking of leaving, you'll have to go now."

I closed the door and went back to find her silently dressing. All of a sudden, the encounter was over, and we could no longer return to the bed or remain trapped in the room. Curses on Bastawisi and the hotel owner both. We slipped out of the room on tiptoe. Bastawisi was sitting on his chair pretending not to see us. We went out quickly, not stopping until we were far enough away. The town was quiet, with few people in the streets, but we were now open to view. I said, "I want us to have breakfast together."

Scared, she said, "That's impossible. It's enough what we've done. I'll go to my aunt's house now and I'll stay there for the next couple of days. I don't want to leave any room for doubt."

She wrapped the shawl carefully around her face to obscure her features. She waved goodbye to me without hiding her contented smile and I watched her walk away, taking part of my soul with her. I went to the bank of the Nile and sat still by its quiet waters, trying to pacify my very self, to convince it that what we had done wasn't simple adultery, that it was desire turned into passion—a passion that had to be concluded in its natural place, in bed, where a body could express its deepest and sincerest longings, pure desire without falsehood. Her husband was nothing but a passing shadow, a trivial connection, a partner not invited into her bed. I repeated these phrases to myself as I took a breakfast of beans and eggs at a small eating house, I repeated them in the offices of the Health Directorate as I completed the order for the medications, and I repeated them again as I sat aboard The Fairest of Them All, crowded with people and animals. Could they smell her on me? What had happened was a dream that should never have ended. I watched what was going on around me carefully. Had anyone seen us? Did anyone know what had occurred in that miserable hotel that had been witness to the best time of my life?

The bus chugged along in the same old way, as if the world had not changed. The tops of the palms showed up bright green as though washed in the sweat of our lovemaking. Insane feelings rolled around inside me, as reality revealed the houses of the village—where her husband was, and her world, and all the obstacles that stood in the way of our relationship. We stopped in front of the line of men forever sitting against the wall. Some of them stood to receive the arrivals while others stayed as they were, heedless of the bustle around them. Even in the crush, I caught sight of him next to the wall—her husband, Eissa—peering at everyone, searching for someone, for her no doubt. But his gaze fixed on me and he followed me with his eyes. I avoided looking into his face, as I didn't want our eyes to meet so as not to feel any sense of guilt. I ignored him and turned my back, heading for the clinic, but in my peripheral vision I could see that he was walking behind me. What did he want? Was he carrying a knife? I didn't want to speed up, which might make me look scared. He continued following me, maintaining the same distance between us. At the door, I saw Desougi standing in anticipation of my return—he had appeared at just the right time. I sighed with relief and entered the clinic without looking back. I paused to talk with Desougi, expecting Eissa to stop or turn back, but he kept on coming, climbed the steps of the clinic, and approached us decisively. It was a decisiveness I didn't like, as though he wanted to expose me in front of Desougi, to make a scene right there in the clinic, so I turned to him and said sharply, "What do you want?"

I wanted to startle him. He recoiled at my harsh tone and stammered, "Medicine . . . I want medicine."

I realized at once that he knew nothing or else he would not have been so weak and confused. I said, "Go to the examination room. I've just arrived back from the town. Sit there and wait for me."

He sat, obediently, on a chair outside the room, curled up into himself, wanting to disappear. I was being aggressive, even rather overbearing, as befitted a secret lover. I went upstairs, threw down my bag, stripped off my clothes, and stood under the stream of water. I didn't want him to smell her scent on me—if he truly loved her his instinct would guide him to it. I used more than one kind of soap, leaving him to wait for me as long as possible. Then I went down to see him, totally alert and feeling superior: I had taken possession of the woman I wanted, while he thought he owned her. He may have been a step ahead of me with her life, but I was steps ahead of him with her body. I took care to hang the stethoscope around my neck and gestured for him to follow me into the examination room, far from Desougi's ears. In a businesslike manner I asked him, "What's the matter with you?"

"I want to sleep," he pleaded. "Any medicine to help me sleep without nightmares."

I resolved to give him something, anything, so that he would go away, but I found myself taking the conversation further without really wanting to. "You don't have children, right?"

He stared at me, but I didn't back down, and he said, "We're trying. We're still very young, and . . ."

I interrupted him. "Have you been to see a specialist?"

He shook his head and I said, "So you don't know whether the problem is with you or with her?"

He stood up, and I realized I had gone too far. I said, "Sit down, I'll bring you the medicine you want."

I hurried to the dispensary. Of course, I had been impertinent, but I wanted to know everything about the woman who had been in my arms just a few hours earlier. I brought him some pills, some harmless sedatives, which he took while muttering a few unclear words before leaving. I followed him as he went off in a hurry, almost falling on his face. Desougi watched me watching him, and said, "We should have charged him the consultation fee."

I answered without caring. "There wasn't much wrong with him."

I slept deeply, feeling that there was nothing clogging me up inside—no disturbing dreams, nor any hint of a guilty conscience, not even any thought about next steps. I took a light breakfast and went downstairs. Everyone was there except her. The two other nurses regarded me—with women's intuition they knew that things were different with me when she was not around. I moved away in a mechanical manner. Eissa wasn't there as I had thought he might be and this seemed a cause for comfort. I wanted her and naturally didn't want him. I was not a villain, but she had chosen me. The patients thronged in with their various symptoms, and Desougi arrived carrying the shipment of medications. I heaved a deep sigh as I opened the window and saw their pale faces crowding before me. I finished with them all and sat alone after everyone had left. It was the middle of the day, and I didn't want to go upstairs, I wanted to go out into the sunlight and see everything. I wanted to see The Fairest of Them All coming to the village, perhaps with Farah on board. Desougi sat on the steps talking, without me listening to what he was saying. The bus didn't come, but another vehicle arrived in a cloud of dust. It was a pitch-black paddy wagon, tearing in, heedless of anyone leaping out of its way. There must be some problem in the village, but no, the van turned sharply to head for the clinic, and directly toward me, fast as a snorting beast. I stood up, worried—the sudden arrival of a police vehicle at such a speed was alarming. It stopped right in front of me, enveloping me in a halo of exhaust fumes. Somebody jumped out, and I didn't recognize him until the dust settled: it was the ma'mour, the superintendent of police himself, in person. I was anxious, as if he had caught me red-handed this time too. He stood adjusting his uniform and his cap and signaled to some figures sitting in the back of the van, who all went into action to drag something out of it. A body fell on the ground in front of me, emitting a cry of pain. Not just a body, it was a woman that had been thrown roughly down, a pile of dark rags. But she was still alive. She moved with difficulty to collect herself. She raised her head and pulled away the hair that covered her bloody face. I was in shock, while the ma'mour stood erect and self-important, bragging, "I brought her to you, so there's no need for you to go to her."

I didn't know what he meant. I looked again at the face of the woman sprawled on the ground, swollen and covered in abrasions and bruises, and recognized her with difficulty—she was not the Jazya I had watched dancing and telling stories, overflowing with vitality; she was a battered creature trying to cling onto the last fringes of life, barely wresting her breath from the dust-polluted air. Taking no notice of the vindictive stance of the ma'mour, I gestured to Desougi to help me pick her up. I didn't want any of them to touch her. Together, we carried her wrecked body into the examination room and laid her gently on the table. She wasn't unconscious, but her vital signs were on the point of vanishing, and every time she tried to move, some part of her body hurt her. I quickly gave her an intramuscular injection to relieve the pain, then inspected the rest of her body, which was covered in bruises. She had been brutally beaten and every part of her was covered in small cuts, which I cleaned and treated with antiseptic cream. I bound the wound on her leg with sterilized gauze, but her whole body was soiled and giving off a foul smell, and I didn't want the cuts to become dirty and inflamed. Her breathing eased a little and she peered at me with her wide eyes as I was dressing her wounds, but I couldn't tell whether she recognized me or knew exactly where she was. Her glazed eyes were lustrous and unreactive and she was finally able to close them; her breathing became regular. Strangely, she fell asleep, and didn't feel me examining her body. She looked like a small child who had finally found a safe refuge. She shivered a little then relaxed. Without my asking, Desougi wiped her face to remove the dust and congealed blood, then brought a clean sheet and spread it over her. She needed quiet to free herself from the terror she had gone through. We left the room and closed the door on her. I was relieved to find that the police vehicle was gone. I was rid of the ma'mour, and I could treat this poor woman, and then let her go on her way as soon as she had regained her strength. But the nightmare continued. I stepped outside and there was the ma'mour, sitting in my very chair, stretching out his legs in the sun, and contentedly exhaling the smoke of his cigarette. I brought another chair and sat facing him. He drew in his legs slightly and threw his still lit cigarette on the ground. He contemplated me for a while, then said, "You don't think I came here just for the sake of this Gypsy woman."

Surprised, I said, "I assumed you didn't want her to die in your prison cell."

He was unconcerned. "She's not that important, alive or dead. She's of no value, and no one will ask after her. In these parts, most people are of no consequence."

He paused to light another cigarette and went on. "My reason for coming here is much more serious."

I felt uneasy and had no intention of having any dealings with him, but I asked, "What is it?"

"You know that in theory we have no president of the Republic. Since the last one was assassinated at that unfortunate military parade, we're without a head of state. Not in practice, but in theory."

I didn't know what he meant. "I thought the vice president had assumed authority in his place and the matter was settled."

"The matter is settled, certainly, but the regime needs a cloak of legitimacy. That's the role of the election game and the justification it provides."

"I understand that, but what does that game have to do with me?"

"This time, you're going to be part of it. This clinic will be a polling station and you will be supervising the casting of five hundred votes."

I objected. "And how is that my business? I'm employed by the Ministry of Health, not the Ministry of Interior."

"I know that, but this is a presidential election, so it's above all our heads and it must be scrupulously free, with no interference from the Ministry of Interior. Doesn't that appeal to you?"

He gave me a meaningful look—did he know something about my history? Had he conducted his investigations into me, in typical police manner? What did his tone convey, mockery or threat? I said, "Do these votes have any weight? Will they really affect the outcome of the election?"

He laughed as he stood up. "Nobody wins through the ballot boxes. As I said earlier, it's a game, and we all have to play our part."

He signaled with his hand in the air and I realized that the paddy wagon was still there, parked at a distance under a tree. The engine started, and it approached. I said, "And this woman, what should I do with her?"

His laughter doubled. "She's yours. Do what you like with her. If she dies, throw her in the street, someone will bury her, even without a shroud. And if she lives, her Gypsy family will come for her, they'll smell her out wherever she is. Don't worry, consider her a gift from me."

As he climbed into the vehicle he gestured to me. "In a few days you'll receive the boxes and the voting sheets. You'll have to close the clinic on the day."

The van snarled and raised more dust, leaping out onto the main road with no care for whatever people or animals might be in its path. I stood there staring after it, feeling genuinely foolish. Desougi followed me as I went back into the clinic. I opened the door of the examination room to look in on al-Jazya. She was still sleeping, in a heap on the examination table, snoring quietly. I closed the door again, as Desougi said, "What are we going to do with her?"

"Let her sleep, but leave some food by her side. Perhaps she'll wake up, eat something, and go."

I suddenly felt tired. I went up to my quarters and tried listening to music or distracting myself with the sunset behind the palms. I did not rest easily. I knew that al-Jazya would hold out until the morning: she was strongly built, she just needed some care, and a restful sleep without fear. I drifted off, I don't know for how long, but when I woke it was still dark and I remembered that she was still under the clinic's roof. Desougi must have locked the door and gone home. What had happened to her? Was she still alive? It had been rash of me to leave her in the building, but I hadn't known what to do with her. Was I to have thrown her outside in the state she was in? I lit the lamp, stamped my feet on the floor to scatter the rats, opened the door carefully, and went downstairs. Entering the examination room, I lifted the lamp high to shed light on the place, and paused, startled, the lamp shaking in my hand: I saw her wrapped in the white sheet, sitting on the examination table like a ghost risen from among the dead. She turned to me, a look of great alarm on her face, and screamed, "Who are you? What do you want?"

I stood where I was, shone the lamp on my face, and said, "Don't be afraid. It's . . . me, just me."

She stared at me with bulging eyes. I remained standing there, allowing her the chance to comprehend where she was. Then I slowly moved closer to her, placed the lamp between us, and said gently, "You're out of the police station now."

She closed her eyes. "You're the physician, now I remember."

"You're far away from their clutches now and you're free to leave whenever you want."

She said sadly, "I don't think I'll be able to walk for a long time."

I reassured her, "You're going to be fine."

Close to tears, she said, "You don't know what this body went through. He let all the sergeants and the conscripts and the security agents violate me. They all took their share of my body."

I was stunned. "Unbelievable!"

"Bring the lamp closer and see for yourself."

She lifted the end of the torn dress she was wearing to reveal her legs full of bruises and scratches. She raised it higher, above her thighs. She was not wearing anything to hide her private parts, but there was a patch of dark, dry, blood that covered this area, and I was unable to distinguish its anatomical form. She said, "Keep your hand away, don't try to touch it—that would be more than I could bear."

"It must be cleaned. Are you still bleeding?"

"No. I no longer feel anything, I no longer feel pain there. That part of me is numb, perhaps dead. After they went on raping me, I stopped feeling anything. Even when they were lying on top of my breasts, panting like hungry dogs, I didn't feel them. As soon as they entered the cell, I went into an intense darkness where I saw and heard nothing."

Her words were stinging and painful. I said, "You're safe now. I'll have the nurses clean you up in the morning. They'll put moisturizing creams on and I'll give you some antibiotics. And I can have you transferred to the hospital if you like."

She was on the point of crying. "There's no need for that. My people will come and take me and take care of me in their own way. We face rape every day—the women, the children, sometimes the men—so we're good at using herbs to treat these injuries."

I pitied her. "Why do you live under such difficult circumstances? What compels you to live this way?"

She sighed. "Destiny and fate. We are under a curse that has lasted for all time. Our forefather, the father of all Gypsies, fought with his brother over a flock of sheep, and in a burst of rage killed him. So, heaven was angered and placed the curse on him, and since that time he and his offspring have roamed the face of the earth."

I looked at her in wonder. I didn't have much faith in legends, but without knowing it she was relating the story of humanity. And despite all that had happened to her, she had still not lost her powers of narration. I said, "Regardless of what they did to your body, your mind is in good shape."

I lifted the lamp up and found a loaf of bread and some cheese placed on the table. I said, "Here's a little food, and I can bring you more from upstairs if you want it."

"This will be enough for me. I'm more in need of sleep."

Feeling for her, I said, "I'll leave you to rest. Shall I leave you the lamp?"

"No. . . . Gypsies are like cats—they're only themselves in the dark of night."

I took the lamp and climbed the stairs. I didn't know why what I had done for this woman had made me feel less guilty, but I slept deeply for the first time in days.

Early in the morning, I woke to the sound of Desougi's knock on the door. "The Gypsy woman's relatives are here," he said. "They're filling up the place and want to take her away."

I was surprised. "How did they find her so fast? They must have eyes everywhere."

I went downstairs and saw their strange faces tanned by the sun, their clothes burdened by the dust of the open roads, and a single brightly painted wagon with an image of a young woman that looked like al-Jazya on one side. A large man approached me, saying, "We want our queen." It was the first time I realized she held an important position.

"Let me ask her first."

In the examination room I found her awake, still wrapped in the white sheet, the blue bruises still covering her face, but she had regained some of her old features. At once, she said, "I didn't want to go with them without thanking you."

I said, "You're still not well. Do you really want to go with them?"

"My only place is among them."

I beckoned to Desougi to open the clinic door wide. Some of the men and women came in and surrounded her, holding back their tears. The women adjusted her robes and arranged her hair, placing small flowers of clover in her tresses, then stepped back as three of the men came forward to shift her body gently and prepared to carry her, but she raised her hand to stop them, commanding instead, "Bring me a stick."

They hurried to the wagon as if they had been expecting this demand and fetched a branch that had been trimmed to make a sturdy walking stick. Leaning on it, she climbed down from the examination table. She was a little unsteady but didn't stumble. It was clear from her face that she was in pain, but she didn't complain or make a sound. She walked slowly, as they all placed their hands on their hearts in supplication, praying for her that she would not fall. At the door of the clinic, she stopped, and grimaced. I said, "Can I at least give you some medication to help you bear the pain?"

She smiled in exhaustion. "Do, physician."

I went quickly to the dispensary and chose things that would bring down her fever, reduce the pain, and help her wounds heal. I returned to find her waiting for me, resting her weight on the stick. She took the bag of medicines from me and gave it to one of her followers. Then she said to them clearly, "Leave us a little—I want to talk with the physician."

They all backed away, leaving the forecourt around us more or less empty. She turned to me and I saw her bright eyes full of tears. Lowering her voice, though I heard her well, she said, "I consent. Any time you want me, anywhere you want, I consent. If you want me to share your bed or just to sit with you through the night, I consent. Whether you share your food with me or leave me hungry, I consent. Use my body as you please or make me a slave to act out all your desires, I consent. Treat me gently or leave marks on my body, I consent. If I'm enough for you or you take another lover, I consent. If you want me now or wait until my wounds heal, I consent."

I wanted to kiss her head in front of everybody, but I wasn't bold enough. I merely put my hand on her shoulder—gently, because I knew it was hurting her. I stood back and waved her goodbye. She walked on, as the other Gypsies slowly approached and surrounded her. She stopped beside the wagon: the women went up its steps as the men came and took the stick from her then lifted her and hoisted her up, the women receiving her with the same gentleness and tenderness. She looked in my direction and gave me a smile through the pain. Certainly, her whole body was hurting her, but she continued to bear it. I wondered whether they would be able to care for her, or whether they would lose her during their long travels. They cheered with joy once they were assured she was lying comfortably, and the wagon began to move off. I watched them until they disappeared from view, and then the villagers began to appear, as though they had not wanted to mix with the Gypsies. And Farah appeared too.

My heart jumped when I saw her crossing the forecourt. I looked at her face and found it neutral—neither smiling nor frowning. She greeted me with a nod of her head before going into the clinic, as if we were two strangers passing on the road. Perhaps she didn't want to reveal what had happened between us. Desougi finished cleaning the examination room and Farah threw me a quizzical look, but the patients left us no time for explanations. She kept her distance, determined to treat me formally. I tried to read signs in any of her gestures or in her words, and finally, more than two hours later I found a brief opportunity to ask her, "What's wrong?"

She replied quickly, "Why did you talk with him?"

I was taken aback. "Who?"

"My husband. You interfered in what's not your business and you made him suspicious."

A patient came in, cutting off the conversation, and her words remained hanging in the air. The patient went out, and none came in. I said, "I wanted to know you were all right. We must talk."

Decisively, she said, "Forget everything. What happened will not happen again. I don't want to ruin my life."

8

Three men—tall, broad, their huge mustaches forming one continuous line across their three faces—stood in front of me in the examination room casting angry glances at the rest of the patients and causing them to draw back. They held thick sticks, which they restively struck on the ground. The tallest of them approached my desk. "The lady requested you by name. We want you to come now and take a look at her."

I didn't know who they were, and I was uncomfortable with them standing there like this—I felt there was some kind of threat involved. "What lady?"

The same man, as if he were the one authorized to speak, replied. "Madame Jalila. You remember her, of course?"

Farah, standing far away in the corner of the room, turned toward us. So, the woman was still alive—I had heard nothing about her since the scandal of Abanoub the tailor—but was she still unwell? Was she living her life as normal since her secret lover had been expelled? The three men stood, blocking my field of vision, their looks alone ensuring that the patients kept their distance.

I recalled what had happened to the unfortunate tailor. "Consulting hours have just begun and there are many patients to see."

He persisted. "We won't take too much time, and the patients aren't going anywhere. And the lady's condition is serious and urgent."

I was reluctant to go with them, even though it was broad daylight. Farah slipped out quickly and headed to the Family Care room: she was afraid my choice would fall on her—as if she had not been anxious to accompany me on every other expedition. Desougi intervened and asked to have a private word with me. "They're her husband's relatives," he said. "And they're hard men. We won't be able to get rid of them easily. We'd better go with them, or else they'll stay here in the clinic all day."

I brought my bag, and Desougi walked behind me. There was no mount, but I had no intention of riding anyway. The three men walked ahead while Desougi and I followed. The village appeared quiet and expectant. I knew the men were in the fields, but where were the children? Why were they not outside playing, and why could I not hear their voices? We reached the drainage ditch at the edge of the village and crossed the dilapidated bridge, following the same route I had taken with Farah. That was just a few weeks ago, but many things had changed since then. The redbrick house appeared amid the crops. One of the men went ahead and pushed open the iron gate. I knew my way into the house, but the three insisted on going in with me. The furniture was as it had been, and the pictures were still there on the walls. We passed through the rooms, and I thought they would take me to the main bedroom, but to my surprise they led me to the same out-of-the-way, unfurnished room as before, where there was nothing but the lone mattress that she had lain on—and she was still lying there, in the same position. They all stood outside the room and left me to go in alone. Was she still suffering the effects of the abortion? The room was unchanged, stark and airless. Had she been here all this time? I went closer. Her body was completely still: she didn't sense me coming in, nor did she hear the voices of the men. I leaned over her and called her name, but she didn't answer or stir, and she didn't appear to be breathing. I shook her gently, but she didn't respond, so I pulled the cover back a little in order to see her face. And now, for the second time, I saw her stained with dried blood, not on her private parts this time but on her chest, near her heart. I looked at her pallid, shrunken face and her frozen, startled eyes. I felt her cold hands and placed my fingers on her carotid artery—there was no trace of any pulse, she was quite dead. She had been stabbed to death, and no one was bothering to hide it. I lifted my head in confusion, looking at the three faces that were staring at me. I stood, facing up to their deathly inflexibility, and said through my teeth, "Why did you insist on bringing me here from the clinic when you knew she was dead, murdered?"

"She's just dead," said the tall one. "That's what it looks like."

I was incensed by his brazenness. "And what about all this blood all over her?"

"We don't want you to bring her back to life. We just want a death certificate."

"I'm not the one to issue a death certificate. Only a coroner can do that."

Their angry voices rose, the room became darker, and they were blocking my exit. One of the others came toward me—I didn't know their names, the only thing that stuck in my mind was their varying heights—and said, "Let's talk in another room, Doctor."

There was nothing that could be said between us, but I wanted any excuse to be out of that room, and away from the dead body. We crossed the corridor to another room. Many women were sitting silently on the steps to the house, neither wailing nor lamenting. I went with the man into the other room, which seemed to be Madame Jalila's main bedroom, with a luxurious bed, a wardrobe with mirrors, and a dressing table. The half-open wardrobe door revealed many dresses on hangers; the man closed it firmly before turning to me and saying smoothly, "We don't have a coroner, and we don't need strange eyes coming among us and uncovering our secrets. You are all we have, and you have to make things easy for us."

"This is a murder," I said. "You know that. It's beyond my specialization, and it's also enough to lose me my job."

He didn't seem to take much notice of my words but went on talking. "You know the scale of the scandals this woman caused. Her relationship with that Copt made us unable to hold our heads high until now. She deserved to die more than once."

I recalled Farah saying that in this village no one forgets, and no one forgives. I said, "You weren't able to forgive the man, so you killed the woman."

He objected. "We didn't kill her, and we don't know who did, but it was God's will."

He reached into an inside pocket and pulled out a bound stack of banknotes—and not the small denominations that I received at the clinic. He said, "Better you than a stranger. The coroner will come and sign what we want, but rather than the scandal and the police, you're one of us, and you can make use of this money."

"A small report from one of her relatives will be enough for the authorities to come and exhume the burial, and everything will be exposed. I don't want to be the victim—let the coroner take that on himself."

I hurried from the room. Desougi was waiting for me, signs of fear on his face, as the two other brothers stood in readiness. I went quickly down the steps, the black-clad women making way for me; if they hadn't been there, I might not have known my way out. As we passed through the iron gate, Desougi said, "What was all the argument about? We didn't get a single pound out of them. Why didn't they pay the consultation fee?"

I didn't reply, hearing his words like tinnitus in my ears. We walked through the silent village, with no children to be seen, as though everybody knew that a murder had taken place. Perhaps they had heard her screams in the middle of the night, but they were all colluding in silence. All except Desougi, who was determined to keep up the ringing in my ears. I walked a few paces ahead in order to avoid listening to him. The clinic came into view, full of the patiently waiting sick—I was amazed that not one of them had left. I threw my bag down and went into the examination room. Farah came to help me, mechanically, and with a different face, worried and tense. I knew the question she wanted to ask, and I hastened to tell her. "They killed her." She gasped aloud, trembled, and leaned against the wall. The patients looked on in surprise and Desougi took a step toward her, but she dashed out of the clinic, not wanting anybody to see her cry. I didn't know just what kind of friendship had been established between them, but suddenly an awful thought occurred to me: Did she see herself in Jalila's place? Was she comparing what had happened between us to what had happened between Jalila and the tailor? Did we both have to expect our punishment?

The police came only on the following day, the black van tearing into the narrow streets of the village, leaping up and down with the uneven road surface, people and animals alike jumping out of its way. I watched it from my balcony. They would go to the house, begin their investigations and their searches, and end up with nothing—I knew this in advance. Farah didn't come to the clinic in the morning, nor did any patients. The unfamiliar presence of the police had set terror in the hearts of all the villagers—they inhabited a small world ruled by the umda and his guards, but their problems began when they were exposed to the wider world of higher authority. The presence of strangers was an existential threat—they didn't want the village to be seen in such a direct and harsh light.

I thought someone from the police would come to interview me, or that I would be called in to answer questions, but this didn't happen. The policemen were scattered around like black crows. Desougi felt it his duty to bring me the news: nobody was talking, nobody was giving out any information, and the coroner had indeed signed the death certificate—"a sharp drop in blood flow"—and issued the burial permit. Everyone was persuaded it had been a burglary, carried out by someone from outside the village for sure. The funeral was held the next day, and I stood on my balcony to watch. Not many people attended, as I had expected, and the three brothers were not there. There were women, a number of them, walking without any outward expression of grief. There were no men to carry the bier, which was large and covered by a green shroud embroidered with Qur'anic verses, but it had been placed on a cart that was pulled by a lean horse more sorrowful than the rest of them put together, which trudged slowly with bowed head, and there was nobody there to give Jalila a genuine farewell. Abanoub could have been hiding somewhere, but she seemed so alone it broke the heart. A line of policemen walked behind the women—I thought they had turned out for the funeral because of the lack of men, but then I realized they were just on their way out of the village for good. The farmers' silence and the substitute narrative made the burial of Madame Jalila and her story both makeshift and quick. In the end, the authorities pay little attention to someone dying in these remote villages. When the cart disappeared from sight, I felt a crushing grief, thinking that it had been in my power to do something to ease her painful fate, but I hadn't been able to.

The next day the ma'mour came to the clinic for the second time, an unwelcome visit as always. I had finished seeing patients, Farah had come and gone quickly. He seemed to know my routine well. He left the paddy wagon at a distance under the shade of a tree and sat smoking and drinking the tea that Desougi had prepared for us. "Did you know her well?"

I gathered he was talking about Jalila and I had no need to hide anything. I told him about my first visit, and half the story about my second. I didn't want to get myself into trouble, or be the only one to talk. He fixed his eyes on me as he said, "Experience tells me it was the three brothers who killed her. That's what always happens, but we always face a wall of silence. The motive is crystal clear, but there are never any witnesses, either direct or indirect. No one has uttered a word that would give us something to hold onto, or an accusation that we could build an investigation on. We have no choice but to close the case, like dozens of others that leave us in despair."

He stopped talking and lowered his head, then raised it again as he continued, "Did you see the inside of the house?"

"Her house?"

"Of course, her house. What was it like?"

"I didn't take a tour of it, but from what I saw it was a prosperous house, wealthier than the houses of the other villagers, apart from the umda of course. It was full of furniture, curtains, and chandeliers, but she left all that behind to sleep on a mattress in an isolated room."

"That's what I thought, but we found nothing."

I didn't understand and looked at him in confusion until he went on. "The house was totally empty, down to the bare tiles—no furniture, no carpets, no beds, no chairs. We only just managed to find a seat for the public prosecutor to sit on."

I was surprised. "I saw one of the rooms, I think it was her bedroom. It was fully furnished, and there was a wardrobe full of all kinds of dresses—where did all that go?"

The ma'mour made to stand up. "It happens a lot, but this is the first time I've seen a house completely stripped to the marrow."

He stood. "We've finished this matter quickly because the elections are at the door. In a few days you'll receive the boxes and the ballots. In the end, the village is clean."

9

I suddenly found the posters everywhere when I was returning from a house call. They were all over the village: attached to palm trunks, pasted on the mud walls of the houses, nailed to telegraph poles—there were even some on the inside walls of the café built of reeds. There was a relatively large one stuck to the wall of the village's only mosque and I stopped to contemplate it: a new pharaoh preparing to take his place on the throne. He didn't wear a golden mask like his pharaonic forebears, but his features themselves were a living mask, assembled by a clandestine priesthood that had been anticipating this moment and readying him for his reign: the slightly thrust-out nose, the prominent lips, the jutting chin—all coming together in an imaginary vertical line on the face, a construction marked by the customary proficiency of those people. I pondered his eyes, their sparkle preserved in the photograph: clear ambition and the desire for absolute power. "He'll last a long time," I heard a voice say from behind me, and I turned to find Senior Arabic Language Teacher Mr. Omar standing next to me, tall and straight. I had seen him before at the school, and once or twice at the clinic. My first impression of him had been that he was the usual kind of schoolteacher—critical and fractious, but above all fearful of the principal, and likely to sicken if his salary was docked. His comment took me by surprise. "Are you talking about this picture?"

"Isn't that the next president? Why is he putting up his picture and setting up elections when he already rules?"

With a touch of cynicism I said, "Elections are important, even if they're unnecessary."

"It costs us to stage them, and we never stop faking them. Even the ancient Egyptians, when they erased the image of the old pharaoh and substituted the new one—this was the oldest form of falsification."

He studied the picture again carefully, trying to see through to what was behind the inscrutable features. "In spite of the bad printing, I can see this man well. That wide brow will never know wrinkles, the careless smile will stay like that, meaning nothing: neither happiness nor pain, no emotion or compassion or sympathy. And that's the secret to a long life. And those prominent lips, with their lust to possess and guzzle down the pleasures of life . . . he'll be rich, this man, the wealthiest king of Egypt."

He looked at me for a long time and I looked back without expression, the face of the gambler playing his last hand. He backed away apologetically, saying, "I didn't mean to implicate you with my talk. You heard nothing from me."

He went off hurriedly, turning to head into the village. I thought he was going to fall on his face, but he stumbled on. I waved to Desougi, who had been standing at a distance, and as he walked beside me, I asked him, "When were these posters put up?"

Uncertain, he said, "They must have gone around in the dark. They've put them up everywhere, even on the walls of the clinic."

"The walls of our clinic? How did I not notice that?"

And indeed, I found many of the pictures on our walls, underscored by the usual slogans about a new age dawning, about dreams to be realized now that this historic man had come, because destiny would follow wherever his footsteps fell. I walked to the entrance of the clinic with my head down, so I was startled by the great frame of the ma'mour blocking the doorway as he watched me approach. "That man you were speaking with in the village street, you shouldn't talk with him. He's a troublemaker, and he'll cause you problems."

I looked at him, stunned. "Are you having me watched? In any case, we didn't talk about anything significant."

"You're not being watched. Not yet, at least. But he is. Even in this remote village there are eyes. And he knows he's being watched and will be arrested."

In alarm I objected, "Why would you arrest him? He's just a regular teacher."

The ma'mour replied coldly, "We know, but we have to do it. It's a part of our police rituals: on every important political occasion that kind of person has to be arrested so that the elections run smoothly. Don't worry—we'll release him as soon as they're over."

He was silent for a while. "You won't tell him that. A simple matter like this doesn't call for a tip-off. And you need to make us trust you again."

He was frighteningly serious and made me feel I was in the grip of something that did not want to let go of me—I was in their clutches. I looked at him in exasperation. He played his role well, acting with terrifying cordiality, but he nimbly and cleverly cleared his face of its frightening mask and added merrily, "Anyway, you shouldn't leave the clinic in these historic times."

Changing the subject, I said, "These posters, when were they put up like this?"

"You see?" he said proudly, "The work of professionals. They can reach the most distant places—even the walls of your miserable village."

"But so many of them!"

"We're in a new world. This image has to be imprinted on everybody's mind, to erase the picture of the last president. That's how things go: everyone new who comes along wants to impose his presence on the memory of all."

The teacher's words about the erasure of ancient Egyptian reliefs came to mind. The ma'mour made a cryptic gesture with his hand, and the black police van appeared from nowhere, snarling and raising dust before coming to a stop in front of the door. I gazed at it in surprise, but he said, "I've brought the goods: the ballots, the box sealed with red wax, the bottles of indelible ink, the wooden partition for the voters to stand behind—all the props for the performance are here."

My astonishment was apparent. "The performance?"

"I told you before, the ballot boxes don't choose the president—it is God alone who chooses. He brings him from obscurity to rule and rise up, before choosing to take him to His side. Everything else is just theater."

I could only follow him open-mouthed as he revealed a hidden side to his character. I wanted to debate him, but I was afraid of him, afraid of all of them. Some conscripts jumped down from the van, carrying the boxes. He said, "These boxes are your responsibility now. Keep them somewhere safe until polling day."

"What? Are you worried about fraud?"

Cheerfully, he said, "The play must be tightly plotted. Take custody."

I led the conscripts to the dispensary, the only place I could be sure of keeping locked. The ma'mour watched me, before sighing with relief when I padlocked the door. "The elections are at the beginning of next week. Of course, there will be no work that day, and we don't recommend any of the employees from the village should be around, to avoid suspicion."

For the first time he laughed, and he placed his hand on my shoulder. "Remember the plot of the play."

He jumped into the vehicle, which growled as it churned up the dust. I stood there until it disappeared from sight, then went back to the dispensary, my head spinning. I contemplated the boxes and felt a sudden, heavy weight settling on my shoulders. The game I had positioned myself on the other side of and had been imprisoned as the price of my opposition to, I had now become a part of. I should set light to these boxes now, but that wouldn't change anything and would send me back to prison. I went upstairs feeling that the clinic had become compromised, and that these boxes were full of equipment for spying on me and my life, so I didn't dare to even think about Farah. I was unhappy because she had been my one joy in this place and my relationship with her had been cut short.

The day before the elections I gave everyone in the clinic the next day off—I didn't need any of them to turn up. Farah gave me an inquiring look. I wanted to ask her alone to stay on. Perhaps we could reach an understanding with each other, come to a mutual agreement, and to hell with the elections, but I didn't find an opportunity to speak with her on her own—or rather, she didn't allow me the opportunity. I woke up feeling depressed and found two policemen at the main door. They stood erect and silent, but they didn't refuse the food and the glasses of tea I brought them—I was sure they had arrived on empty stomachs. I took out the two boxes. One was empty and sealed with red wax—this was the one that the ballots in the other box would be placed into. I put it on my desk and placed the wooden partition across a corner of the room for anybody casting their vote to hide behind. As I came downstairs again the little radio was playing nothing but nationalistic songs, appropriately conferring an atmosphere of artificiality on the elections. I took up a fat English novel and sat reading it, or pretending to. I didn't know exactly what it was about, because my eyes were flitting between the lines on the page and the road outside the village to the fields. I saw nobody—neither people nor animals. The Fairest of Them All didn't come, not even a single motorbike passed by. There was nothing but the emptiness and the wind playing on the crops. There were plenty of flies, which came back as soon as I drove them away, and there were small birds that alighted on the wall and peered around with worried and bulging eyes before flying off. For a while I watched the egret standing on one leg and searching in the mud for its lost worm. The sun spread its light, then withdrew as the shadows grew, and the shadows became weary and still nobody came, even by mistake. No one was suffering from an upset stomach, pain, injury, or headache. There was no fighting, no one assaulted anyone, or beat his wife, nobody tripped or fell down the stairs, or was bitten by a dog or a rat, or stung by a scorpion, or bitten by a snake. Nothing. A village quiet and still, as if living the first moments of creation, powerless to move, or to determine its destiny. I stood up, walked to the main door of the clinic, and looked at the two policemen standing there. We exchanged brief glances full of embarrassment. Were they commiserating with me for the fact that nobody was paying me any attention? No, the villagers came to me every day with their pains and their worries, but today they were afraid of these boxes and ballots, as well as of these two policemen, and of those who ruled heedlessly over them. I stopped again and asked the policemen to leave, but one of them answered, "It's orders, sir. We have to keep standing here, not talking to anybody, not harassing anybody, just remain standing."

They stayed where they were and no one came, even after the sun had begun to decline behind the row of palms. I looked at the untouched ballots and shook the empty box in case it had suddenly filled with invisible ones. I sat down and folded my arms, feeling the cold pervading my limbs. I wished somebody would come, throw me a greeting, and sign their name, but the silent stillness remained heavy. Not forever, though: the sound of a vehicle's engine broke the silence and the dust that accompanied strangers swirled up. The dark vehicle appeared, stopping right outside the main door of the clinic. The engine was kept running as a number of policemen jumped down from the back and took up attack positions—or at least that's how it seemed to me. The door opened and the ma'mour sprang out. Of course, he had to come. The two policemen at the door raised their hands and stamped their feet in salute. The ma'mour practically leapt from the middle of the forecourt to the middle of the room. Slapping a thin stick against his leg, he stood in front of me happy and beaming, calling out in his strong voice, "Everything in order?"

"No, not exactly. Nobody came."

His face changed, the beaming replaced by malice, and he stared skeptically. "What do you mean? There was no voting at all?"

I nodded my head and pointed to the box. "Look at it—empty."

He still couldn't believe it. "How so? The posters are all over the village and the timing was well known. And the only thing these people are good at is doing what the government tells them to do. What made them disobey this time?"

A meaningless question without answer. He went on looking at me suspiciously. "Did you have something to do with this?"

"You can ask the two policemen at the door about that."

He turned around, exhaling in exasperation, paused, then yelled, "So, what are we waiting for? Let's get to work!"

I thought he was going to signal to the conscripts to take the boxes away—perhaps to dump them in the canal—but he didn't. He went to the first box and tipped out the ballots it contained, spreading them out on the surface of my desk. "You will fill in the ballots, while I mark off the names of the voters. We have to record that they all attended and voted."

I objected. "That's forgery."

"Of course it's forgery. What are we supposed to do when these peasants fail to perform their obligations? You and I are just going to do what they should have done. We have to hurry, in order to get the boxes to the town."

I thought about it wearily as I picked up the ballots. I had not imagined it would reach this point. I examined one of them: one red circle, one black—did choosing between them matter, or was the next president a fait accompli? I saw the ma'mour go through the lists with a sigh, signing for attendance against every name. It didn't matter if they were alive or dead, knew how to read or not. He panted ardently as he completed each list and turned to the next page. I began marking "Agree": it was easy, except for that choking feeling at every stroke. It wasn't realistic that everybody would assent; there must be opposing voices. Unconsciously, my hand went to the black circle, as if I were taking private revenge, avenging myself for the ma'mour's arrogance and superiority. My hand moved in spite of myself: for every few checks on the red circle, I appeased my soul by marking the black circle, dropping the ballots straight away into the box sealed with red wax, leaving the ma'mour no chance to review my work. I was certain I was doing the occasional right thing among all that wrongdoing. The ma'mour finished with all the signatures as I dropped in the last of the ballots. He sighed with genuine victory, while I felt crushingly defeated inside: he had imposed his will on me once more. He banged on the box and the conscripts rushed immediately to carry everything to the paddy wagon in silence. I breathed out, feeling a weight lifted from off my chest. But the ma'mour, still staring at me, was troubled. "We don't have much time. We have to go to the town to hand these boxes over to the judge."

Irritated, I exclaimed, "What town, what judge? I'm finished here and have nothing more to do with all this."

Calmly, as if explaining to a schoolchild, he said, "The judge is the head of the constituency and you are now the head of one of the polling stations, so it's your responsibility to deliver the box yourself."

I felt he was trying to embroil me further, so I said, "And why can't you deliver it?"

"The judge will refuse. He'll accuse me of forging the ballots and I'll swear on the Qur'an that I didn't touch them—and indeed I didn't touch them."

He was a professional policeman: who was I to be able to keep up with him? He touched my arm in a friendly manner and lowered his voice a little. "Don't worry, we'll go quickly in the van, and come back even quicker. This will improve your standing with the authorities. No one knows how long this president will live—perhaps a long time. Anyway, I promise you, you'll sleep in your own bed tonight."

There was no choice but to follow him the whole way. He sat in the driver's seat and I sat next to him. He spun the vehicle in a rapid half-circle that almost tipped it over, but he set it straight, and suddenly the village was behind us. A green carpet of clover fields stretched before us, the bent stalks waving constantly in the wind. Many of the villagers were to be seen out in the fields, dark specters doing work of some kind, as though unable to leave their crops. Another field appeared without cultivation: the dark brown earth looked sad, yearning to be planted and irrigated. A rounded lump of soil moved fitfully in the wind, trying to expel the remains of the old roots within it. And even though it was the day's end, there was a farmer working in the middle of the field, raising his mattock high and bringing it down into the soil. There was a woman with him, perhaps his wife, wielding a small mattock to break up the lumps of earth and even up the furrows. At the edge of the field were two children, a boy and a girl, hunched over and pulling up weeds, working together, silent and engrossed.

That peculiar ma'mour must have read my thoughts. Raising his voice, he said, "They work patiently, and they work hard, but they're stupid."

He was harsh on them, which was typical, but his comment bothered me. "Stupid? How so?"

"Because they live on crumbs, and they're used to it. All this land, as far as you can see, is under the control of five or six businessmen—I know them by name—who buy at the price they impose, and what they don't want they leave to rot."

Half-cynically, I said, "So why haven't you stopped them? It should be up to you to save these people from exploitation."

He laughed drily. "Who do you think I am? In spite of this uniform, I'm just an employee. Those people are stronger than you can imagine—they could have me banished to the ends of the earth."

I was determined to stand up to him. "You have the strength of the law, and its power too."

"But I can't change history. Ever since God created Egypt there have been three classes: pharaohs, priests, and peasants. Each class lives by sucking the blood of the class below. It's always been like that and it always will be."

"You forgot about the businessmen, the source of the problems."

"They're part of the priestly class, and they're the ones who finance the pharaohs."

We spent the rest of the journey in silence. The last light of day faded and the road fell under a darkness that the vehicle's headlights had little effect on, giving me the opportunity at last to ponder this strange man without him noticing me. He was full of contradictions, unlike the other police officers I had encountered during my prison time, but he was definitely one of them. We left the dirt road, and the van whipped along the asphalt as he continued to drive at great speed, other vehicles evading us in terror. Finally, the lights of the town appeared, and our mission—frivolous and pointless as it was—would soon be over. I said, "Where are we going?"

"To the secondary school, to the principal's office. That's the headquarters."

The vehicle plunged into the night of the town and its muddy streets. The school wall came into view, plastered with hundreds of posters, the manifold picture of one man who was not in need of any kind of elections. The ma'mour pointed to the pictures in admiration. "He's the man of destiny, as they say. It's God who has chosen him, the boxes have nothing to do with it."

As usual, this infernal man was reading my thoughts. We entered the courtyard of the aging building, which looked like it had not been renovated since the British Occupation. We climbed out of the paddy wagon and the conscripts followed us carrying the boxes: it was as though we were on our way to present offerings to an unknown god. From the school corridor we entered a hall crowded with tables, boxes, and many clerks sitting, as if embalmed, behind old, faded desks. We headed for the largest desk, in the middle of the hall. It was dark brown and shiny, the only one that reflected any light in the hall's general gloom. Behind it sat a large man, apparently half-asleep, his hands clasped over his belly as he watched us approach. The ma'mour stopped directly in front of him, stamping his feet as he gave a military salute. "Sir!"

The judge shook slightly, as if waking up, and said offhandedly, "Finally. You're the last box. We were about to close the constituency without you."

"Doctor Ali, head of polling station number 40," the ma'mour intoned officiously, "is pleased to present to you the final box."

The judge didn't bother to look at me. He signaled to one of the clerks. "Remove the red wax and open the box, count the ballots, inspect a sample of them, and write the report so that we can finish up."

He didn't invite us to sit down, so we remained standing in front of him like a pair of suspects. He sat still and the sound of his breathing became audible. The clerk started by removing the seals and emptying out the contents of the box, sorting them speedily into five piles and counting them quickly and carefully. Another clerk came to work beside him, and they began to examine a sample of the ballots, screening them rapidly. I was bored and wished that I could leave them and go. I would spend the night in any hotel—I didn't want to ride in the paddy wagon again with that unpleasant ma'mour. Suddenly, the clerk cried out, "There's one marked Disagree!"

The judge woke up with a start, while the ma'mour shuddered with the enormity of the shock. Despite his great weight, the judge stood up quickly and snatched the ballot from the clerk's hand. He peered at it closely, then screamed, "Check all the ballots!"

All the clerks sitting at the faded desks came to life, phantoms rising from the dead. They pounced on the ballots, as I watched them in silence, and the judge remained standing. I turned toward the ma'mour, who was giving me furious looks and seemed to be having difficulty breathing in his excess of wrath. He surely wanted to kill me, but he couldn't do that in front of the judge and all those witnesses. Another of the clerks held up a ballot and shouted, "This one has Disagree too!"

Not a moment later another clerk held up a third ballot: Disagree . . . Disagree . . . Bedlam! It was a nightmare visited on them all, and everyone was screaming hysterically. I was the only one who was calm, but the whole situation was on the point of erupting. The judge turned to me with fire in his eyes. "How did this happen!?"

I shrugged my shoulders dismissively. "It's normal. Like any election, not everybody has to agree. There must be a minority who disagree. That's the natural way of things and that's what makes the result more authentic."

"Are you sure of that?"

"It's a tiny number of votes that won't have any effect on the final result, or on the absolute majority."

The judge exhaled and sat down again in his place—whether convinced by my logic or tired from standing up for so long. Panting, he said, "Let's finish with this. Count all the votes and record the number of Agrees and Disagrees in the official report. I want to sign off before I leave."

For a minute, I thought the crisis was over as quickly as it had begun, but I was mistaken. The ma'mour's voice rose to a screech. “This will not stand! Not while I’m ma’mour of this district!”

He turned, poked a finger into my nearest shoulder, and went on angrily, “No one will pull the wool over my eyes or make a fool out of me!”

I moved my shoulder away from him and said, “I only did what had to be done.”

“Wrong!” he screamed. “What you did was totally wrong! There’s no substitute for an absolute majority, for complete consensus! This is what I have to accomplish. That’s my responsibility as a loyal officer.”

The judge paid no attention to his refractory tone, only saying coolly, “This doctor did the right thing. It’s logic.”

This further inflamed the ma’mour’s outburst. He immediately reached and pulled his pistol from its holster, waving it high in the air and shouting, “To hell with logic! I decide what’s right . . . and what’s logic.”

Suddenly, the place was in uproar. Chairs hit the floor; ballots fell from the table. I stepped back in alarm until I was pressed against the wall. I could see that all the clerks had dived under desks. The judge didn’t move, but his face had turned pale. More than once, he opened his mouth to speak, but no sound came out. The ma’mour turned in a circle, pointing his gun at everybody, probably looking for me. I retreated farther to disappear into the shadows. Finally, the judge found his voice. “Calm down and tell us what you want.”

Firmly, he said, “These Disagree ballots will be torn up, completely obliterated. They will be replaced by others marked Agree. I want the report to be one hundred percent Agree."

The judge signaled to the clerks, who emerged cautiously from under the desks. With trembling fingers, they went through the ballots again. I felt I was in danger and there was no longer any reason for me to be there, so I began moving slowly toward the exit. But I heard the ma'mour's voice call out, "Stop right there! We're not finished with you yet. Come back to where you were."

I went back to stand against the wall, while a feverish activity was ignited in the hall—opposing ballots were torn up, new ones were brought out and inked as Agree, and the final report was written up—all as he gripped his gun and looked daggers at everybody. He didn't let go of his anger, even though things were going as he wanted. The clerks came and placed some papers in front of me, which I signed without knowing what was in them. I watched the judge as he signed every sheet before finally raising his head and looking in my direction. He avoided looking at the ma'mour. At last, my voice escaped my throat. "Is everything finished?"

The judge was still panting. "You can leave now."

The ma'mour muttered in objection, but I continued on my way out. I could barely believe I had left the hall and the courtyard and reached the school gate. I walked blindly in the tenebrous streets. The alleyways twisted and turned as I walked, and I felt I was going around in circles. It was a part of the town I didn't know and hadn't been to before. I came across the picture of the president everywhere, mocking me and my disorientation. No one had chosen him, but he would rule over the fields, the palms, the mud villages, the restless river, the children infected with bilharzia. A man whose face nobody had seen except in badly printed posters plastered on walls would rule over all these houses, over the women and the old folk within them. I walked without knowing where I was heading. After much puffing and panting I stopped a passerby to ask the way to Station Square, the point from which my knowledge of the town began. I turned to look behind me, afraid the ma'mour might be following me. I was terrified of him and I tried to find a street that was well lit and crowded with witnesses.

I breathed with relief when I reached the broad square and saw the old buildings, and I was hit by the memory of my one tryst with Farah. I looked for somewhere familiar that would serve as a refuge until the morning and found myself walking toward the little hotel that we had spent the night in together, the only night in my life that I had experienced utter pleasure. There was Bastawisi, the hotel concierge, with that same insincere smile. He looked at my face with curiosity as he wrote down the details of my ID card, then asked, meaningfully, "Are you on your own? Or is somebody with you?"

"No one," I said sharply.

He raised his eyebrows in surprise. "A blessing in disguise, perhaps. I hate to see you spend the long night alone."

I looked at him without understanding and he went on, "There are plenty of girls who stop by and leave their telephone numbers with us. Would you like me to call one of them?"

I shook my head. He persisted, but I stopped him and went upstairs to the same room. I threw myself on the bed—perhaps I would find a trace of her perfume and then my trembling might quieten a little, the specter of the ma'mour might stay away, and I might fall asleep.

10

There was rain—a mercy from the sky. Drops were falling that were strange for the time of year in that desiccated corner of the earth. They fell on the crowns of the palms and on the fields, and the walls of the houses and the piles of straw on the roofs soaked them up. They stormed the clinic balcony I stood on. Faint sounds were stilled and the sparrows and other birds disappeared. I felt alone in the midst of a vast emptiness, without friend or lover. Even Farah had closed the narrow door she had opened to me. I recalled the words of some poet about the sadness that rain arouses in the soul and the feelings of solitude that more than anything else lead to self-pity. The rain hammered relentlessly on the walls of the clinic, but it couldn't tear away the president's picture. It only removed the dust that was stuck to it and made it clearer and more effective. The election result had been overwhelming, not a single vote slipping away: he acceded to the throne, and destiny alone knew when he might leave it and another ruler come. On the occasion of his ascension, from which there was to be no fall, today was an official holiday. The employees had not come to work and the clinic had not opened its doors. It was a good time for me to withdraw into myself. I didn't play any music, I just wanted to listen to the sound of the rain and nothing else, without disturbance. Nature's rage was like no other sound. I don't know how long I stayed sitting like that—perhaps for hours, while the rain poured without pause, punctuated only by the claps of thunder and the lightning that lit up the sky over the village. In a fleeting flash, the palm fronds appeared an unprecedented brilliant green. But amid the rain and the thunder came a sudden and unexpected sound, a knocking on the main door of the clinic. It reached me like a muffled echo coming from another world and for the first instant I thought it was the sound of the wind causing the doors to bang. It came again. Who would venture out in this weather? Was it an emergency case—a shooting, a difficult childbirth? Whatever it was, the knocking continued, and I had to go downstairs. I was annoyed, it had disrupted my enjoyment of the sound of the rain. I went down, preparing to explode at whoever it was, but when I opened the door, I saw the dripping face of Farah, at a rare instant when all thunder crashed and all lightning flashed. I reached out quickly to pull her inside. She didn't say a word, because I lunged at her mouth and kissed her with all the yearning and longing inside me. She tried to resist me in vain. I hadn't imagined she would finally come to me, and in spite of this weather and the cold, and the alienation they had imposed on me, I couldn't believe that I was once again holding this body full of warmth and kissing those soft, sweet lips. It was a moment I had not dared to picture or dream of. Her tense body relaxed. She was unable to resist my kisses and the strength of my desire, so she reciprocated. But after a while she pushed me away, freeing herself from my grasp. Panting, she stepped back until she was against the wall and raised her hand to stop me from rushing at her again. I knew her weakness to my touch and it was this that impelled me to move closer, but she put her hands up to block me. "Don't come any nearer. Don't try to touch me. Let me speak."

I held back, feeling that I had been more of an animal than was right, that hunger had turned me into a harmful creature unable to act with love—I had wanted to defile her drenched body, instead of taking her into a kind embrace, and gently stroking her hair. I held back my breath and said, "I'm listening. I won't move."

She put her hand to her breast to calm her gasping, and said, finally, "I'm pregnant."

The rain outside came on more heavily, or so it seemed. I wanted to come a little closer and place my hand on her belly, but I feared that would startle her. I said, "And is it mine?"

"I haven't been with another man."

I hesitated. "Could it have been your husband?"

"He hasn't been near me," she said firmly. "I haven't let him anywhere near my body, he hasn't even touched a lock of my hair since I was with you."

I remembered her words to me in our final moments there on the dirty hotel bed and I said, "But that was what you wanted from the beginning, and it was the reason we went to that hotel together, wasn't it?"

I had given it much thought and had not come up with any other explanation for her sweeping passion followed by her remoteness. She said, "Yes. . . . At the time it seemed simple, just a wish that I was determined to see come true, a burning desire. But now I feel it's a bigger matter than I can cope with. I can't bear what's happening in my belly. I feel there's another life there, another body growing inside me."

I moved toward her and took hold of her hand. She was shaking, cold, and wet. I led her without resistance to the examination room and helped her to sit on a chair as I sat facing her. On the verge of crying, she burst out, "I'm not a whore, I just wanted a child."

The word stunned me and I had no idea where she had produced it from to slap me with. "Who would dare to say that of you? I never thought of what happened between us like that at all."

She went on in tears, "That's what I would be if I lied to my husband all these years to come, if I made him raise a child that's not his. Only whores do that."

Without thinking, I said quickly, "That won't happen. The fetus inside you belongs to me just as much as it belongs to you."

She shook her head, scattering her tears in the air. "No! No! I'll carry the guilt alone. If Eissa says it's a bastard, I won't be able to contradict him."

I held her hand and squeezed it to quieten her. It was time for me to talk and for her to listen. "I won't allow my son to be born a lie. Or anyone to raise him but his father. And I won't allow anyone to call him a bastard."

She raised her face to look directly into my eyes. "What do you mean?"

"We'll marry. Free yourself from him, and we'll marry."

"Even if I could free myself, which would be difficult, we couldn't marry—we're from different worlds, you and I. That man is my cousin, I couldn't get away from him easily. Where would I hide my face from the villagers? They're all my family and relatives."

"God's lands are broad. My posting here will come to an end, and we can move to another town where nobody knows us. We can marry and raise our son like any husband and wife."

She stopped crying, but she couldn't hide her surprise. Her mouth was open as she stared at me, then finally, she whispered, "You're dreaming, for sure. Or perhaps you're toying with me."

I still held her hand, which she left in mine without pulling away. I said, "I want you so much. In the beginning I thought it was just a passing physical desire, which would die down if I could just draw you to my bed, any bed. But what happened between us awoke a strong feeling inside me. Making love with you didn't put out my fire: instead, my feelings for you deepened, creating a bond between us, and the way I viewed you changed totally. I loved you even when you made it clear you were refusing me. I loved you despite knowing you were only sleeping with me in order to have a baby. And what made the feeling stronger was that your choice had fallen on me, that you embraced my seed. There is now a tie greater than you or me that will bind us together in spite of everything and despite all the differences that you say stand as impediments between us. Because I have come to know that I love you."

She looked at me doubtfully. "How do you know that? I mean, how did your passing desire turn into love? Isn't that strange, especially as that desire was the only thing that brought us together?"

"Don't undervalue desire, Farah. It was desire that allowed me to discover my love for you inside, and it was desire that made you gift your body to me. I'll tell you something. When I was in the town a few days ago I had to find somewhere to spend the night, and I found myself going to the same hotel that we had our single night together in. The hotel concierge recognized me—I had given him a generous bribe, so it was natural he would remember me—and he even asked after you, in an indirect way. And when he knew I was on my own he offered to bring me a woman to spend the night with me."

Farah gasped, and asked, "What woman?"

"A professional. This happens in a lot of the cheap hotels. Anyway, I refused, and went up to the room, the same room we spent our night in. I remembered the number and asked him to put me there, I wanted something to remind me of you. After a little while I heard a knock at the door. I thought it must be the concierge, but it was the woman he had spoken about."

Her interest grew. "Hadn't you refused? Was she attractive? Did you invite her in?"

"I looked at her, and at the bed in the room. She had large eyes, surrounded by kohl, which made them deeper.

They took up most of her face. Her bosom stood out and was half-exposed, begging to be touched and played with. Her lips were full and slightly open, ready for kissing. All this was there in front of me, easily obtainable in exchange for a few pounds. But you were inside of me. At that instant, I knew it. I didn't want or crave another woman as I wanted you, and I'll only find pleasure in my life if you're with me. I asked her to leave, and when she insisted on staying and began to raise her voice, I gave her some money to keep her quiet. I was buying my soul, certain in some mysterious way that at some time there would be a chance for us to set things right between us, and I would be able to come to you true and blameless."

She held my hand and looked into my eyes as the rain went on falling outside. "And what am I supposed to do? What happens if I go along with you? That man is my husband and my cousin, I can't hurt him."

Decisively, I said, "It's too late. From the moment you chose to carry my son in your womb you made me a partner, a part of your life. We're in a dilemma, Farah, and we won't all be able to emerge from it unharmed, only with minimal damage."

She was at a loss. "All that, and you haven't told me what I'm supposed to do."

"Before your belly grows and becomes obvious to everyone, you must convince him to agree to a divorce."

"Then I'll be all on my own."

"I'll be here, I'll be at your side."

A gamble—she knew we were embarking on a gamble. She stood up suddenly, and I didn't know if she was planning to leave, or what she was doing. But when she went out of the room she didn't head for the main door but into the clinic, to the Family Care room. I could hear her rummaging in drawers, then she returned quickly, panting, and carrying a copy of the Qur'an in her hand—I realized right away what it was from its gilt-edged pages. She placed it in front of me and said, "Put it to your eyes and swear you'll never leave me."

She watched me, wide-eyed and breathing heavily, as I picked it up and placed it over my face. "I swear on this holy book that I will not leave you whatever happens."

Her breathing eased, and she raised her face to me. She wanted to be certain of my sincerity, but at that moment I meant it. I thought of al-Jazya, who never stopped roving across the surface of the earth—I didn't want to be like her, I wanted to plant my roots somewhere. Blind chance may have played its part in my finding this woman and sowing my seed in her, but could things work like this, and could we slip away from here together? Could this child be the bond between us? I put my arm around her shoulders and felt her trembling under my touch. I said, "I'll put in a request to the Health Directorate for a transfer, and before anyone discovers anything we'll be well away from here."

She looked at me unconvinced. I said, "I know it will be difficult for you to leave the place you've spent your whole life in, but this is the only option we have."

She shook her head and buried her face in my chest. "I won't let him come near me; he won't touch me from now on."

I kissed the top of her head, as her warm body remained in my embrace. She said, "The rain's stopped, I have to go."

I placed a light kiss on her lips and walked with her to the door, which I opened carefully before looking in all directions. There was nobody about. She wrapped the shawl tightly around her head to hide her features and set off through the mud until she disappeared from my sight.

The rain had ceased, but the mud sat on all the roads for several days, and as always all means of communication were shut down—the village was cut off from the world. The transfer request remained folded in the pocket of my coat. I had sat up for an entire night composing it and preparing the appropriate answers if I were to be questioned about it, but it was three days before I could find transport to take me to the town. For those days, I kept busy examining patients whose symptoms all resembled each other's, but at the end of the third day, a different sort of patient came to the clinic. He was not from the village and was not even a farmer: he was one of the Arab Bedouin who only rarely appeared in this area. Desougi brought him to the examination room and introduced him to me with a kind of pride. "The noble sheikh wants you to examine him."

He was a large man, who moved like an untamed steed, puffing through his nose, treading with overlapping steps, and striking the ground with his staff. Hesitantly, I invited him to lie on the examination table, unsure that there was anything wrong with him. I looked questioningly at Desougi, but he gave me no response.

I put the stethoscope to several places on his chest. His heart was beating strongly, as if it wanted to leap out of his body. I sat down and said to him as he stood in front of me, "There's nothing wrong with you as far as I can see, and I don't think you have anything to worry about in the future."

He stepped back a little and took Desougi to a corner of the room, taking out a rather large banknote and handing it to him. Desougi tucked it away and looked at me to indicate that this was the consultation fee, even though it was substantially more than usual. The man came and sat in front of me, sighing. "I know there's nothing wrong with me, at least at the moment, but I often suffer from severe stomach pain and a head fever, and I'm about to embark on a long journey."

I didn't know whether he was being serious. I said, "Where are you going?"

"A rough trip across the desert, to my tribe near the border."

In surprise, I exclaimed, "From here?"

"This is the closest point," he said definitively.

Desougi approached and in his most suppliant voice said, "Help him, Doctor. He has a hard trip ahead."

I couldn't be difficult, so I gave him some medicines. Desougi pestered me to give him more, but I didn't want to yield to the color of the money of somebody who wasn't ill. As I watched him leave, I asked Desougi, "What does this man do for a living?"

"He trades in all sorts—in livestock, in cattle, in camels. Sometimes in people."

I was shocked. "You mean he's a human trafficker?"

He turned to me anxiously. "What's a human trafficker? Is it something bad?"

I left him as I saw Farah coming down the road. She was late for work, but I didn't say anything, and she no longer took any notice of the other nurses' comments. She waded through the mud, wary of slipping. I felt for her, as she looked at me with a slight smile; the whole village had turned into a morass, and I worried she would fall and soil her white clothes. I lifted my head and saw him—Eissa, her husband—standing at a distance and watching her progress, keeping an eye on her. It would be difficult to remove him from the picture; the expression on his face gave the impression that he owned her. She reached the door of the clinic, threw us a glance, then stood to one side to take a pair of shoes wrapped in plastic out of her bag, and left her muddy shoes by the door. She entered the clinic as clean as the morning bird, barely touching the floor with her feet. I felt my heart quake. The request was still folded in my pocket, and I had to do something to get it to the Directorate. The day wore on and we didn't speak, just exchanged warm smiles, not caring whether anybody noticed. Slowly, I became certain that this was the woman I wanted, but when she went off at the end of the day, I caught sight of him standing there watching her leave and cross the mired ground, going to him while I would remain the rest of the day and all the night alone.

Life returned the next day. From my balcony I saw The Fairest of Them All coming along the road between the fields. I went downstairs quickly without finishing my breakfast, calling out to Desougi that the clinic was closed for the day. I grabbed a small bag, checked that the transfer request was in my pocket, and walked across the dried mud to where the bus was standing. As usual, there was a crowd of people and their animals, but this time the driver stood at the door, regulating the boarding, deciding who he wanted to allow onto the bus, and preventing anyone with animals or poultry, which meant there would be room for me. I nodded to the driver, but somebody else stopped me from climbing up—Eissa stood in my way, saying, "I want to talk with you."

His tone was cold, and a little threatening. I was stern. "Can't you see I'm on my way to the town? Wait until I come back."

"I don't know when you'll be back."

Sarcastically, I said, "Do you want to come with me?"

"Yes!" he shouted in affirmation, and he moved his feet to climb onto the bus before I could. I followed him, disconcerted, and uneasy. We didn't find adjacent empty seats, so we sat apart. I kept glancing at him cautiously as the bus bumped up and down with us, stopping occasionally to avoid a pothole full of water, then continuing on its way. What did he want from me? Had Farah told him anything? Did he want to fight with me, preferring to do that away from the village? I was sure he didn't have it in him to kill me, his personality was too weak. I tried to prepare scenarios in my head for everything he might say to me, but there was only one scenario that my thoughts came back to, however much they spun around: divorce. I wanted to be bold, for my sake and for hers,

I wanted this to be my opportunity to cut short all the tedious and painful details, and I wanted to take possession of my unborn son. Whatever happened, I wouldn't let anyone else be his family or raise him. We continued to exchange silent glances. Our bodies and our thoughts convulsed uselessly, and perhaps a spirit of animosity was growing and rising without our realizing it. The Fairest of Them All emerged onto the asphalt road, the ride became smoother, the hubbub diminished, and the town, with its dusty houses that the rain had not managed to wash clean, appeared beyond the wild plants. I was aware that the moment of confrontation had arrived, but I wanted to put it off: since he had decided to come with me he could endure waiting a little longer. He came up to me as the journey reached its end, but I said to him, "I have an appointment at the Health Directorate, and I'm afraid the staff might leave. Wait until I finish there."

I didn't wait for his answer, or for his agreement. I headed for the iron door without looking back—perhaps he would go away of his own accord—ran up the worn steps, and plunged into the maze of functionaries crouched at their desks. In spite of their great numbers, as always, the particular clerk I wanted was not there—off sick, out on an errand, on training . . . whatever, nobody knew anything about him. There was nothing for it but to go and see the manager and enter into a pointless argument with him. "Why do you want a transfer, after all the special privileges we've given you?" I didn't know what those special privileges were, and he didn't enumerate them for me. "We gave you the best clinic in the district, with hardly any problems, so what are you complaining about?" I wasn't complaining—my submission was not a complaint, only a transfer request, just an attempt to find a new beginning in a new place. He laughed. "Beginning? New? The whole of Egypt is an old country, and there's nothing in it that's new, neither places nor positions. You're fortunate to have found the position you have, and you should be thankful to God instead of submitting requests."

He didn't offer me a coffee, or even a glass of cold water, and he accepted the request irritably, wagging his finger at me. "But approval will be suspended until we find a replacement for you."

I left the room in a hurry, knowing it would not be an easy matter, but time was on my heels: her belly would grow, and her husband was waiting for me downstairs. I went down to him, there was no avoiding it. I hoped he would not be there, but there he sat, craning his neck, his gaze fixed on the door of the Directorate, his eyes tracking me as I passed by him without turning in his direction. He followed me without a word. I cast my eyes around the small square until I saw a café with a tree in front—it was better to meet in a public place like this. I sat down, and he hastened to sit opposite me, silent and stony-faced. I clapped my hands and ordered two glasses of tea. He remained as he was, not looking at me, even after the waiter brought the tray. "So," I prompted, "what is it?"

He raised his face to me and adjusted his neck so that his voice would come out stronger. "I want money."

He didn't say more. Did he want to blackmail me? What did he have to blackmail me with? I didn't yell in his face, I just sat there staring at him. I wanted to know how far he would go. I took a sip of tea. “How much do you want?”

He looked at me, uncertain whether I was agreeing or not. “I want two thousand pounds.”

It was a huge amount, and I didn’t know how this half-educated, unemployed farmer would be able to manage it. “What would you do with such an enormous sum?”

“I need it.” He stopped, and I continued to stare at him. “I need to turn my life around, and that’s the least that will help me do it.”

He hadn’t given me a clear answer, so I went on staring as I sipped my tea. He said, “You’re not saying anything.”

I said, “I’m waiting to hear something specific. Why do you want the money?”

He reached out to take his glass of tea and drank from it for the first time. “I’m going on a journey. I’m going to cross the desert, to the country next door. I’ll find work there and I’ll pay back every piaster of your money.”

I scoffed. “And how will you pay it back if you’re in another country?”

“My wife works with you. If I fail to pay, she will.”

“Does your wife know about this expedition?”

He was hesitant for a while and couldn’t meet my eyes. “I haven’t told her yet. You know what women are like. I won’t tell her until I’ve got everything organized. Please, don’t you tell her.”

He stressed the “you” in that sentence, but I persisted. “You ought to have talked with her before talking with me.”

"She wouldn't understand. There's been a tenseness between us recently."

Rashly, I said, "Has she asked you for a divorce?"

I realized immediately that I had made a mistake. He looked at me sharply, though he didn't stand up, or leave. "Did she tell you that?"

I shook my head firmly. "We don't talk about anything outside of work."

He looked at me skeptically. "Of course I can't divorce her. Nobody leaves their own flesh. She's my cousin and she's all I have. And my situation isn't good—who would accept me in this state?"

There was silence. The shoe-shine man came along, clacking his brush against his box. Eissa said nothing for a while, then his patience ran out. "You haven't said anything. Will you give me the money or not?"

Taken aback, I said, "Why are you in such a hurry?"

"Now is the right time to go. The weather's not too hot or too cold. And the man's in the village now and he won't stay long."

"What man?"

"The Bedouin sheikh, the man who'll lead us across the Sand Sea. He knows a trail that cuts through the dunes and takes us straight to the border, where we can cross the barbed wire. Nobody gets lost when they follow him. I have to get myself in order before he leaves and takes the others with him."

Putting other considerations aside, I felt I had to warn him. "It's dangerous. Are you sure you can trust this man?"

Practically begging, he said, "Please, it's my only chance to get away from the prison of this village. It won't come around again for another year, if at all. I can't sleep at night thinking about it. I don't want to sit any longer against the wall watching the people coming and going."

Obstinately, I said, "But you're not going to tell your wife you're going."

He raised his voice slightly. "Forget about my wife now. It's me who's talking to you, it's me who needs the money, and it's me who will pay you back, double if you want."

Was this my opportunity to be rid of him? What difference did it make if Farah came to me as a widow instead of a divorcee? Could I be that evil? But I wasn't determining anything for him, he was choosing his own fate for himself, though it could go either way: death and perdition in the desert, or dreams of wealth when he reached that oil-rich neighboring land. He looked at me as I sat there wavering. His quandary was less than mine—he was torn by only the one impulse, to travel, while I was torn by more than one: an all-encompassing feeling of selfishness, and a fearful feeling of complicity. His eyes narrowed as he continued to peer at me. He was likely to explode if I said anything that went against his expectations. I had humiliated him enough, having made him follow me all this way, and having deposited the fruit of my loins in his wife's womb. There was nothing left but to nod my head and say, "Yes, . . . I'll give you what you want."

11

Life went on as usual, it seemed to me, as a disquieting stillness reigned over the village. I saw Farah every morning: she met me with a neutral face, expressing neither rapture nor loathing, but she shone with a quiet and rather fragile smile. We moved around each other as if performing a hidden, endless dance. Only formal talk passed between us, wrapped in uncertain glances. It didn't seem that her husband had told her anything, and he hadn't left the house yet—had he been playing me? The money wasn't the problem; it was the unsettled situation I was in. I should have taken her aside and told her the whole story, but there was no opportunity, and besides she remained silent and rather distant, bearing the burden of our covert pact on her shoulders, and in her belly carrying another secret that she could not reveal. I had the feeling that everyone was watching us, including the patients. Why didn't it rain, so that the roads would become impassable, Farah could come to me at any time, and we could talk together without prying eyes? But the weather stayed dry and the sun kept shining. I didn't dare to speak with her, but there was room to take risks, and talk with Desougi. As if apropos of nothing, I asked him, "That man who came to the clinic that time . . . the Bedouin sheikh, has he left? Has he gone to his tribe?"

"He's still here. He can be found at every village gathering. Why do you ask?"

"No reason. Just that he seemed in such a hurry to leave."

"He'll go, for sure, but he plays his cards very close to his chest. He listens to everybody but doesn't say a word."

He stood there, expecting me to take the conversation further, but I had nothing more to add. Our exchange dried up, but he kept looking at me. I didn't know why I had this feeling inside that everything I did aroused suspicion in others. Perhaps it was the feeling of guilt that never left me, whether I was alone, or surrounded by a crowd of patients. I didn't know what was going on with her at home—there was a blank wall between us, impenetrable without causing a scandal. She was absent from the clinic for three whole days, without sending a message, and without even her husband appearing, a silence on her part that was absolute and perplexing. The entire village hushed up in front of me, but on the Friday, the day that the clinic closed its doors and Desougi finally went home, at sunset after everybody had returned from the fields, in those moments when everyone was quiet and the smoke rose up from the houses, and after I had become bored with reading and listening to the radio, a knocking resounded loudly on the main door. I tried to ignore it, but it went on, and the barking of the dogs reached a crescendo too. I went down and opened the door. Farah stood there, alone and trembling. I quickly pulled her inside and shut the door. She was crying, her eyes red and swollen, the kohl drawing black lines down her cheeks. What had happened?

"He's gone!" she shouted.

I paused to take in what she was saying—in the end he had done it. I knew what she meant, but I hadn't expected this reaction. Just to be certain, I said, "What do you mean?"

"My husband, Eissa. He's gone, without a word. I just found out today."

I still didn't understand how Eissa could have slipped away. She sat on a chair and continued through her tears, "He told me he was going to visit his relatives in the next village, and he didn't take any clothes because he was coming back the same day. But he didn't come back, he's gone across the desert."

"How do you know that? Perhaps he's still with his relatives."

I was being dishonest—I knew he had gone. She said, "He didn't go alone, he went with ten others, led by the Bedouin. Their names are all over the village. I was the last to know."

"If he had told you, would you have let him go?"

At once, she said, "No!" Then she said, "I don't know."

"Maybe that's why he didn't tell you. He wanted to take the decision himself."

She was genuinely bewildered. "He just suddenly abandoned me, I don't know why. Did he find out what

I did with you? Is he angry because I tried to have a baby with another man? It must be my fault."

I felt a cruel pang of regret. "Don't talk about that—that's our secret. If you didn't tell him anything, he certainly doesn't know anything. And nobody else needs to know about it."

"So why did he do it? Everybody else talks about going away all the time, but he wasn't like them. He had his difficulties, but he never thought at all about going anywhere."

Surprised, I said, "Are you upset that he's gone?"

"Yes!" she burst out. "I never imagined he would do something like this. The house is like a tomb without him."

I pondered her silently. So why had she run the risk of coming to me, then? To tell me our pact was off, and that she missed him? What about what was mine, being formed in her womb? She raised her head and looked at me with widened eyes. "But where did he get the money from? I asked our relatives and the people who know us, but nobody gave him a piaster, and he didn't ask them for anything either—maybe because I would find out. But it's still baffling."

I went on gazing at her in silence. I was under suspicion and I didn't want to make my position any worse, but nevertheless I started to feel deeply guilty. I didn't try to approach her or touch her, I left her to cry and whimper, but she came back perplexed again to the same question. "Where did he get the money from? That Bedouin man wouldn't do something for nothing."

I felt a rage sweeping through my chest, and through my clenched teeth I snapped, "All this wailing over a man you were planning to leave?"

She raised her head, opened her eyes wide, and stared at me as though seeing me for the first time. "He's my husband, and my cousin. I spent my childhood and most of the days of my life with him, and he's thrown himself into the unknown. Do you know what it means to cross the Sand Sea?"

I felt the ground quake beneath my feet. "But we have an agreement, we're going to leave everything behind us to build our family and raise our son."

She stood up and came toward me, a fierce look on her face. "And what about when you tire of me? When you get bored of my body and fall for another, younger nurse? What about when you leave me for her? Where do I go after I've burned everything behind me that I could go back to?"

With all the passion of my heart, I cried, "I will never leave you!"

She didn't seem to believe me; didn't want to believe anything. "It will happen. Right now, you think it won't, but it will. I won't be the woman who sells everything and loses everything."

She paused to catch her breath, as I also tried to fill my lungs. Together we gasped, and there was no air in the place fit to breathe. I was the one who had given him the money, wanting to sweep him out of my way, but it was he who had swept me aside—he had vanquished me without knowing it. He had left us standing face to face, shaking, unable to act. I didn't try to embrace her or even touch her. I looked at her belly, which had grown a little. It stood as a barrier between us, adding to the great distance that separated us though it was no more than a few inches. Defeated, I said, "Is this the end?"

"I want him to come back. I want him to find me waiting for him in his house."

She turned around and went toward the door. I couldn't stop her, but before she opened it, she turned to me and asked, "Did he come to you? Did you talk to him? Did he tell you what he was planning to do?"

I knew where she was going with this and I had to lie. "It wasn't me who gave him the money. You can throw your accusations at someone else."

I was upset and angry. She turned and left quickly. I couldn't believe this conversation had taken place and that everything was finished—there had to be something left. I felt I was suffocating. All the air in the clinic was mixed with her angry breath and the remains of her tears. I hurried upstairs to my rooms and threw together some of my clothes, wishing I could gather everything and just leave. Quickly, I went out to the road, just in time to see The Fairest of Them All passing by on the last trip of the day. I yelled at the driver to stop, but he didn't, and I kicked at the ground until the bus disappeared from view. I didn't want to go back and spend the night alone, but to find transport was near impossible. I stood there resigned to my situation, but even on a bad day like this, little miracles can occur: a motorbike stopped right in front of me and the driver asked, "Are you heading for town?" I climbed on behind him without a word, and without agreeing on the fare. There was a rush of air and I suddenly felt liberated. The cold, dust-laden wind hit my chest, but it was bearable, and it didn't matter if the bike leapt up and down so long as I was holding onto the man's galabiya, and so long as it didn't plunge into the water channel. The man said something, presumably about the fare—they always did this once the customer was in their hands. I breathed easier once we reached the asphalt and we stopped bouncing about. The Ibrahimiya Canal ran alongside us, still and sparkling, but ready to swallow us up at any moment. The horrific journey continued until the houses of the town, and its streets that were in need of a good sweeping, appeared. I jumped down and gave him what he asked without discussion. I had escaped from the village, but to where, and until when? It is hard to feel at home in a place void of friends. My feet took me to the same old hotel, as if there were no other hotels in the town. As usual, I found Bastawisi behind the reception counter, and the hotel owner only in the portrait on the wall. Bastawisi called out, "You're on your own this time too, even though you refused my gift!"

I took the key from him and said, "This time, I won't refuse it."

He looked at me in surprise as I carried my bag to the room, which was just as it had been, not very clean, but empty and waiting for me. I sat on the cold bed. It had lost her smell and her warmth, and I had to live with that. I took off my clothes and lay on the bed. What had I done wrong? Was it because I had tried to steal another man's wife? Had I really stolen her, or had she come to me, and offered me her body on this bed? How had that appetite inside me turned into love? I should have restrained my self, my soul, from getting caught up in the tattered ropes of emotion, liberated my body from my desire for her, in order to liberate my soul. I heard a knock at the door, light and hesitant, like a whisper. I didn't bother putting my clothes back on and opened the door to find the same woman there: the big eyes surrounded by kohl, the prominent breasts and the décolletage that allowed a partial view of them. She perused me with a cynical smile. "I see you're ready."

I opened the door wide for her to come in, and she deliberately brushed against me to let me feel the softness of her body. She stood in the middle of the room looking at me for a moment. "Are you in such a hurry?"

I tried to move closer and touch her, but she stepped back a little. "Business first. . . . The money, sweetheart."

She stretched out her long fingers. I pulled my wallet from the folds of my clothes and put a few pounds in her hand. She kept her fingers stretched out toward me, so I added more. She didn't seem satisfied, but I closed my wallet, and she closed her fingers around the money, saying, "Not to worry. Special first-time price. Next time you'll have to be generous."

She put the money away in her bag and closed it carefully, then turned around and began to take off her clothes. I sat on the edge of the bed watching her. She did it slowly and theatrically. I discovered that her body was larger than I had imagined, and the marks of time were apparent all over it. Before I could make any observations, I felt her jump on me and cover my body with hers. "No kissing," she announced, panting. "I don't like customers' slobber. The business is better without that." She went about removing my underwear—she was expert at this. I felt her naked flesh sticking to me, she was sweaty, and her breath was ragged. I heard her cracked voice. "Don't squeeze my breasts, they mustn't sag." They were already sagging. Did she give all these warnings to other customers? I remembered Farah giving me her body so generously, responding with joy to my every touch, I recalled her kisses and the wonderful taste of her saliva. The woman's hair was in my mouth, coarse and covered in oil—I pulled it out before I threw up. She said, "It's better if I'm on top. I want you to relax and let me take charge." I couldn't tell where her body started or ended. She certainly appeared to be in charge of the rhythm. She sat with half of her naked body on my thighs, and pointed at me in admonishment. "All fluid outside. I'm still in my prime, and I don't want to get pregnant willy-nilly." I felt I was suffocating, and I shouted at her: "I don't want to have sex with you like this! No woman's going to take charge of me from now on." I pulled myself out from under her, grabbed her wrists in one hand and held them over her head, and twisted her body so that it was under me. She was stunned. "What are you doing? Why this roughness?" I didn't reply, or take any notice of her objections, and I squashed her breasts with my other hand. I had no desire to kiss her, but her body had to submit to me. She yelled, "I don't like violence. It's just sex, not a battle!" I wanted to pour out all the accumulated rage inside of me onto her. I pushed her body around as I wished. She tried to resist, which only inflamed my rage the more. I pressed my weight on top of her more forcefully, wanting to curb any resistance and subject her to my rhythm. She warned me, "My body won't take it. I'm getting up, and I'm leaving. I don't like this painful way of doing things." I raised my hand as if to slap her face. She closed her eyes and cried, "Please don't!" Her body shook—I didn't hit her, though it seemed she was recalling all the men who had—her body shook, and she stopped resisting. The pleasure was lost, but the animal atmosphere lingered. Was I striving for relief or for revenge? There was no point in that with a stranger's rented body. I stood up and moved away from the bed, away from her. I saw my reflection in the mirror on the wardrobe, was struck by a sudden shame, and looked for something to cover my nakedness. She raised her hand and shouted, "It's enough! Never again!" I wanted to apologize to her, but I couldn't. I handed her clothes to her, I couldn't stand to see her naked any longer. She pointed to the bruises on her body. "You have to pay me compensation." I looked at her and she stopped, afraid, but I gave her some more money to go away. I wanted to stand under the shower, to rid my body of her smell, and of what remained of the moment of weakness that had come over me. She took her clothes and left the room before putting them on. The bed looked disheveled and skewed, incapable of prompting any sweet memories in my soul. My whole being shuddered as I faced the first bursts of cold water. I scrubbed my body thoroughly with soap, but even so her smell remained in my nose, and on the bed too. My body was unfamiliar: my reflection in the mirror brought to light a stranger amid all the furniture, the walls, and my bag of clothes. It was alienating to be in this place. I curled up on the bed, taking up the smallest part of it possible, and leaving myself prey to all kinds of nightmares.

In the morning, Bastawisi greeted me with his unctuous smile, but when he saw my disgruntled face he whispered, "I'll send you another woman."

I shouted at him, "Don't bother!"

I dived into the town's alleyways and took my breakfast at a small restaurant on the Nile, observing the cliffs on the other side of the river, standing silently with their tombs and their secrets. How had I collapsed so suddenly and my world been demolished? I was now sitting at some isolated eating place when I should have been sitting at my desk in the examination room, Farah in her bright white uniform standing at my side to assist me, giving me a smile whenever I turned to her. Everything was wrecked, and here I was, unable to face the empty clinic, guilt-ridden over an insignificant husband who would return from his journey ruined or laden with sand and find his place in her arms, and they would laugh together and dandle their little child while I was turned into a distant memory of no importance. And I had done this to myself.

I wandered around the muddy byways of the town all day, and sat for long hours watching the sun descend in the west until suddenly the light was extinguished and darkness reigned. I didn't take anybody back to my room—even the bed felt hostile to me. I had lost the sweet memory that she had left behind, and I was unable to sleep for very long. Early every morning, I sat watching the sun rise and the white doves stir, following them as they circled over the surface of the river—small, scattered patches of cloud that had strayed down from the sky, unable to ascend again after being soiled by the dusty atmosphere. An old fisherman approached in his boat, his net empty—luck had not been on his side. He said, "Do you want to cross over to the other bank?" I said, "And what's over there? Nothing but desert hills." He said, "Every hill has its secrets, standing there for thousands of years past and thousands more to come." He struck his oars in the dark water. The river appeared vast and endlessly tranquil, lacking fury though it harbored ancient grief. The fisherman went on rowing as he complained to me about his state. "I've lived with this river for a long time, but it looks like it's angry with me—it doesn't let its fish come anywhere near my nets. I'm going to implore it from the other bank. Maybe it will relent."

The other shore came slowly nearer, and the rocks of the desert hills appeared like motionless animals lurking in wait for us. The fisherman climbed up, as I followed in his wet footprints. There were many sharp edges to the rocks, not worn down by people passing over them. The fisherman pointed to the summit of the hill, where there was a cave that was a refuge for all: for brigands, for fugitives from the law, for a few madmen and failed lovers. The cave was dark and cold. In its entrance were the remains of ashes and burned branches, next to a pile of bird bones, and on the walls full of hollows and protuberances were drawings and faded colors. And deep inside, was a long, smooth rock, like a bed of stone, which must have welcomed many fleeing and weary bodies. It was an unbearable, rough place of exile and I went out from its damp darkness into the hot sun. The fisherman was sitting on the edge of the cliff, his legs dangling, nothing beneath him but the river and space. I sat down beside him. He said, "Now we're sitting at the end of the world."

"Which world?" I said. "What end?"

"This is where hunger resides. Hunger means the Day of Reckoning. If the river had been pleased with me, I wouldn't have climbed up here, nobody would climb up here."

We started down. More than once I thought I was going to fall, and the sharp edges tore at my clothes and cut my legs. I saw myself in a trap, as I always did. The fisherman took me to the other shore, where I realized that my journey of flight had come to an end: I had to return to the place that was mine, even if only temporarily. I went back to the hotel, picked up my bag of clothes, walked to where The Fairest of Them All stood waiting, and insinuated myself among the passengers on the last shuttle of the day. I didn't find an empty seat, and I didn't know why nobody gave their seat up for me. I swayed with them, and bore the jolts of their bodies as they chattered non-stop and yelled in my ear, "Where have you been, Doctor?" or "Why has the clinic been closed all this time?" I said any old thing and made any excuse. They besieged me until I promised them that from now on the clinic would not close and even then, they continued to castigate me with their looks as they crammed around me. The bus slowed down as darkness began to fall, and I silently prayed that we would stay well away from the edge of the canal. As it continued on its way, all trace of daylight was extinguished. I sighed with relief when I saw the crowns of the palms, and the road that led to the village appeared clearly in the bus's headlights. The moments passed slowly until the bus stopped and everybody surged off as I surged with them. The doors of the clinic were closed, and its windows were dark as though nobody lived there, but I found my way to my rooms. I took off my dirty clothes and let the water stream over me. With difficulty, I got rid of the grime of the town and its smell, then I sat quietly on my bed. I realized now that my plan had miscarried, that having a body next to me and the sound of a child crying in the next room were not to be. Nothing so beautiful could come so easily. If I hadn't had my experience with Farah, this village would be just like dozens of other forgotten villages over thousands of years, but that fleeting experience had given me a glimpse of the dream that had been squandered.

The silence was broken by a forceful knocking on the clinic door. Was it one of the chronic patients? Or had Farah let go of her anger? I couldn't pretend not to be there: the light was shining from my window, and the whole village could see it. The knocking went on, and the barking of the dogs grew louder. I carried the lamp and went downstairs. I pulled the huge bolt and pushed open the door to find the last face I had expected to see: the glowering, irate, droopy-mustached face of the umda. I regarded him in surprise, enduring the piercing looks he was directing at me, and said, "Are you ill?"

He was on the point of erupting, shouting roughly at me, "Where is she?"

I stared at him as I tried to understand what was going on, but he moved quickly to shove me out of the way and rushed inside. He turned around in a circle, then stopped when he saw that everywhere was dark, and stared hard at me. He was not just angry, he was also weary, and I asked him again, "You're really not well, right?"

He didn't reply, but lunged at me and snatched the lamp from my hand. Fearing it would break or fall, I let him take it without a struggle. The shadows shook because of his trembling hand as he went into the Family Care room, and the examination room, moving around looking for something. Then, he found the stairs leading to the upper floor, looked at me without saying anything, and began climbing. There was no room for discussion, or questions. He moved with a kind of hysterical agitation, and it would have been difficult to stop him without a scuffle. I stood in the dark, with no wish to follow him, and I heard the sound of his steps going from one room to another. I didn't know whether he was inspecting the wardrobe or opening my bags, but my quarters were too cramped to hide anything. The light of the lamp appeared after a while and he came downstairs exhausted, his eyes wandering. He looked at me unable to speak, or to apologize. I took the lamp from him and led him gently to the examination room, where we sat on facing chairs. I didn't need to ask him what he was looking for—I had seen something of the beginning of the storm, and we were now at its end. I said, "Have you looked anywhere else?"

Wheezing, he said, "I've looked everywhere. I've searched the houses of all her relatives and the people she knows. You're the last one. You're the only man in the village that she talked to without me knowing what she said. I thought she'd hidden at your place."

"Perhaps she's not anywhere in the village. It's more likely she left for the town—you should go to her family's house."

He lowered his head. "I did. She wasn't there. Her family are very poor and live in the poorest part of town. She married me to get away from that house. She just wanted a room of her own, away from the crowd of her sisters."

The bird that escapes never returns, and this woman in particular I didn't think would come back to him. I thought to myself she was a desperate woman, who would seek refuge anywhere but her husband's hell. He was silent for a while, then said, "I don't know how she got away—there are several guards around the house, who kept me informed about all her movements, everyone who came to the house, everyone who talked to her. She certainly didn't abscond alone. She had a big bag with all her gold and her valuable clothes. How did no one notice her in the alleyways of this tiny village?"

"When a woman wants something, she's capable of doing anything."

Objecting, he insisted. "She's not a woman, she's just a child, and that's how I treated her—sometimes I gave her love, sometimes I taught her manners. I was waiting for her to reach maturity, when she could give me an heir."

I had no sympathy for him. He was too ignorant to recognize the moment when she matured and transformed. He had bought a closed box without opening it to look at what was inside, and there was no way he could see how much hatred she concealed for him.

"Why don't you sit at home in silence? You're the umda, and you have to preserve your reputation."

"And leave her like this to do what she wants?!"

"Maybe she'll come back of her own accord," I said dishonestly, "and maybe not. But you'll have held onto yourself and minimized your losses—the loss of your reputation at least."

"I wanted to report her to the police," he said in despair. "I could accuse her of stealing."

The umda was still an umda, even if he was brokenhearted. I said, "In a small community like this, I wouldn't advise you to do that."

He stood up, frustrated. "I thought you would give me something."

"I haven't given you what you want because there is no connection between me and your runaway wife."

He stared at me. "I won't take your advice, and I won't give up searching."

Then he turned and left quickly, and I watched him until he plunged into the darkness. I shut the clinic door and went up to my empty rooms. The barking of the dogs rang in my ears all night.

12

The telephone in the clinic rang. The old black telephone that I had thought was out of order. I had only heard it ring a few times, and the Health Directorate never relied on it to convey any instructions, but now it was ringing continuously and insistently. I wanted to ignore it, but I had been away from the clinic for a while, and I didn't know how many catastrophes might have taken place without my knowledge. The telephone was connected via the umda's residence, one of the few lines in the whole district. I finally lifted the receiver, and the hoarse voice came through. "At last, I found you! I was about to tell all the authorities you'd disappeared."

The ma'mour spoke with his distinctive gruff voice, sending powerful pulsations down the line of the dead phone. I didn't know what to do except say, "All's well, I hope?"

"I sent an official notification to the clinic, didn't you get it?"

I hadn't asked, and Desougi hadn't handed me any notification.

"Time's running out. You have to get ready. You shouldn't have been absent from the clinic without letting me know where you were."

Who was this man? Did he think I belonged to him? He took no notice of my silence but went on talking. "We're on a rescue mission. It will begin tomorrow morning. The police cars will be at the door of the clinic early. There are lost souls we have to save."

His voice disappeared, and there was nothing but a beeping on the line. He had hung up without saying anything that made sense. I shouted for Desougi and asked him about that notification from the police, and he quickly brought a sheet of paper with several signatures and stamps on it. It was a dry, official document with nothing but the same mysterious words—"mission to rescue some lost individuals"—without any additional information, nothing about where these people were, or how many. I went into the dispensary and began to prepare some medications that could be useful: some for bringing down fever, some to counter infection, some serums against snake bites and scorpion stings, and a few other things that might help. I fretted all night, then rose and went downstairs in the gray morning, before Desougi arrived, to go through everything again. I sat near the door watching the road and looking at one of the muddy patches in front of the clinic and the small birds that stood at its edge—they drank, then lifted their necks high so that the water ran down over their bodies. Desougi came and was surprised to find me ready so early, but I couldn't hide my worry.

The birds flew off in a fright when the quiet was broken by the sound of engines. The dust blew up, and through it I could make out two police vehicles coming toward me—two large, black vehicles, each bearing the image of an eagle with outspread wings surrounded by two bows of olive branches. I stood waiting until the dust died down and the engines stopped. Then the ma'mour jumped out, as he always did, with his full frame and his shining gold stars, and stood in front of me striking his short stick against his thigh. "I see you're up early. Are you ready to depart?

"Where to?" I wondered.

He went inside and sat on a seat in the examination room. "To the desert—is there anywhere else in Egypt? It's the beginning and it's the end. We're going to look for the people lost in the Sand Sea."

He talked breezily, as though he were going on a picnic. The last scene of him in my memory was when he held up his pistol and forced everybody into a blatant falsification of the elections. He was neither a gentle nor a light-hearted man. I asked him, "Who are they?"

"A bunch of imbeciles. What rational person throws himself into that labyrinth?"

I looked around, perplexed: I hadn't realized it was like this—my medicines might not be enough.

"We have jerricans of water," he affirmed, "and some canned food. We have to save whoever can be saved."

He seemed unconcerned, however, and sat relaxed while the conscripts stood to attention. No one made a move, as though the rescue operation was to take place in the clinic forecourt. He took out his cigarettes and lit one. Desougi looked in my direction, as if to remind me that I had completely forbidden smoking inside the clinic, but I kept my mouth shut—what was I supposed to do? How could I object? I said, "Shouldn't we get moving?"

"Patience, Doctor. As I said, the desert is a labyrinth, and before we set foot in it, we must have a guide. We're now waiting for that guide."

It was like he was talking to a small schoolboy. Lord! This was the one man that I couldn't stand to be with, and yet our paths were always crossing—or perhaps he put himself in my way deliberately. I sat on a chair at some distance from him, keeping an eye on the road. How would this guide arrive? On foot? By camel? Desougi went off to make tea. I turned to the ma'mour, my exasperation coming out of nowhere. "Why me? Why didn't you use any other doctor, one from the police? I'm just a junior doctor at an out-of-the-way clinic."

He regarded me for a while. "Isn't it obvious? All those lost men are from this village, or they left from here. It's your responsibility, one way or the other."

I didn't say a word, but I immediately recalled Eissa, the last moments as I gave him the money I knew I would never have back. Was that the price of perdition and death? There was a lump in my throat. Desougi placed a glass of tea in front of me, but I couldn't reach out for it. I remembered Farah's face staring into my eyes as I denied being involved. She didn't believe me, of course she didn't. I looked apprehensively at the ma'mour sipping his tea—did he really know the extent of my responsibility for what had happened? I woke from my abstraction as I heard the sound of an engine and dust rose on the road. Another vehicle approached, a large, black flatbed truck, also belonging to the police. It stopped in front of the door, but the ma'mour didn't move—he seemed to know what was in it. Two policemen climbed down, went to the back of the truck, and pulled out and threw to the ground a shackled figure. I stood up. A shackled woman—it was al-Jazya, in humiliation as always. She tried to stand but couldn't. Her hair was disheveled, her face soiled with filth. The ma'mour stayed where he was, holding onto his tea, but I noticed a strange gleam in his eyes as he looked at her—was it desire, or vengeance? He ground his teeth as he spat out, "What have you done with her, you idiots? I asked you to bring her, not arrest her! Release her immediately!"

Two policemen came and helped her to stand up and untied her bonds. She tore herself away from them and came angrily toward us, screaming, "What are you doing with me? How can you order them to snatch me from among my people like that?"

Of course, it didn't occur to the ma'mour to apologize, and I didn't think it was something he would ever do. He made do with saying, as he inspected her, "We had need of you—imagine? And finding you wasn't easy. That's why I assigned the security agents to search for your good self."

She took no notice of the sarcasm, but placing her hands on her waist she yelled, "And what do you want from me? You want me to dance at a wedding? Or wail at a funeral?!"

The ma'mour growled angrily. "Hold your tongue! Do you think we're going to beg you? You're coming with us on a small excursion into the desert. We want to reach the track that the traffickers use through the Sand Sea."

Something in her stance changed when she knew she was needed rather than accused of anything. She stood more erect and thrust out her breasts. Scorning submission and servility, she became antagonistic. "I'm a Gypsy, not a trafficker, and I don't know any tracks."

The ma'mour spoke threateningly. "You think we sleep with our eyes closed? We know you and your people are always going into the desert and crossing the border. That on its own is enough to have you all thrown in jail."

He stood up and put his hand on his belt. Looking like a looming giant, he wagged his finger menacingly. "Listen, girl, I don't have time to discuss or argue. We know it's you who leads them every time. If you don't guide us to this track, I swear to God, neither you nor your family will see the sunlight again."

Al-Jazya remained silent. To my surprise, she didn't seem the least bit affected by the threat. Her eyes flicked between me and the ma'mour. I couldn't do anything for her—what was happening in front of me was new and unexpected. She brushed the dust from her dress, pushed her hair back to reveal the round, copper pendant suspended from her ear, and said, "On one condition."

"Are you out of your mind? Who are you to impose conditions on me?"

Resolutely, she said, "I don't want any of your men to interfere with us, assault us, or confiscate our money."

He signaled to one of the conscripts. "Make her wake up."

The conscript came up and slapped her hard in the face. She hit the floor but didn't groan. I leapt up in alarm. "Sir, with respect, this isn't right!"

He remained stone-faced. Al-Jazya levered herself off the ground and stood up. She tried to stand firm in front of him, brushing the dust from her face again, and wiping away the string of blood that drooled from her mouth with the back of her hand. She resumed her defiant stance and said, "Is that all you can do? Order them to beat me? Come on and do it yourself as well!"

She wasn't intimidated by his large build, by the shiny stars on his uniform, or by his aggressive posture. He looked around, as a large part of his prestige melted away. "How can we leave you alone when you're outside the law?"

She stood there, her hand on her hip. "That's my condition. Keep them away from us, we've seen enough of them."

The ma'mour said nothing for a moment, then spoke. "Agreed. None of us will bother you—so long as you stay inside the law."

She didn't seem satisfied, and added, "I want it in writing."

The ma'mour looked around, at a loss. He knew he couldn't order another beating. "And how am I supposed to provide you with this undertaking in writing now?"

We all stood there silent and stumped, but Desougi came up with the solution: he emerged from inside the clinic with the prescription pad in one hand and a pen in the other and gave them to the ma'mour, who heaved a deep sigh of irritation, placed the pad on his knee, and began to write while reading aloud: "I, ma'mour of the district, have commanded that the tribe of Gypsies, present in the area, will not be interfered with, beaten, abused, or thrown in jail, except in the case of crimes punishable by law." He tore the sheet from the pad and handed it to her, saying, "Will this do you?"

She took the piece of paper, kissed it, and placed it to her forehead—a sign of respect that caused the ma'mour's anger to abate a little. She folded it, but instead of placing it in her bosom, as I had expected, she turned to Desougi and gave it to him. "My family will come looking for me. Give them this and tell them where I've gone."

We all knew it was a worthless piece of paper that even the most junior security agent in the district would not be bound by, but she felt she had achieved a victory and had washed away a part of the abuse that she experienced every time she had any dealings with the police, and with this ma'mour in particular. She was gradually regaining her dignity as leader of the Gypsies, and her ravaged body was reclaiming its special energy, again becoming full with femininity and overflowing with life. She said, "Before we leave, I want to go to the bathroom."

The ma'mour said scathingly, "And since when do you need an enclosed space for that?"

She was defiant. "I can't do it in front of all these men."

I intervened and signaled to Desougi to show her to the clinic's toilet. She gave me a grateful glance as she followed him. The ma'mour went down and began organizing his men, saying to me, "You'll sit next to me in the back seat of the jeep, and that woman will sit next to the driver. The truck will follow us with the rest of the conscripts."

Finally, I picked up my bag and climbed into the back seat of the vehicle. From the corner of my eye, I caught sight of some of the Gypsies watching us from a distance, fearful and tense, but none of them attempted to come closer. Some of the villagers gathered too. We waited, as the ma'mour snorted angrily, then al-Jazya came at last—she knew her place without being told and sat next to the driver. We moved off.

We cut through the alleys of the village, which woke up in alarm. The dogs barked in our wake and the children watched us as they yawned in front of their houses. The chickens ran out of the way and the geese jumped into the canal. We followed the road in the direction opposite to that which led to the town. Had we passed Farah's house? Could she be aware of the mission we were on, and that we—I in particular—were off to search for her missing husband? We crossed the dirty drainage ditch and followed a narrow track through the fields. The wheels of the vehicles flattened the crops, without bothering to stop. Al-Jazya sat upright next to the driver, not turning back to us even once, while the ma'mour's gaze was aimed at her back, almost boring into it. His shoulder kept chafing against mine, and I was uncomfortable with such proximity. If he had sat next to the driver and left al-Jazya to sit next to me, it would have been preferable: we would have been able to talk, as a change from the sound of the engine bursting our eardrums. Nevertheless, I spoke to him. "I still don't understand exactly what happened, how these men got lost, and how you knew about it."

In a low voice, so that al-Jazya wouldn't hear and join in the conversation, he said, "It happens all the time now. This is the closest area to the distant border, less than five hundred kilometers, especially for anyone traveling on foot. There's a way that only the Bedouin inhabitants of the desert know. The Bedouin of the Awaysa tribe exploit this and lead people across the desert to enter our neighbor's land through the barbed wire. They call them the Wirers. But this time their money wasn't enough to persuade the Bedouin sheikh to complete the journey—he left them in the middle of the way, without them knowing which direction to take."

I was astonished. "How did you know all that? Were they spotted by an airplane?"

"How could an airplane see a handful of lost people? Nobody would be able to distinguish them from the rocks. That despicable Bedouin told the tale to one of his relatives, who unbeknown to him was working with us as an informant. So it was only by chance that we knew what had happened, and despite our best efforts the story reached the top. You know . . . there's a new president and a new government, and at this stage they both need to appear concerned for people's welfare. When the tale spread, it could no longer be ignored, direct orders were issued to begin a search, and we all got stuck with this expedition."

The ma'mour stopped speaking. I took in the route we were following: the palms had disappeared, then the trees, the cultivation had thinned out, and lines of yellow sand were imposing themselves on the receding dark soil. The other face of the valley was showing itself, the parched face, and the air was becoming hotter, the sun fiercer. The flat land receded and the small stones grew larger the farther we advanced until they turned into solid rocks, great blocks carved by the wind into the shapes of fabulous animals frozen in time. The vehicle skirted around them and cut a path leading we didn't know where. It picked up speed, our route extending in no clear direction. The sand and stones slipped away under the wheels, and the ground seemed fragile and unstable. It was as though we were about to be transported to another world with only the most tenuous connections to the ancient black land. I looked at al-Jazya's back as she sat silent, only her hair moving in the wind—but after a while the ma'mour, unable to stand the silence, reached out and poked her in the shoulder rather roughly, shouting, "We're in the middle of the desert, why aren't you saying anything?"

She moved her shoulder out of the way without turning around to him. "I haven't recognized the track yet. This is not the way we go into the desert, we have our own routes far from here."

"Secret routes?"

"Perhaps to you, but to us they're familiar."

The driver hesitated a little and almost stopped. The ma'mour struggled to hold back his curses and ordered him to keep going. I leaned back, suddenly remembering

Eissa, lost in this yellow-gray wilderness. I hoped she could recognize some better landmarks, and we could quickly reach the place where the Bedouin had duped them and find him alive. Perhaps by some miracle he had been able to chew on dried plants and eat snakes—the instinct for life could drive him to anything—and if so I would immediately return him to his wife and not try to interfere or spoil what was between them. The jeep stopped suddenly, and the ma'mour roared, "What happened?"

We heard the wheels spinning. Al-Jazya turned in various directions without answering him, climbed out of the jeep, undid the red band on her head, and let her hair flow long, as if freeing her thoughts. She bent down to examine the sand and crumbs of rock, uttering some words under her breath like an ancient incantation, then climbed back into the jeep and pointed the driver in a different direction. The large truck followed, but the sand rose around us and its labyrinth stretched to infinity. The sky was empty of birds or clouds, and the shrubs that appeared every now and then were spindly and desiccated. We crawled along amid an emptiness devoid of life. All at once, the sound of the jeep's engine rose higher than normal, the wheels chafing against the ground without moving, sending up clouds of sand. The conscript at the wheel shouted, "We're stuck!"

We all jumped out of the jeep at once and saw that the sand was up to the middle of all four wheels. The ma'mour shook with rage and turned to al-Jazya, screaming, "I was sure we were going the wrong way! This can't be the sand track. You've got us lost, girl!"

He balled his fist and moved toward her, but she dodged him. She didn't seem afraid, she just evaded his attack and the bloodthirsty look in his eyes. She held up her hand and raised her voice. "Get back! Don't you dare touch me or abuse me. We're not in the police station, and I'm not a suspect to be ordered about by you. I could leave the lot of you here in the middle of this nothingness and walk away and you'd all be dead."

The ma'mour dropped his fist, stunned, confronted now by a different woman, one who was not cowed or submissive as she and all the Gypsies usually were. She drew her strength from that infinite emptiness. I tried to intervene, in order to calm things down, by asking, "So what do we do now?"

Unworried, she said, "Get his men to put some stones under the wheels while I scout the route. I'll look for a different way to go."

She paused a little then said, as if talking to herself, "First, we have to reach the Roc's Eggs, to the north, then after that the Desert of White."

I gaped. "What eggs? What roc?"

"You'll understand when we get there," she said firmly.

Was she misleading us? She turned away from us without paying the ma'mour any heed. I worried about her, feeling she had been quite reckless in challenging him—out here in the middle of nowhere, his power was absolute. But it was clear that her threat had kept him at bay. She walked toward a high rock, and I observed in wonder as she lifted her feet to deftly and lightly scramble up it, like a desert creature scurrying over its familiar territory. The ma'mour watched, astonished, then tore his eyes away from her and turned to signal to the conscripts in the truck to dismount and help shift the jeep, and they began shoving stones under the four wheels. Al-Jazya reached the top of the rock, spread her arms, and turned around in a circle, catching the wind, sniffing its scent to know where it was coming from and uttering words I couldn't hear, then she sat down on the rock and buried her head in her arms. The men pushed the jeep until it was out of the pit of sand, while she continued to sit motionless. Everyone stood still, and all was silent except for the sound of the wind. I glanced at the ma'mour, expecting him to be seething with rage, but he wasn't—he watched her bug-eyed as she slowly rose as if waking from a swoon and descended from the rock with the same lightness, barely touching the stones. She went to the jeep and sat next to the driver, pointing him in a different direction. We got in behind her, and we set off again. We were hungry and thirsty, but we carried on. This time we didn't push on into the sea of sand, but kept to a line parallel along its edge, between the sand and the gravel. The rocky landscape went on, with its forms carved by the wind, an open museum created by the unforgiving forces of erosion. I was aware of the ma'mour fidgeting beside me, but he didn't speak. Al-Jazya signaled to the driver to go a little deeper in behind the dunes. There were clumps of dry vegetation here and there, and the sun blazed ever more strongly, almost setting the sand on fire. I felt we had lost our way for good, the dunes all murderously alike and hard to distinguish, but it seemed she saw them with different eyes. She asked the driver to stop, jumped down, and announced, "We've reached the beginning of the track. Here are the Roc's Eggs."

We all alighted, walking as if we were on the surface of a strange planet. She pointed to a group of rocks, and I went closer, fascinated: they were an odd shape and gleaming white. I touched their smooth, rounded surface, which emitted faint reflections as though following the movement of the sun—giant spheres sculpted in limestone, shot through with tiny pieces of crystal that took on color with the light, as if they teemed with an internal life. There were a number of the eggs scattered around, some of them half-buried in the sand, some about to roll away though fixed in place. It was a mythical nest awaiting the imaginary birds that would emerge from the depths of old tales to sit on it. I walked around the largest of the eggs, lost in amazement, and encountered al-Jazya coming in the opposite direction. She fixed me with her profound eyes and whispered, "I always hoped we would meet, but we always meet in the wrong place."

Boldly, I said, "What? Do you still want me?"

"Now, yes. . . . Later, who knows? I'm like al-Jazya of the Banu Hilal, I can't stay in one man's bed for long."

Her directness didn't surprise me, I knew she was a free spirit. "I still can't believe that we're meeting at the nest of the roc, the ancient bird of Sindbad—do you know that story?"

"Of course. I know all the stories of the world, but even so I live forever on their margins. This trail that stretches away before us, I've walked it dozens of times, without finding a place to settle."

"Perhaps everything will change. Perhaps we'll come out of the desert and find a suitable place."

I sensed that there was much in her of the woman I was searching for. She didn't have the elegance and hauteur of Faten, or the innocence and spontaneity of Farah, she was a wild woman who had emerged matchless from the putridity of the world she inhabited. Her body was somewhat tarnished, but she made up for that with a primitive energy from the basic nature that lived within her like an unquenchable ember. The ma'mour approached, not angry to a great degree. In principle, she had passed the test of finding the way when we were lost, proving that she knew the hidden secrets of the desert well, and might be the means of us all surviving. He said, "Where's this trail you're talking about? I can't see anything but endless rocks and sand."

"You may not be able to see it clearly in front of you, but it's there. Some rocks may block it, or traps of shifting sands, and its path may be altered by the sandstorms, but it always connects. We are the only ones who know it and hold its topography in our heads from traveling it so many times."

"How many days does it take to reach the border?"

"Five or six on foot, if nobody collapses."

He was annoyed. "I thought we'd be able to finish up this damned expedition today."

"I don't know how many days they were following the Bedouin for, but we'll find them on this track."

The ma'mour was still irritable. "Even though I don't see any track! But we have to keep going."

Al-Jazya looked around her, appearing to be listening for something. Everything was silent apart from our own voices. Abruptly, she said, "It's best we go back. Enough for today."

"What?" he shouted angrily. "Have you lost your mind? Do you think we're playing with you? We're on an official mission, and we must find those people."

She was firm. "Most of the daylight is gone, and there's a sandstorm approaching."

The ma'mour looked around skeptically, and barked, "There's no sign of any storm. Everything's quiet, and there's still enough light."

I was surprised, and I went up to her. "How do you know there's a storm?"

"Perhaps you can't hear it," she affirmed, "but its sound is echoing around the dunes like the faint beating of a drum."

We strained to listen for a while: we heard the wind and the flapping of passing birds' wings, but we heard no hidden sound, nor sensed any stirring. The ma'mour said, "Nonsense. Even if night falls, we have enough blankets, water, and canned food. We don't want to waste time."

The signs of dread were clear on her face, and she turned dubiously in a circle. But the ma'mour was furious again: he glared at her, his chest rising and falling in rage. She shrank in fear and walked silently to the jeep. We set off once more, moving forward with nothing before us but a tortuous and obscure trail. Up until now al-Jazya had read the language of the sands well—but would that last? We were far from any oasis, from any point of civilization, and the sun had slowly begun to withdraw its light. We needed to stop for a rest or a bite to eat, though I wasn't certain whether we had food with us—but the ma'mour said nothing and was determined to push on, as if on a sacred quest. Al-Jazya directed the driver to skirt around a high plateau with a few gaunt shrubs; beyond it was an extensive plain of dark sand. I was shocked to see a number of skeletons, the bones of large creatures—some articulated, some broken up and in piles. I said, "What's this?" "The bones of camels," she said. "They also fell along the way, and the hyenas didn't spare them. The desert has no mercy for those who fall." The wind picked up, and the still sands began to shift in ripples that chased one another. The jeep swayed, beginning to lose its purchase on the ground. For the first time, al-Jazya turned around to us, alarm in her face. "The storm has started. I don't know how strong it will be, but it's coming."

"Just like that, out of nowhere?" said the ma'mour.

She peered around and said, "That's what the desert's like—quick to anger, quick to calm. We need to find somewhere to shelter."

She pointed to the driver to park the jeep behind a large rock, and the truck came and parked next to us, but the rock wasn't big enough for the two vehicles. The wind grew stronger as the blue disappeared from the sky and the air turned yellow. We could no longer see what was around us. Waves of tiny particles blocked out the sky and the horizon, and the desert turned into a perfect trap, with us in it. The ma'mour climbed out of the jeep, but when he felt the strength of the wind he was forced to return, in a funk. We closed all the windows and vents, but the hot sand continued to seep inside the vehicle like stinging flames. "What an abominable mission!" he yelled in a rage. "What are we to do now? We can't go on and we can't go back."

Al-Jazya said, "We have no choice but to spend the night here."

The situation was becoming worse. The driver suddenly said, "Sir, we won't be able to stay where we are—the sand will cover us. I'm from Upper Egypt: once these storms hit, we could be buried here."

For the first time the ma'mour's face showed signs of panic, and he shouted to al-Jazya, "Could that really happen?"

She stared at him wide-eyed and said nothing. "Say something!" he screamed. "There must be somewhere we can take cover."

Her face remained composed. Despite the sound of the wind battering the vehicle I heard her catching her breath with difficulty, and I felt she was hiding something. I put my hand on her shoulder, and she didn't attempt to move away, although she was shaking; she must have been aware that I was trying to support her. "It's getting worse, ya Jazya. We really do need to find shelter."

In a low voice she said, "They don't deserve it."

The ma'mour must have heard her, but he made no sound. I said, "This is different. We're on a rescue mission."

"I'd be betraying the Gypsies' compact," she said for all to hear. "We've spent our lives avoiding the police, living far from their sight. How could I lead them to our hideout myself?"

The ma'mour said, "In a place like this, in this weather, do you think we'd ever be able to find your damned hideout again?"

I said, "Don't let us down now, ya Jazya. Take us to the hideout."

She was silent for a moment, then signaled to the driver to move ahead. He drove slowly, and the big truck behind followed us. She could barely see a thing: the combination of the sand and the darkness that had come on suddenly veiled all from sight. The jeep shook violently, and we heard the sound of the storm like the howling of hungry wolves. I don't know how she discerned the way, but she kept on guiding the driver, who followed her commands while grumbling noisily. After a period of stopping and starting, I felt the jeep beginning to go downhill. The driver objected, but she went on urging him forward. His nervousness spread to the rest of us. The ma'mour growled, fear apparent on his face—he realized he had put us all in danger by not listening to her earlier warning. I felt like we were entering a bottomless pit, and the blood rushed to my head. For the first time in his life, the ma'mour seemed defeated. I could hardly believe my ears when I heard al-Jazya shout to the driver, "Stop! We're here."

Turning around to us, she said, "We'll go down in the dark, but I know the way well."

The ma'mour's voice was cracked. "We have some flashlights, and some blankets too."

He was smarter than I thought and had come prepared for a multitude of eventualities. He reached into the back of the jeep and pulled out a large bundle, which he quickly opened, throwing each of us a blanket to put over our heads and yelling to the driver, "Tell the rest of the men to follow us."

We opened the doors of the jeep with difficulty, as the wind fought against us with its force from above, hot as high noon. I wrapped the blanket around my head and helped al-Jazya to wrap hers. The visibility was better outside, the darkness not as dense as inside the jeep, and in spite of the hot flares of sand I could make out a huge mound of rocks, with the narrow path on which we stood descending under it. The ma'mour switched on his flashlight, revealing a slope of limestone scree beneath the swirling vortices of sand. We carried on down until we reached a dark opening in the jumble of boulders, like the mouth of a cave, an underground refuge impossible to locate amid this rocky conglomeration. The wind pushed us quickly inside—walls enclosed us, and suddenly all was still. We stood in a broad hall excavated in the belly of the rock. The ma'mour lifted his flashlight and shone it around the place. It wasn't a natural cave: human hands had intervened to modify it and make it fit to live in. There were traces of peeling paint on the walls, dusty white, with the remains of other obscure colors. Al-Jazya wrapped the blanket around herself to disappear in it, sat down on the ground, and leaned against the wall. The sound of the storm outside grew louder, angrier. Waves of sand blew in from the entrance, bringing with them the rest of the conscripts, tired and scared, carrying more blankets and boxes of water and food, cursing each other, and almost collapsing from exhaustion. They switched on several flashlights, revealing the extent of the space and a number of columns made of rocks piled on top of each other to prevent the ceiling from falling in. When the ma'mour shouted to the men his voice reverberated frighteningly around the place, but then he turned and stood automatically in front of al-Jazya as if awaiting her orders. She didn't disappoint him. "Sir . . . we had best make a fire. They'll find lots of firewood and dry sticks around."

He went back to bellowing at his men. She was the queen here in this place, holding in her hand the rope to save them all. The conscripts spread out, happy that they had survived the storm—and that they would be blessed with light and warmth. They came back carrying plenty of firewood, which they stacked in the center of the hall, away from the flow of angry air, then began to start a fire, blowing on the kindling and flapping the edges of their uniforms in their effort to turn sparks into tongues of flame. Slowly, the fire took hold of the sticks and made them blaze until the whole place was filled with light and dancing shadows, revealing the drawings that were on the walls. They were not intact, and the dark lineaments of the rock still showed through them, but one image was clear despite its flaws: a man with a flowing white beard and a solemn halo around his head. He was a saint, but his face wasn't blessed with a saintly serenity. He held a book in his hand, perhaps the Bible, and stretched his other hand before him as he gazed in terror at a mysterious empty space, wanting to protect himself from it, repelling an evil that was about to overcome him. I contemplated him in a daze, and muttered aloud, "Are we in a church?"

Gently mocking me, al-Jazya said, "Has it taken you all this time to realize that?"

I picked up a firebrand and set off to explore the place, walking around the walls. Other faces of saints all had the same halo around their heads and look of terror in their eyes. There were symbols, and icons, and inscriptions in pharaonic characters, the Eye of Horus, the Key of Life, and cartouches full of mysterious marks and signs. I went back to al-Jazya, who still sat shrunk in on herself, and asked her in wonder, "What is this church, and who set it up here?"

She pointed to a place beside her and said, "I told you before, I know all the stories of the world. Sit next to me and I'll tell you all about it."

I sat down beside her and leaned against the wall. She said, "Come closer. At least let your shoulder touch mine, so that I can feel your presence. We Gypsies are accustomed to tight spaces and don't mind physical contact."

I looked around nervously. In the broad hall we had split into three groups: the conscripts were gathered together near the fire, eating and talking in subdued voices; the ma'mour sat apart in a corner, looking at everyone in unabated anger, and at us in an even greater rage. I felt afraid of him. I said, "That man, ya Jazya, gives you strange looks."

"I know he wants me badly, I'm good at reading eyes. But he's afraid of impotence, he's sure he'll fail with me."

I ignored his glances and moved closer to al-Jazya, to connect with her shoulder. She was warm and strong. His eyes widened and he moved his lips in displeasure, but he didn't stir or utter a word. I asked her, "Are you comfortable like this?"

"So long as I feel you next to me. I'm afraid of them. Can you believe I'm alone among these brutal conscripts, and that old villain, who have abused my body for so long! They're all animals, indistinguishable from each other. You're different to them."

I pondered her for a moment and closed my eyes. How, despite her long experience, had she not seen the animal that was inside of me? What would Farah say about me? I reassured her: "I'll stay beside you the whole night, even if I fall asleep."

She smiled weakly, as the image of the terror-stricken saint stared at us, and she spoke slowly. "Our forefather was the first to lead us here. We were fleeing, as usual, from some ruffians who were hounding us—there's no difference between them and the police, to us they're all thugs. This place was built by the hands of persecuted Copts. At that time, they were running from Roman soldiers, who were arresting anyone who embraced Christianity and throwing them to the lions, which they took care to starve for several days beforehand. Imagine being left to hungry lions to chew on your flesh piece by piece. The Egyptians who professed Christianity fled and came to hide out in this place. The persecution persists to this day, except that instead of lions they use trained dogs, which are no less fierce—they bite and rip and keep on tearing until their handlers call them off, and sometimes they don't stop at all."

"Enough, ya Jazya. You don't want these people to see your tears."

"You're right. But that man sitting in front of me is frightening. He desires me and he detests me. I wish he'd die or just go and sit somewhere else. I'm afraid of being assailed by nightmares with him staring at me like that."

I wanted to laugh, but I couldn't. I looked over at the fuming ma'mour—he must have known instinctively that we were talking about him. She said, "I won't fall asleep unless I can feel your shoulder touching me."

I said, "That's the most I can do with you. No embraces, no kisses." She closed her eyes as she said, "Later. . . . Later."

Her breathing became regular. The conscripts were scattered around the fire, falling asleep and snoring, but the ma'mour remained awake and the storm continued to rage outside. I couldn't bear his fixed gaze and I closed my eyes, feeling that my eyelids were full of sand. And although I drowned in the darkness, a maze of dreams and loss opened up, all centered upon one face that pursued me and would continue to pursue me: the face of Eissa, begging me to loan him money—and when I held it out to him his fingers turned to sharp pincers that grasped my hand and pulled me into a maelstrom of shifting sands. I opened my eyes in a panic to find myself sitting stiffly against the wall. Al-Jazya was asleep, her head having slipped from my shoulder to settle on my thigh, and she breathed quietly. The conscripts still slept around the fire, the sound of the storm had abated completely, the fire had gone out, and daylight seeped in weakly through the entrance, but the ma'mour wasn't there. I turned my stiff neck, but I didn't see him. I didn't think he had died, as al-Jazya had wished. He must be outside, exploring, perhaps not having thought it necessary to yell at the conscripts, who slept like corpses. I didn't want to close my eyes again in case Eissa was still pursuing me—though it was I who had come here in pursuit of him. I sat where I was, careful not to wake al-Jazya, but I heard the sound of the ma'mour's feet stomping heavily, coming in from outside to kick one of the conscripts in the rump and yell, "Wake up, you rabble! We didn't come here to sleep!"

They all shuddered awake with a start, rubbing their eyes, and straightening their clothes. Al-Jazya too raised her head and adjusted her body. She stood up, leaning on the wall and breathing heavily, as though she had been chased all night. The ma'mour threw us a passing accusatory glance, then went out. The conscripts milled about in confusion and went out after him. Al-Jazya stood until she had regained her breath and shaken off the shock of the sudden awakening, then we stepped out into the sunshine together, into the desert that a few hours before had blazed with fury but that had now completely regained its stillness, our voices being the only sounds to be heard.

We climbed up out of the hollow to God's wide-open spaces, where lines of sand lay harmlessly on the rocks, undulating and shining, full of luminous grains. Thorny shrubs that had been torn from their roots lay still in deathly peace. The ma'mour sat alone in the jeep, even the driver wasn't there—it seemed clear that everyone had gone off in different directions to attend to their natural needs. The ma'mour was aware of this, as he sat keeping a cap on his anger until the driver returned—there was no resisting the laws of nature. Al-Jazya climbed up onto a high rock to reconnoiter, while I sat in my previous place next to the ma'mour. We were silent for a while, but then I heard him say through his clenched teeth, "You didn't need to stick that close to her." "I was protecting her." "Who from?" "From all of you." His laughter was scornful. "And did you think you would have been able to? I could have raped her a hundred times without anyone daring to stop me."

I looked at him in amazement: he had made plain his buried desires without realizing it, while struggling hard to keep himself in check. The driver returned, and al-Jazya too, and some time passed until everyone else was gathered. The sound of the engines rose, and we discovered that a number of birds had been sleeping among the rocks—they flew up in a panic when the engines started. What did these birds find to eat here? How did they drink in this arid place, supposedly the driest of the world's deserts? Al-Jazya signaled to the driver which direction to take, the large truck followed us, and the sand, smooth as silk, parted before us. She turned to me and said, "This is a new desert. After every storm the desert changes its form."

The ma'mour said, "Just don't lose your way in it. We don't need to get lost again."

She ignored his sharp tone and said lightly, "Prepare yourself now, Sir. . . . You're going to see something you've never seen in your life."

The jeep drove on, and we were surrounded by dunes and hills of sand, the desert stretching away as far as we could see. I felt we had become the property of this desert, captives in its infinite grasp, and that we would never be able to return to or contact our other world—because there was no other world. After an hour or more, the color of the sand suddenly changed, losing its yellowness and becoming more like ash residue, but ash that was alight, as its grains shone with the shifting sun. The journey seemed to have no end, and the color of the sand kept changing. What were these transformations all in the one place? The sand changed color again, and suddenly became totally white, like hot ice. Al-Jazya felt my surprise and turned to me. "This is the White Desert."

This told me nothing more than I could already see. The jeep proceeded through wave upon wave of white. Even the ma'mour sat stunned and speechless, no doubt sensing how small he was beside the expanse of the natural world. I asked al-Jazya, "Have you seen this place before?"

"It's been here for eternity. This is not just an empty desert, it's a complete world of white, filled with white things. It's clean . . . cleaner than any one of us."

She spoke with childlike enthusiasm. The ma'mour too seemed soberly surprised, unable to speak. He looked around in wonder at this world that had burst suddenly from the nothingness. Rocks appeared, small, quiet eruptions, great piles of white, not solid but sculpted by the wind. The driver stopped the jeep without anyone telling him to. The ma'mour didn't object, and the large truck stopped behind us. The conscripts jumped down and ran around like children, pointing to the rocks of different shapes. We all climbed out, and even the straitlaced ma'mour couldn't contain his fascination. One rock was in the form of a huge chicken with its beak in the air. At a distance was a rabbit, curled up, fearing the hunters' guns. Near them, a horse's head was raised in a silent whinny. Behind them, a towering, petrified tree, a broken-winged bird, a boulder balanced on a thin column as if suspended in mid-air. A world of white magic to intoxicate the soul. We went on a little farther in the jeep and stopped again in front of a whole hill of quartz crystals that reflected the sun's rays and turned them into the colors of the spectrum—the colors of a rainbow soaked up by the sands. Al-Jazya grabbed my arm and squeezed it, and I saw sudden alarm in her face. The intoxication evaporated at once. She pointed toward one of the chalky dunes and I caught sight of the shadow of some animals racing away—I discerned a pair of dogs that seemed to have been disturbed by our presence, running quickly to find a place to hide. I said, "No call for all that panic. They're just dogs."

She shook her head. "They're not dogs, they're hyenas."

"But . . . we're in the desert, it's natural they would be here."

But her alarm didn't subside. The ma'mour approached so that he could hear what she was saying. She went on, "There are no dangerous animals in this area, not even any snakes. But hyenas are the vilest kind of animal, and they only go for carrion. There are bodies here somewhere."

The ma'mour didn't wait to hear more. He shouted to his men to return to the vehicles and told them to drive cautiously and look around in all directions. We crawled along slowly, glimpsing the shadows of the hyenas as they disappeared behind the scattered dunes. The nightmare had begun: we were now tracking lifeless corpses, not lost souls. We looked everywhere. The vehicles drove to every shadow, every movement. They paused, drove around a chalk boulder, carried on. Our driver gasped in horror, and we stopped in shock: there was the first corpse, a black body thrown down on the white sand. We approached it, the ma'mour climbed out, and I followed him. Al-Jazya stayed in the jeep, looking straight ahead, refusing to look at the corpse. I peered at the body, trying to recognize its face. My heart was beating violently, afraid of the face I might know. I couldn't make out the clothes: they were torn, just tatters soiled with sand and blood, as though he had suffered a brutal attack, whether by an animal or by a person, and had tried to defend himself as best he could. I went closer. Death had not gifted the features of his contracted face any rest or repose, as if it had overtaken him only moments before. I went down onto my knees and touched him gently and fearfully. His body was stiff, his skin completely dry, and on his face and his arms were the marks of claws and fangs. His belly was ripped open, the soft part of him that the hyenas had devoured—yesterday's storm had filled it with sand, making it less repugnant. It wasn't enough that he had died of hunger and thirst, his body had also been ravaged. The ma'mour said, "Don't waste your time, Doctor. We'll find them all in the same state. The desert is merciless, and so are the Bedouin."

His voice was shaky—the cruelty of death must have melted a part of his hardness. "There's nothing for us to do now but return him to his family."

He signaled to the conscripts in the large truck, and they jumped down holding a winding-sheet, a pure white shroud, like the sand on which we were standing—they had known from the beginning it was a journey to the dead. They spread their palms as they recited the Fatiha and held up their fingers as they repeated the Shahada. Then, they wrapped the body, with its rags and the sand that was on it, secured the ties around its neck and its feet, and carried it to the back of the truck. I went back to my place in the jeep, as al-Jazya sat there silent and stiff, staring ahead. She didn't want to see the body, even after it had been wrapped in its winding-sheet. Over the whole desert reigned the dread of death. Even the wind seemed to have stopped blowing. The vehicle moved on, and I knew I would shortly meet my destiny, wrought by my own hands. I was shivering, as well as being shaken by the jeep jolting up and down. The chalk sculptures appeared like phantoms, like ancient agonies awoken. I suddenly had the feeling that al-Jazya knew everything, and that she wouldn't talk to me or be able to look me in the face—she would keep on giving me her back forever. We hadn't gone far when we came across the second corpse beside a hollow full of calcareous water and a rock in the shape of a small bird. I jumped out quickly, the ma'mour too, and al-Jazya remained sitting rigidly. Perhaps she had seen these scenes in her past travels and didn't want to see them again. This face too was a stranger to me. Death changed and distorted features, but I was certain that I would recognize him. The conscripts jumped down once more, with a new winding-sheet. How many had they brought with them? And how many bodies would we find?

. . . His corpse was the fifth. I knew it as soon as we neared it and before we left the jeep. I jumped out before the ma'mour, and stood in front of the body stretched limply on the sand as though he were taking a nap. I moved a little closer. His features were not shriveled like the others—he had surrendered to death, as if he had been waiting for it. His clothes were torn, like the others, and his leg was flayed—he too had not been spared by the hyenas. His hand gripped at the sand, as if appealing to it for help. I saw his face, his mouth with which he had begged me to give him the money: the mouth that Farah had kissed—as she had kissed me. Like the hyenas, like the desert, like the perfidious Bedouin sheikh, I bore my part in his death. But I couldn't bear to look at him for long. Shaking, I cried out, "I'm sorry! . . . Truly, I'm sorry!" I turned away and began to throw up, as al-Jazya watched me stone-faced. The ma'mour waited a little for me to compose myself and raise my head, then said, "Do you know him?" "Yes, he called in at the clinic regularly." He said, "I don't know whether we should mourn them or curse their stupidity."

The conscripts came with the winding-sheet, performed the rites quickly, and began wrapping the body. Then they picked it up and threw it carelessly in the back of the truck. I remained where I stood, unable to move. The ma'mour said, "The sun is high in the sky, and we have to finish our patrol." I turned my head to wipe away the tears that had taken me by surprise and went back to my seat bitter and exhausted. I didn't know what I had been hoping for: that he would survive this trap, that he would succeed in crossing the border? The jeep went on circling around amid the white sands, the wind whipped up, whirlwinds of sand spun in front of me. I heard her voice whispering in my ear, "Murderer! . . . Murderer!" and I looked around me, afraid someone else would hear it too. We discovered more corpses, pulling some of them out of the folds of drifted sand: the storm had swallowed their helpless bodies without resistance. We no longer left the jeep—the conscripts knew their role and carried their winding-sheets. We picked up more bodies, some of which might have been old ones, perhaps belonging to earlier lost wretches. One of the conscripts stood and stamped his feet on the ground in salute. "Sir!" There were no more winding-sheets, and the day was nearly over. Finally, the ma'mour decided: "We'll go back quickly in a straight line." Turning gravely to al-Jazya, he said, "Lead us by the fastest route. We have enough bodies."

I breathed in relief. The jeep turned around, and the truck followed us. The sound of its engine reminded me that it carried a body that mattered to me, no doubt lying next to the body of someone else, with perhaps another on top of it, and the rituals of grief would begin only when we reached the land of blackness. Al-Jazya continued to guide the driver without turning around or looking at us. We left the White Desert as the sun dipped to its setting, after casting its red shadows on the hills, and darkness crept on slowly. It was dangerous driving, and it would have been better to stop and pass the night where we were, but no one wanted to spend the whole night next to all those bodies. The vehicles stopped to fill up with the fuel that we had brought with us, then carried on driving in the dark. Al-Jazya could no longer signal to the driver, so she began giving spoken directions. "Drive straight ahead. Watch out for that rock. Go around that dune." We couldn't see a thing, but al-Jazya's cat's eyes kept leading us along the way. The jeep progressed slowly, but without stopping. I heard the ma'mour speaking—not mumbling or talking to himself but speaking to me. He wondered, "What made them plunge into all that hell, just to get to another country? What pushed them so far to suicide? What were they running away from?"

I didn't want to become involved in a conversation with him, but I heard al-Jazya say, "They were running away from your brutality. Life is cruel enough, but you make it worse."

He replied sternly, "We apply the law to people who don't know the meaning of the law: forgers, adulterers, prostitutes, pimps, rustlers, burglars, muggers, hired killers."

Al-Jazya was stubborn. "All of those slip through your hands easily. You only catch the weak ones who live on crumbs, and you want to take a share of their crumbs."

He growled angrily. I expected him to reach out and grab her hair to twist her neck, but he didn't—perhaps because he realized that she alone knew the secret of the way home. Furious, he said, "You're just a wandering dancing girl who doesn't know anything about the law."

"You're right, but I know one thing that my forefather said, the grandfather of all the Gypsies: that all these laws were around in the days of the pharaohs, that times have changed and moved on and the pharaohs have all gone, but the laws remain because you remain, you people, you who created the hell that everybody is running away from."

The ma'mour muttered something I didn't catch and shifted uneasily in his seat. He wanted to do something but couldn't. We had all been through a terrible experience, and there was no way to blame its victims—perhaps he was wondering whether he was responsible for it. I was choking in my silence, in the feeling of enormous sin, and the wind had changed and we began to smell the fetid odor coming from the large truck. Al-Jazya was silent for a long time, then she continued with her directions. After hours of driving, the pitch-black of the night slowly began to lift, and a dark fog covered everything, but there was a change in the texture of the air loaded with sand—it became less hot, and cool currents infiltrated its warm gusts. Even though the fog was like a total blindness, al-Jazya continued to know her way by the feel of the air, and soon it broke up to reveal lines of green on the edge of the horizon. The driver cheered as he gripped the steering wheel, and the conscripts cheered in the truck behind us. I felt relief, and the lump in my throat receded slightly, but I heard the ma'mour say in a rather formal tone, "We must go to the village umda. He's the only one who will be able to identify who these bodies belong to."

I said, "Do whatever you want to do in the way of procedures but drop us off at the clinic first. Our mission ends here."

He looked at me, aware that I didn't want to leave al-Jazya behind for him to mess with. The fog lifted further, and the sun seemed to be looking for a place to rise. The high tops of the palms appeared and grew bigger and clearer as we neared them. We crossed a rickety bridge, over a canal covered in waterweed, and we heard the barking of the dogs, then the muddy bulk of the village appeared, with its tightly clustered houses. The ma'mour pointed to the driver to head for the clinic first. The sound of our engines shattered the peace of the village, but no one came out to see us, and finally, after passing through several twisting lanes we entered the open space in front of the clinic. The ma'mour, faster than us to jump out of the jeep, quickly came around the front of it. I was shocked when he grabbed al-Jazya by the hair, pulled her out of the vehicle, and threw her to the ground, bawling,

"You slut! How dare you argue with me?! How dare you insult the government?"

He kicked her once, but I caught him before he could kick her again, and yelled in his face, "Keep away from her!"

I pulled him away, as he shouted at me, "Didn't you hear what she said?"

I shouted too. "Yes, and I agree with her!"

He looked at me in surprise and anger. "What? I thought you were a little better than her!"

"I'm not better, and nor are you, and you should keep your word to her."

"What word?"

"You promised that you would stay away from her, you and your men."

"How can you defend her like this? She's scum . . . she's just a Gypsy."

"It was she who saved our lives in the desert."

The rest of the conscripts got down from the truck and encircled us, ready to pounce. We were both panting, trying to catch our breath. Al-Jazya still lay on the ground, afraid to stand up. The smell of the corpses had intensified and become unbearable. Struggling to control himself, the ma'mour said, "Anyway, now's not the time for reckoning."

He sent the conscripts back to the truck, went to the jeep, and sat next to the driver. But before he left, he pointed to me. "And you will write a report about these bodies and bring it to me."

He wanted to have the last word before the jeep moved off. Before I could move to help al-Jazya she had stood up and was adjusting her hair and dusting off her clothes. I said, "Are you all right?"

"Of course I'm all right. I'm used to falling down and getting up again by myself."

And suddenly her voice rose in laughter—a clear, ringing laughter that I had not heard before. She said, "Did you see what that ma'mour did? He's afraid, terrified of us. He knows I say what's on everyone's lips. He was stunned you stood up for me and stunned by the repression inside himself."

I stood there astonished. Where had she come by such insight? Had she picked it up along her wandering of the ways? The village was waking up and beginning its trek to the fields. I said, "How will you get back to your people?"

"My people will come to me," she said simply.

I understood her words only when they suddenly appeared, showing up from behind the bushes and the wild scrub. They came toward us with slow steps, as though still asleep. As they usually did, the Gypsies walked up to her and surrounded her. I almost recognized their faces and knew their features. She slipped among them as if seeking their protection, turning to me and saying, "I'm grateful to you, Physician, for defending me. It might be the first time anyone has stood up for a daughter of the Gypsies."

She turned and walked among them, as they walked around her, a single, wretched, but connected throng. I turned too, toward the door of the clinic. I wanted to find somewhere to hide, to find tranquility for my shredded soul. I went up to my rooms, which were as silent as the desert. I took off my clothes and shook the sand out of them, then sat naked for a while, until the heat of the desert left me. I felt neither hungry nor sated. I lay on my back and stared at the ceiling with its peeling paint, listening to the sounds of the village mixed with the roar of the engines that still buzzed in my ears. I sank into a gradual darkness and saw the hyenas lying in wait for me behind the hills of sand. Eissa ran from them, afraid, and I ran with him—we shared the moment of terror. I saw that the desert had changed color, as Eissa grew distant and the hyenas continued to chase me. My veins filled with sand, and I bled sand that was red. The ma'mour placed his foot on my chest and screamed for my execution. He knew that I was an accessory to murder, that Farah was pouring sand on her head in grief because of me, and that the men who sat with their backs against the wall had become the female mourners dressed in black, crying out their proclamations of death. How had I entered the net of the futile rites of sorrow and remorse? I turned restlessly onto my side and found Eissa sleeping next to me and sharing my pillow while hyenas filled the room. I woke with a start. My bed was rough with sand, which I would not be rid of for a long time. There was weak daylight, but what day was it? How long had I lain like this, a hostage to nightmares? A new dawn was breaking over the village, and mist enveloped the crowns of the palms. A hubbub and voices rose from the direction of the village, sounds rarely to be heard at this early hour of the morning, because the people rise quietly and go to the fields in silence. But the hubbub grew louder and the voices clearer—calls of "God is most great" and supplications to the Almighty—and then they appeared on the road. The first bier was carried by a few men on their shoulders. It wasn't covered, and the body was wrapped in layers of yellowish linen, a green cover over the head. He was curled up on himself: death had not taken away his fear of thirst or hyenas. The second bier followed, also open, carried on the men's necks. Then came the third and the fourth, and the rest of the biers, a long line of monuments to the white death, the harvest of bodies that we had collected from the desert. A fleeting, unreal scene repeating itself in front of my eyes, in its slow, sorrowful march accentuated by the mist that descended from the palm tops and enfolded them. In one of those shrouds lay Eissa, capitulating as he always had. The lump arose in my throat. The men of the village appeared, walking behind the biers and crying "God is most great," and "There is no god but God." Then came the women, dressed in black, their hair wild. They slapped their cheeks and screamed terrible screams that tore the heart. I couldn't make out Farah, but I knew she was among them. I was shaken by that wailing; it was like something primeval. I stepped back, afraid she would see me, afraid anyone passing would see me. I went back to sit alone, unable to sleep, unable to wake. I opened the door of the fridge and found some food. I was hungry but couldn't eat—couldn't do what it took to live. I heard noises coming from downstairs—things were starting to happen in the clinic. Desougi had opened the doors, and the patients were thronging in. He must know that I was there, and he was letting them in to force me to go down. Soon, I felt I could not sit like that any longer, so I stood up and dressed. I didn't usually wear the white coat, but today I needed to: I wanted to hide in it, I didn't want anyone to see me as anything but the clinic doctor. I put the stethoscope around my neck and went downstairs, where I found strange faces belonging to another world, or was it I who came from another world? They were the same as always, with their illnesses, their symptoms, their complaints that persisted through time. Desougi stared at me as though I had arrived from the realm of the dead. He followed me to the examination room, exclaiming warmly, "Welcome back, Doctor! Shall I bring you a glass of strong coffee?"

"I'm well awake. What's happened?"

"For three days I've been knocking on your door, and you don't answer."

I was stunned. Had I been sleeping for three days? I looked in the mirror: my face was worn, and my beard was sprouting. In confusion, I said, "Just this morning I saw the funeral for the bodies that fell in the desert."

"They were held in the morgue in town. They weren't released until late last night."

I understood nothing, nor did I want to understand. It was a nightmare I was still living in, and I wouldn't have been surprised to see the dispensary filled with hyenas. I looked around. Farah wasn't there; she must be at the cemetery now. Eissa lost her when he was alive and won her back when he was dead: everything comes around with time. I wound up my conversation with Desougi; there were many patients to see—they hadn't all gone to the cemetery, they had come here and were sitting staring at me. I began work, listening to the usual complaints from everyone who sat there humbly bearing all kinds of degradation. But this didn't last long—I heard a scream coming from outside the clinic, the scream of a woman in anguish. I didn't need to turn and look at her, I knew it was Farah. The time had come to face her. I stood up and went out to her. I saw her standing outside the clinic dressed in black, her clothes ripped and dusty. Her head was bare, her hair was matted and torn, her hands were soiled with mud. As soon as she saw me, she shrieked at the top of her voice, "Murderer! . . . You killed Eissa! You killed my husband!"

All the patients turned to look at her, as did the two nurses, and Desougi, and everyone who was passing by. I didn't move away, as she went on shouting, "It's you who gave him the money! It's you who encouraged him to go to his death!"

She bent down to the ground, took a handful of mud, and hurled it at me. It fell on the white coat. I remained standing, not moving from where I was—there was no use in running away—and she didn't cease yelling. "It's you who killed him!"

She threw more dirt, which this time landed on my face. I didn't move. My face was covered by a mask of mud. Through my weighted eyelids I saw her stagger away in the direction of the village. The patients dispersed quickly. Desougi came up and touched me on the shoulder. I sat on a chair, unable to take off my coat, or wipe the mud from my face. Desougi sat opposite me. There was no sound, and no movement. Still, her anguished scream rang in my ears, and after a long time I heard Desougi's voice coming to me from another dimension. "There's something I forgot to tell you this morning."

I raised my head slowly and saw him in front of me, holding a piece of paper in his hand. It looked plain and empty to me. He said, "This notification came from the Health Directorate two days ago."

"You've obviously read it carefully. What's in it?"

"Your application for a transfer has been approved."

Cairo
26/4/2020
Under Covid lockdown

Translator's Afterword

The Country Doctor's Tale is a welcome addition to the limited coverage of Egyptian rural life in modern Arabic fiction. Tawfiq al-Hakim's *Diary of a Country Prosecutor*, Taha Hussein's *Call of the Curlew*, and Abd al-Rahman al-Sharqawi's *Egyptian Earth* are classics of the genre, all adapted for a second life on the silver screen—and Mohamed Mansi Qandil's novel, with its conflicted and morally ambiguous narrator, its cast of scene-stealing characters, and its richly textured depictions of the beauties and cruelties of life in an Upper Egyptian village would surely also make a great cinematic excursion.

The central setting of the novel is a small, remote village in the Nile Valley of Upper Egypt in the late 1970s and early 1980s, at a time of political upheaval (the assassination of President Anwar Sadat on October 6, 1981 and the subsequent election of Hosni Mubarak) and social inequality, leading many young men, in particular, to seek opportunities in other, oil-rich Arab countries—Eissa's motivation for desperately trying to reach Libya in this novel. Upper (that is, southern) Egypt, both urban and rural, has always been seen as far more socially conservative than Cairo and the north, and is a region of proudly (and often fiercely) upheld tradition and values—of hospitality and great generosity, but also of family honor that when felt to be shamed can lead to dire consequences, as our doctor sees for himself first-hand, amid his own transgressions.

Egypt's Gypsies are a highly marginalized group. Alexandra Parrs, in her 2017 book *Gypsies in Contemporary Egypt: On the Peripheries of Society*, writes: "Middle Eastern Gypsies are called the Dom, as a mirror name to the European Roma and the Armenian Lom, but that name is mostly used by scholars and rarely by Egyptians or by members of the Dom community themselves. They are also called Ghagar, Nawar, or Halebi in Upper Egypt. . . . The terms all have negative connotations in Arabic." Indeed, they are generally seen by the settled population as living outside society and acting outside society's norms. This is reflected in how they are regarded and dealt with by the villagers and the authorities in the novel, while the doctor seems to be the only one to recognize their humanity and treat them with respect.

There is a rich (though now waning) culture of oral literature in Egypt, in which epic poems have been passed down and memorized by successive generations of professional storytellers, traveling around the country and performing in coffee shops and public places. One of the favorite and best-known epics is the *Chronicle of the Hilalis* (*al-Sira al-hilaliya*), in some versions said to number up to one million lines. It is this that the Gypsy queen al-Jazya references and adapts to recount for her audience the tale of her namesake, al-Jazya of the Banu Hilal. In English circles, the legends of King Arthur perhaps occupy a similar position, while Chaucer's *Canterbury Tales* also portray a colorful oral tradition at work. Our country doctor has his own morality tale to tell, and we are his privileged audience.

Translating this novel was a real pleasure, and I was fortunate in enjoying the support and engagement of the author throughout the process. Together, we were able to amend a few minor issues in the published Arabic text to the author's satisfaction, and to mine.

My thanks to all at Syracuse University Press, in particular acquisitions editor Laura Fish and series editors Michael Beard and Adnan Haydar, for their warm welcome and careful shepherding of this project. I am also grateful to Kay Heikkinen and Marilyn Booth, two of the best literary translators of Arabic into English working today, who both reviewed the manuscript and enthusiastically recommended publication. Thanks are also due to Shereen Abouelnaga, who gave me early encouragement to translate the novel, calling it "one of the classics now," and facilitated my introduction to the author. I can never thank enough two special friends, Habiba Ahmed al-Sayfi and Aiman Azabawy, who between them patiently followed the Arabic text line by line as I read my draft English translation out to them, ready to help untie any linguistic knots for me, or stop me if I had missed or misunderstood anything. Their deep knowledge of, and love for, the Arabic language made them invaluable partners in this translation (though of course the responsibility for any remaining errors or infelicities is mine alone), and I am glad to know that they enjoyed the exercise as much as I did. Habiba has now left us, but her inimitable spirit lives on, and to her memory this translation is dedicated.

Tunis Village, Fayoum
April 2025

Mohamed Mansi Qandil was born in al-Mahalla al-Kubra in Egypt's Nile Delta in 1949 and graduated from the Faculty of Medicine, Mansoura University, in 1975. He spent two years working at the medical center in a small village in the governorate of al-Minya, Upper Egypt, before leaving medicine to concentrate on writing. He is the author of several collections of short stories, a number of non-fiction titles and books for children, and five novels, including *Moon over Samarqand*, which won the Sawiris Cultural Award for best novel in 2006, and *A Cloudy Day on the Western Shore*, which was shortlisted for the International Prize for Arabic Fiction in 2010. *The Country Doctor's Tale* is his fifth novel, published in Arabic in 2020. He lives in Cairo.

R. Neil Hewison, born in Yorkshire in 1956, first arrived in Egypt to teach English in 1979. He was later editorial director of the American University in Cairo Press for many years until his retirement. He has translated works by the Egyptian writers Yusuf Idris, Yusuf Abu Rayya, Gamal al-Ghitani, and Naguib Mahfouz. He lives in Tunis Village in the Fayoum.

www.ingramcontent.com/pod-product-compliance
Lightning Source LLC
La Vergne TN
LVHW091108080826
845145LV00008B/1848

* 9 7 8 0 8 1 5 6 1 2 0 2 5 *